ROAD TO RHUINE

Also available in Perennial Library by Simon Troy

SWIFT TO ITS CLOSE

ROAD TO RHUINE *by*

SIMON TROY

PERENNIAL LIBRARY
Harper & Row, Publishers
New York, Cambridge, Philadelphia, San Francisco
London, Mexico City, São Paulo, Sydney

The characters, places, incidents and situations in this book are imaginary and have no relation to any person, place or actual happening

This work was originally published by Dodd, Mead & Company, Inc. It is here reprinted by arrangement.

First PERENNIAL LIBRARY edition published 1982.

ISBN: 0-06-080583-8

82 83 84 85 10 9 8 7 6 5 4 3 2 1

For
ALYS EDWARDS
Dear friend
and good companion.

Remembering crowded
buses, rainy days
and quiet places.

CONTENTS

ROAD TO RHUINE

CHAPTER ONE

OPEN CHEQUE

TEN minutes before Sheila Fabian came in and altered my whole slant on life, I was sitting in my office, wishing there was a Gipsy Sarah somewhere around to foretell my future.

It was a nice day, but I wasn't in the mood to appreciate it. There had been just one letter in the wire basket that morning. It was neatly typed, short, and to the point. It seemed that I owed twenty-eight pounds, fifteen shillings and fourpence for rent, and unless its owners received that sum or a substantial portion thereof within three days, I should be out on my ear.

I sat by the window, looking at the trucks moving up towards Covent Garden Market, which I could smell fifty yards away. I sat and looked, not even thinking. After a while I turned my back on the window and looked at the office instead. It was no more inspiring than the trucks.

I owned a flat-top desk and three hardwood Utility chairs. Besides these, to give the place tone, was a wicker wastebasket, a filing-cabinet (empty), a few books essential to my peculiar and probably unique profession, and a calendar issued by a marmalade firm.

There were four newspapers on the desk, all of the superior type. They had to be for my purpose. For want of something better to do I turned to the Agony Column. Agonies are less agonising now than they used to be. One time it was all *Come Back to Elsie, All Forgiven*, or *Any Person knowing the Whereabouts, etc*. These days, you find paragraphs about superfluous hair removers and bungalows for sale at Henley under *PERSONAL*.

I was reading *Retired Colonel (Indian Army) requires active Gardener-Chauffeur-Houseman, Knowledge of Curries and Hindustani Preferred*, when I heard the honk of a car in the street. Now honks under my office window are ten a minute, but this was a quality honk. It was loud. But it was polite too, like the *Queen Mary's* siren. I crossed to the window again and looked down. The car looked like a cabin-cruiser to me. It moved like one too—slow and dignified, upstream, pushing the bananas and watercress aside in a high bow-wave as it came along.

I was surprised when it stopped at the street entrance to my office. A woman got out. I couldn't see anything but the top of her head. Two children followed her, a boy and a girl. They looked, respectively, about six and four.

I didn't start frantically tidying up the office, because mine isn't the only place of business up those stairs. She could just as well have been on her way to see Levi Cohen (Money up to £10,000 Advanced on Note of Hand Alone), or Jimmy Rideout (Non-Arsenical Flypapers), or even the Rev. Theodolphus Haltwhistle, who ran the Brotherhood of Light on a non-profit footing, so he claimed.

So I sat with my head cocked on one side, listening. The stairs creaked. So it wasn't Levi. They creaked again. It wasn't flypapers. They creaked a third time. That meant me. I crossed my legs and waited. I often wish I could look tough and efficient. But I'm neither.

There was a tap on the door and I called, "Come in." She came in. Nothing quite like her had ever come through that door before. I stood up, the way people do when they hear

2

God Save the King played, and for the same psychological reason. She was only an inch or so shorter than me (I'm not a tall man) and she looked as if she had been made that morning. A prototype model.

She wasn't wearing a hat, and her hair, a dark brown with all kinds of hidden lights in it, was taken back smooth as an egg-shell and broke loose somewhere at the back. She was wearing a short jacket and a green linen blouse, and round her neck hung a pendant, a platinum chain thin as a hair, with a single diamond drop in the hollow of her throat.

"Can I see Mr. Vaughan?" she asked.

She must have taken me for a secretary. That showed how little she knew about the state of my business.

"I'm Lee Vaughan," I said. And as I spoke, the two children came through the door and stood beside her, the boy on her right, the girl on her left.

"I thought you would be older," she said. "From Gwendolen Morris's description I expected . . ." She looked me up and down. "I don't quite know what I expected, but not—not anyone like you."

"I'm not responsible for my age," I told her. "So Gwendolen Morris sent you?"

"Not exactly. She recommended you. She said you could be trusted."

"That's nice of her," I said. "Will you sit down?"

She moved to one of the Utility chairs. The two children stayed just where they were, not even moving closer together when she came from between them. It irritated me, that. It was too perfect. I'd seen things happen like that on the stage.

"I found Gwen Morris's daughter," I went on, "at a time when it wouldn't have been easy for them to go to the police."

"I know. She's still terribly grateful for everything you did. So when I realised I needed a—a private agent . . ."

"I'm not a private agent," I said.

3

"No?"

"No, but we can go into that later."

She didn't look very comfortable in that chair. I perched on the desk, so the two kids, if fancy took them that way, could sit down also. That seemed as little as I could do, considering the size of the car down below. I swung one foot, waiting.

"My name," she said, "is Sheila Fabian."

"Miss Sheila Fabian?"

"Mrs. Fabian."

"Sorry," I said. "I thought perhaps you were their nurse or something." I nodded towards the children.

"I'm their mother." She looked at them, thoughtfully. She added, almost with a note of apology in her voice, "They are not—they are not my present husband's children."

I waited a decent period.

"Their names," she said, "are Peter and Ninian Charles."

I nodded. "That isn't a surname you often strike. And now you're Mrs. Fabian. Live in London, Mrs. Fabian?"

"No. I did at one time. Willesden. But now I live at Rhuine. Probably you haven't heard of it?"

"Or probably I have. I wouldn't mind living there myself, Mrs. Fabian. That is, if someone would provide me with three or four thousand a year, tax-free. I should say you need it there. Must be difficult to make a living."

She smiled. It wasn't a hard bright smile. It was certainly not an amused one. It was as though she had to smile to relieve something inside her. I got the impression that Sheila Fabian was just about as tight-strung as an overwound watch.

"I don't have to worry about making a living," she said, letting the words come on a long sigh. "You see, I own Rhuine."

I blinked slightly. "Like the Dame of Sark owns Sark?"

"Almost like that."

"My congratulations," I said. "To Rhuine."

She looked at me a moment, "Thank you, Mr. Vaughan."

"And what does the Dame of Rhuine want with a bankrupt Personal Relations Officer?" I asked.

She looked steadily at the marmalade calendar.

"For twelve months," she said, "my husband has been making life intolerable. For me and for the children. I need help before he—"

She stopped there, biting her lip. I wasn't looking at her any more than she was at me. I was watching the children. They hadn't stirred. I'm not easily embarrassed, but they embarrassed me. She shouldn't have brought them, I thought, if she wanted to discuss things like that. It seemed indecent to be talking about their mother's second marital adventure in front of the two products of the first.

She probably guessed what I was thinking.

"Peter and Ninian are very well trained," she said. "Not by me—by circumstances. They won't repeat anything they hear, Mr. Vaughan."

"Useful to have children like that," I remarked. "I wasn't worrying about what they'd repeat, though. It's simply that I'm not accustomed to talking in front of innocence."

"Innocence?" she repeated, and her thin brows lifted wryly above those green-glinting eyes. "Oh, *innocence!*"

I didn't like the way she said it. I was still looking at the children. They were both slight and straight. Their hair was blonde, unlike their mother's, but they had her short nose and good, firm mouth. It was the boy who interested me. The girl was just a pretty little doll, but he looked as if he'd seen things he shouldn't have. His eyes were old. His silence wasn't respectful or shy. It was guarded.

I didn't understand it. I might have if Sheila Fabian had been a good specimen of the hard-boiled type, all cocktails and Freud. But she wasn't. There was warmth under that cool, lovely crust. I didn't understand why she treated Peter and Ninian like the children of a brother she hadn't seen for

5

a long while.

"Sorry I haven't anything for you to play with," I said. "No dolls or woolly bears. Not even a comic."

"Peter imagines he's rather past that stage," Mrs. Fabian said.

When anything puzzles me, I'm apt to show my resentment more than I should. I nodded towards the books on my desk. "If they're as advanced as all that," I said, "perhaps they'd care to glance through Whitaker's or the Classified Directory."

The boy's eyes turned a darker shade of blue.

"If you talk to my mummy like that," he said on a sharp high note, "I shall kick you and break your knee-cap. Jonquil says you can easily break a man's knee-cap if you kick him right."

I took one quick glance at Mrs. Fabian. I saw something in her eyes that gave my heart a jolt. I looked down at the boy and said, as if I'd been talking to an adult:

"I'm sorry you got the wrong idea, Peter. I was only joking with your mummy. You can take it from me that I like her very much."

I went to the window. "There's plenty to see from here if you like a grandstand view.'

They came over, both of them. The little girl gave me a wispy smile. I looked to see that the window was secure, then went back to their mother.

"And what do you want me to do," I asked, "before your husband does something else?"

She thought that over. "Mr. Vaughan," she said, "how well do you know Rhuine?"

"Not at all. I've never been there. I know it's half a day's run from Paddington. I know it's a show-place and a dollar-earner. After that I pass."

"Can you imagine it," she asked, "with half a dozen luxury hotels, a pier and an icedrome?"

"I can imagine anything," I said.

"Those are my husband's plans."

"You'd better tell me from the beginning," I suggested.

It took her quarter of an hour to do that. To save a lot of quotes and interruptions, this is what she told me. I had the impression that it cost her a lot to talk about it at all. She had a low voice with husky overtones. She used short words, short sentences mostly, and thought a lot, as if she wanted to get everything exactly right.

She was twenty-seven. She was born in North London and christened Sheila Margaret Cardew. Father a doctor. Parents both died young. She had been brought up by her father's sister, a Catholic. Sheila herself wasn't a Catholic, though she had been sent to a convent school for her later education.

At eighteen and a half, after six months at a business college, she had gone into a factory office. Shortly after that, being good at languages, she had been sent to Lisbon. There she met a man called Godfrey Charles, a naval officer, and they were married. She didn't tell me precisely what she was doing in Lisbon, or why Charles was there. But Lisbon, I gathered, was European clearing house Number One in those days, a hotbed of everything from straight commercial competition to espionage.

She knew little or nothing about this man Charles when they were married, except that the family was rich, that his father was dead, and that his mother was an American citizen domiciled in England for the previous twenty years or so.

Peter was born in 1943. Ninian, two years later. And in 1947, with the War safely over, Godfrey Charles was killed in a gunnery accident.

Sheila had met her mother-in-law only once, in London, but had been impressed by her. She had the address, which was Edward's Bounty, Rhuine, via Shilstone, and wrote there.

But the letter wasn't answered.

When she made enquiries, she learned that Mrs. Charles, at the end of the War, had gone to America and presumably stayed there.

In 1948, therefore, Sheila's position wasn't too good. She was twenty-five, had a small pension, no home, and two babies to fed, clothe, and educate. And a man named Stuart Fabian wanted to marry her.

Fabian was no millionaire, but he held two or three guinea-pig directorships of provincial firms, owned a comfortable home at Richmond, up-Thames from London, and wore a good school tie. Also, he was sufficiently infatuated with Sheila to say that her two children would be well cared-for if she married him.

But something made her hold back. What it was, she didn't tell me till later, much later. She wrote to Mrs. Charles again. At this point in her story she gave me a copy of the letter to read. This was it:

> *Rackworth's Hotel,*
> *Bloomsbury Square,*
> *LONDON.*
> *Oct. 17, 1948.*

My Dear Mrs. Charles,

I wrote to you at Rhuine some months ago, but my letter was returned and I was told that you had gone away without leaving a forwarding address. I have not heard from you since Godfrey was killed. I think you must have written to me, but so much mail has been lost. Or perhaps my own movements have made me difficult to find.

Now, however, I am making another effort, through your lawyers, to get in touch with you, because I would greatly appreciate your advice. Peter and Ninian are your grandchildren. I am not asking for any help—I can look after myself and the children too if necessary—but Godfrey always gave me to understand that the Charles family are wealthy and enjoy a good social position. And I think it is only right

8

*that if you wish the children to have the kind of education
I could never afford to give them, you should be given the
opportunity to help with their future.*

*I do so wish I could see you. There are so many things I
would like to say, about you and Godfrey and myself, that
can't be put down on paper. On that one occasion we did
meet, I felt it would be easy to know and love you as Godfrey's mother. And I feel I can write to you in this way and
be sure you won't misunderstand my motive.*

*Peter and Ninian are mine, and I wouldn't give them up to
anyone. But if you want to see them and would like to help
me give them the things they should have, I shall be glad to
hear from you.*

> *Your daughter-in-law,*
> *Sheila M. Charles.*

Reading that letter touched me. It was the sort I would
have expected her to write. I gave it back and waited till
she went on with the story.

Still there was no reply, and as the weeks passed, she
wondered if ever there would be. The woman might be dead.
Or, having lost her son, she might feel she wanted nothing
further to do with the girl he had married or with that girl's
children.

Meanwhile, the man Fabian was still worrying her.

In the end she married Fabian. She married him at Clerken-
well Register Office in February, 1949. They sent the children to Sheila's aunt at Willesden for two weeks, and went
honeymooning to Brighton. Fabian had suggested going
abroad, but Sheila's Lisbon experiences were still fresh in
her memory, and she preferred her native shores.

And then came the shock.

About the beginning of May, there arrived a communica-
tion from a firm of lawyers at Raleigh, North Carolina. They
said Mrs. Charles was dead, and had left a letter to be forwarded to Sheila. As to certain financial matters referred to
in that letter, she would be hearing at an early date from

their colleagues in London.

She showed me the letter the lawyers had forwarded.
Here it is:

> Willoways,
> Arrowville,
> N. Carolina, U.S.A.
> March 14, 1949.

My Dear Sheila,

I received your letter four months ago, and should have
answered it right away, but I didn't wish to enter into a
transatlantic correspondence—and a rather emotional one—
during the last weeks of my life. I hope you will understand
this and forgive me.

By the time you read these words I shall be dead. My health
has been failing for some years. I thought there might still
be time to come over here, see the friends and scenes of my
early life, and return to England to die at Rhuine, the place
I love better than any other on earth. But it is not to be so. I
shall never see home again.

I must tell you now (perhaps Godfrey has already done
so) how we came to be so nearly English. Godfrey, of course,
actually was English by birth.

My husband was a wealthy man, the son of Senator Eldon
Charles, of Raleigh. He frequently visited England on business trips, and on one of these occasions I came with him. We
stayed at Rhuine with English friends of his—the Maldwyches, who then owned Rhuine and lived at Edward's
Bounty, the manor house. I knew the greatest happiness of
my life at that house, for our return to the States was delayed,
and Godfrey was born there.

But a few weeks later, my husband contracted infantile
paralysis while visiting London. He was taken to a hospital,
and later brought back to Rhuine, where he died. . . . So I
am bound to that little place by ties both of birth and death.

All my life since then, I have never been able to forget the
kindness we received from everybody. I can see the little red-
headed nurse who cared for my husband in that London

hospital. I can see the porters carrying him so gently down the steps and putting him into the ambulance. I remember the day we buried him in the little churchyard at Rhuine, among the sailors and fishermen, near to the sea that had claimed so many of their lives.

But these are sad memories, and you are too young for sadness. Only let me tell you that when the Maldwyches fell on evil times, like so many old English familite in those days, I came back again from America to see what could be done.

I found the villagers in tears. Since the day when Edward the Fourth gave the Manor and Lands of Rhuine to Gervease Maldwych, the family had owned every stick and stone in that enchanted valley. By accident of birth, it had been preserved unspoilt for five hundred years, one of the most beautiful places on earth. But who knew what might happen now that the estate was to be broken up?

For the first time in my life I felt truly grateful for the power that wealth still gives. I was able to buy Rhuine as one estate, and guarantee that for another generation at least it would be preserved as I had first seen it. And after me there would be my son.

Need I tell you that when he married, before I had ever seen the girl of his choice, I wondered and pondered. . . . And need I tell you that when I met you, I thanked God that you were everything I had always hoped for him.

And now, like so many others of his tragic generation, he is dead, and I am dying far away.

But you are Godfrey's wife, a Charles. Your children are Peter and Ninian CHARLES. You are beautiful and strong and intelligent. And so, without any condition or qualification, Rhuine is yours as it would have been Godfrey's and yours, in trust for those who live there and for your children who will one day own it in your place.

Kiss Peter and Ninian for me. I leave their education to you; I know it is in safe hands. No one can tell what the future may bring, for these are troubled times in which we live. But as far as you are able, keep Rhuine as it is, as it has always been. You will find it an asset rather than a liability.

It is well-held by good tenants who will be your loyal friends because you are a Charles, and, I believe, a good woman in your own right.

Waste no tears on me. Live your life to the full. I don't ask you to remain a widow to my son's memory. If you find a man you love, and who loves you, and bring him to Rhuine, it will only be my very friendly ghost that haunts you. A ghost you need never be afraid of.

And now, goodbye and God bless you.
Your loving mother, Mary Louisa Charles.

I dropped the letter and went over to the window. My throat felt dry and tight, and something was pricking and burning at the back of my eyes. I should be tougher for the job I chose.

Peter said to me, "Do you live here?"

"No," I said. "This is just my office."

"I'd like to live here," he said.

"Better than Rhuine?"

"Course he wouldn't," piped Ninian, speaking for the first time.

"I would," said Peter. "There's plenty to see here."

By the time I turned round, Sheila Fabian had picked up the letter and was putting it back in her bag.

"Meanwhile," I said to her, "you'd married Fabian."

"Yes."

"Nice for him. So he left the Richmond house and took up residence with you at Rhuine. Or is my slant on human nature all wrong?"

"Your slant's pretty good, Mr. Vaughan."

"There's something I'd like to know. Who's this Jonquil who told Peter you can crack a man's knee-cap if you kick in the right place?"

She looked quickly at Peter, then back again to me.

"There are two brothers. Luke and Isaiah Jonquil. Luke has the Liquorice Gardens, Isaiah has a share in a trawler

12

and hires out pleasure-boats. It would be Isaiah."

"And when Isaiah imparted this useful information to your son, whose knee-cap had he in mind?"

Her mouth tightened like a string bag when you pull the tags. It was Peter who answered that question from the window.

"Old Horny's," he said.

Now Sheila Fabian's voice came, thin and lost.

"We have a Christmas Mystery at Rhuine. That happens to be one of the characters."

"Old Horny's the Devil," said Peter. "Old Horny is mummy's husband."

"Well-informed, these children of yours," I said.

She didn't speak. Her hands were clenched. She put the white, strained knuckles up to her mouth, biting them. It was a childish, pitiful gesture. Her eyes were wide as she looked at me. She slowly shook her head.

"When I grow up I'm going to kill him," Peter told me dispassionately.

"That's interesting," I said. "How?"

"I'm going to throw him over Yeo's Jinkin."

"Where's that?"

"Into Mrs. Crummett's back-yard. I'm going to break his neck."

I eyed him with some respect.

"I suppose Old Horny's a pretty hefty specimen?"

"Twice as big as you."

"Then you'd better go steady till you've had a lot more rice-pudding," I advised, "or maybe it'll be you who finishes up in Mrs. Crummett's back-yard."

I sat down again on the edge of the desk and pulled a piece of string out of the waste-basket and started tying knots. I tied knots for a long time.

"Old Horny," I said at last, "is twice as big as me. So what are you trying to hire me for, Mrs. Fabian? If Old Horny is trying to maltreat you physically or mentally, there's the police-station and the divorce court. If he's up to monkey-tricks with the property left to you by Mrs. Charles, I can send you to the best lawyers for that job in London. If he's ill-treating the kids, there's a society specially chartered to deal with him."

"Yes," she said. "The police and the divorce court and lawyers are sometimes useful." She added after a pause, "But not always."

I went on tying knots.

I said thoughtfully, more to myself than to her, "Though I don't see how he can monkey with the estate. Lawyers know how to tie those things up."

"He can't. But Rhuine is very small, Mr. Vaughan. A strip of land a mile-and-a-half long and half-a-mile wide. And my husband has money enough to buy up land here and there, all around, and—and develop it." She took a long breath, smiled that odd, safety-valve smile. "Think of West-minster Abbey with a factory over the road."

It was a good point to make. I tried to imagine it, and though I've no personal interest in the Abbey, having no near relatives buried there, it wasn't a picture I liked.

"He's already bought up a thirteen-acre strip on the north side. It goes down to the beach. I think he's interested a financial group in the idea. There's some talk of a lido. . . . And Luke Jonquil's Liquorice Garden is next on the list. It happens to be just outside my property, you see. I can't do a thing about it."

She leaned forward. "Rhuine has stayed this way for five hundred years, Mr. Vaughan, because the local people have been proud of it. It's been a matter of local goodwill. But now, anything may happen."

"How can you be blamed," I said, "for something that takes place outside your territory?"

"Legally I can't. But these people look to me for protection. Rhuine hasn't outgrown its feudal ways of thought."

"What about the local Rural Council?" I asked. "What about the National Trust and the Council for the something-or-other of Country Amenities?"

"I seem to have heard of them all," she said. "But I'm too near breaking-point for all that. I want someone to help me. Not lawyers and societies. Someone who will fight back without being troubled by legal quibbles. Someone who will fight as hard to keep Rhuine safe as my husband is fighting to destroy it."

"But what's in the man's mind? Why, is he doing it at all?" I wanted to know. "It must be costing him a lot of money. And hard-headed business men don't usually part with pelf on a big scale unless they stand to make a profit or else they're getting some personal satisfaction for their outlay."

"With my husband," she said, "it's personal satisfaction. By destroying what means so much for me, he destroys me as well."

She took a cheque-book out of her bag, wrote in it, and dropped the result on my desk. The cheque was for two hundred pounds, and she'd left it open. I smiled and left it where it lay.

"I'm no Galahad," I said, "but I wouldn't take money even from a rich woman unless I thought I could give value. And I don't see how I can."

For the moment, I'd forgotten the children. But Peter must have been listening. He probably judged it was time to throw his weight in the scale.

"Tell him about the coach-house," he said.

I looked at him, then at his mother. I didn't know whether she would. I didn't know whether I would in her place. I don't like taking advice from anybody, much less a seven-year-old.

"The coach-house was burnt down," she said. "Two

15

months ago."

"Things like that happen."

"It's attached to the house. No one ever used it. There isn't even a road now, for coaches to run. Nothing was ever stored there, even rubbish. There was nothing to catch fire."

"You'd be surprised what a cigarette-stub can do."

"On a stone-flagged floor? The insurance adjustors said it had been done deliberately."

"Well," I said, "those boys usually know their stuff. So who did it?"

Sheila Fabian shrugged. "Who has a grudge against my husband?"

"Don't expect me to believe that worries you."

"It doesn't. I'm not a hypocrite. But a blow against my husband might fall elsewhere. On me or the children. On the people of Rhuine. That worries me."

"I can understand that," I said.

I could. But there were other things I didn't understand. I had the feeling again that pages were being flicked over too quick for me to read. I was getting a good story, but not the whole story. Arson is a police matter. You don't travel three hundred miles to ask a man you don't know to find out who fired the coach-house.

I was thinking this over when Ninian fluted, "Mummy, tell him about Lora."

"You leave Lora out of it!" flashed Peter. "Lora's a smasher."

"Lora isn't. She's a baggage. She's a whore. Phoebe says she is."

I pondered that curious word with its emphatic aspirate for a moment. Sheila, I noticed, had flushed slightly.

"Phoebe," she explained, "is one of my maids. In Rhuine, people rather pride themselves upon their forthrightness."

"Calling a spade a spade and a whore a whore," I said thoughtfully. I turned from the two astonishing children.

16

"Anyway, smasher, baggage, or worse, who is Lora, what is she?"

Sheila put the cheque-book in her bag. She didn't meet my eye.

"When Mrs. Ruddan died, her cottage on North Score was empty. I had a long waiting-list, but Stuart put Lora in."

"Legally, he couldn't," I said.

"A man can go a long way beyond legalities when the only barrier happens to be his wife. I think he brought Lora from London."

"It's an interesting situation," I said.

"I'm glad it appeals to you."

"It doesn't." The string was practically full of knots by this time and I started to undo them. "Suppose I decide to take a hand? What would you want me to do?"

"Come down to Rhuine and stay at Edward's Bounty."

"As a sponging relative recuperating from something?"

"I have a cousin in Australia," Sheila Fabian said. "His name is Harry Cardew. My husband has never met him. And Harry is due for a visit to England."

She carried it no further than that. She left me to sort it out.

"You make it sound tempting," I said. "Once, I spent three months in Sydney. I could answer questions about Sydney and sound intelligent. So Cousin Harry pays you a visit. Maybe. What comes next?"

"Next, deal with my husband. Whatever it costs and whatever means you have to employ, stop him."

"Just like that," I said. "I appreciate the faith you have in me, Mrs. Fabian. But I still think there are simpler ways. I think so more than ever since you told me about this woman Lora. She's your emergency exit, not me."

"A divorce would make him worse. You don't know him."

I picked up the cheque, looked at it and put it down again.

"If I start up any active opposition against your husband I shall be thrown out. If I don't, I shall be wasting your money. Either way, it isn't a very satisfactory prospect."

I thought she seemed to sag. As if that over-wound spring inside her had snapped.

"I can't make plans for you," she said. "I can't even offer suggestions. I only know I'm alone and I need help. I've fought back till I'm tired out, Mr. Vaughan. I want to foil these crazy schemes he has for Rhuine. I want to prevent him inspiring these dreadful thoughts in my children's minds. If he thinks that someone else belonging to my family is in the house, it may influence him."

I could feel myself slipping. But before my discretion took its final plunge overboard I made a last protest.

"I still don't see why you can't come into the open and fight him on legal grounds. You've a good case. The Press would soak it up like blotting-paper. Before you knew it, there'd be a national fund to preserve the outskirts of Rhuine from defilement, there'd be an Act of Parliament sterilising land, there'd be such an outcry that your husband would be glad to crawl into a dark place and lick his wounds." I scowled at her. "Rhuine's a national institution, remember."

She didn't move in the chair. The diamond drop nestled in the hollow of her throat, a little lake of fire.

"I can't," she said.

"So there's some other reason?"

She said nothing.

"And without knowing what I'm up against, I'm to stick my neck out? I suppose that's the reason you throw me a cheque for two hundred pounds when you probably know damn well that twenty would tempt me?"

"I won't argue about that," she said. "Just say yes or no. I've no one to help me. And I've been told you can be trusted. That's all."

"I can't say yes or no to a thing like that," I told her.

"I'll have to think about it. I've got your address. Give me your phone number in case I need it."

"Shilstone one-nine."

"Thanks." I scribbled it down. "You're going back home now?"

"This afternoon."

"I'm not promising anything," I said, "but post me a dossier on Harry Cardew of Sydney. Send a photo if you have one. Age, occupation, what he knew of you in years gone by, mutual family links and anything else you can think of."

"I'll do that," she promised.

She didn't try any more persuasion. I liked her all the better for that. She got up and called the children from the window. And that reminded me of something.

"Suppose I decide to come?" I said. "What's going to be the position with these two precocities?"

"Peter!" she said quietly. "Ninian! If this gentleman comes to stay with us, have you ever seen him before?"

"Not on your sweet life!" piped Ninian.

"Don't know him from Adam," said Peter. "Is he coming to kill Old Horny?" He looked up at me. "He's big. You want to knife him when he isn't looking."

I went downstairs with them and waited till they got into the car. It moved off. Sheila Fabian looked up from the wheel and smiled. The children watched me through the rear window. But they didn't smile. They didn't even wave.

You could have thought it was the charming wife of some wealthy professional man, out for a morning's shopping with her two beautiful children. I imagine many an envious glance followed them as they went towards Long Acre.

I went upstairs and took a bottle out of the desk cupboard. I keep it there for emergencies. This was one. Then I sat down and started to think.

After half an hour's thinking I shut up the office and went to the public library in St. Martin's Lane. There I got hold of a guide-book to Shilstone and District. There were twenty pages about Rhuine, several photographs, and a map. I studied them all as if they were Darkest Africa and I was a student missionary. It was probably going to be something rather like that, anyway.

Then I reached down *Who's Who* and looked up FABIAN, Stuart Durward. Born 1900. Educated Longchester and Christ's, Oxford. Director of So-and-So and Such-and-Such. Served on Allied Industrial Relations Committee, 1944–6. No mention of matrimonial contracts, either with Sheila or any before her time.

I sat there staring at the library assistant's face until she must have thought I had intentions. Then I went back to the office and started telephoning. I rang up everybody I knew who might give me a line on Stuart Durward Fabian.

I wasn't lucky at first. It seemed we moved in different circles. But after half an hour I got on to a fellow whose second cousin once removed had been at Longchester with Fabian, and kept in touch with him through the Longcastrian Old Boy's Association. After two more blanks I was given a slant on his industrial activities from an old acquaintance in the City. Last of all, I contacted a friend in the licensed trade who had known Fabian as a more or less worthy citizen of Richmond.

None of them had much to say against him. Nor did they display much enthusiasm. And all three agreed that as far as the opposite sex was concerned, he was what is commonly known as warm. I didn't have to ask for that information; it was volunteered.

I went back over everything Sheila Fabian had told me. Her story held water, in spite of the gaps I was sure she had left in it. The letters she had shown me proved what she was, even if I hadn't felt it in my bones. The Charles woman,

20

her mother-in-law, must have been impressed by her character to leave her the whole place as it stood, just on the strength of one meeting. And, I noticed, there had been no come-back. If there had been anything wrong with Sheila Fabian—morally, mentally or legally—it's a safe bet that some disgruntled member of the Charles clan in North Carolina would have been ready and eager to contest the will.

But it seemed that she had accepted the responsibilities as well as the privileges of owning Rhuine, and I could understand the way she felt about her husband's anti-social behaviour.

I could also understand Fabian's attitude up to a point. He was fifty; Sheila was twenty-seven. Twenty-three years is a big gap. It's bridged every day, but you need the right people to do it. I didn't wonder that Fabian's inferiority complexes had wakened up under present circumstances.

But I wasn't any nearer to understanding the things that had started me guessing in the first place. Those pages Sheila had skipped. The queer business of the coach-house. And those long thoughtful silences. . . . People often tell you a lot more when they keep their mouths shut than when they're tumbling over themselves to be communicative.

My mind wasn't any clearer next afternoon, and by that time the sheer physical pull of Sheila Fabian wasn't so strong. If a nice straightforward job of work had turned up, I should probably have posted back her cheque with a covering note and that would have been the end of it.

But all that came by the two o'clock post was a bill for electricity, the telephone account, and a reminder that my endowment premium was overdue.

I propped the cheque in front of me. I thought about Rhuine, very nice at this time of year. I thought about Peter, and Old Horny, and Mrs. Crummett's back-yard. I thought about the girl in the deceased Mrs. Ruddan's cottage. Not so nice, any of it, whatever the season.

Then I stopped thinking. I'd done too much already. I took the cheque to my bank, paid it in, and drew all but ten shillings of my previous balance for current expenses. It came to seven pounds fifteen shillings. Back at the office I wrote cheques for the outstanding accounts, post-dating them all, and addressed the envelopes. I put them in the OUT tray, though later, being my own office-boy, I should have to mail them myself.

Then I pulled the phone across the desk and asked the operator for Shilstone one-nine.

The call didn't take long. I thought Sheila Fabian would take it, but a man's voice came the three hundred miles across the wire. It was a clipped but not unpleasant voice. I asked who that was, and said I was Harry Cardew wanting to talk to Mrs. Fabian.

The voice said that Mrs. Fabian was out, but he was Mr. Fabian, and had I said Harry Cardew?

"I don't know you," I said, "so I can't expect you to know me, though you've probably heard Sheila mention my name. I'm her cousin. Haven't seen her for years. In fact, I only came over three or four weeks ago."

"Over?" he said. "Where from?"

"Sydney, New South Wales," I said. "And if this is the climate you still keep over here, I don't care how soon I'm on my way back."

The voice laughed. I had the impression that he thought hard for a moment before letting himself be pleasant.

"I remember Sheila saying something about you. Why didn't you drop in instead of ringing?"

"From here to Rhuine's a long drop," I said, "and it's a long time since I saw her. I didn't even know she'd been married. But it seems she has, twice. I started looking for her under her own name, then her first husband's. It was only this morning that I heard the name of Fabian. I wasn't sure of my welcome. What's she doing in that God-forgotten hole, anyway? Running a rooming-house?"

The voice laughed again, this time not so pleasantly.

"You could call it that. With one principle lodger in the best apartment."

That, I thought, was cutting near the bone. I didn't make any reply, and after a second he went on: "Shall I tell Sheila to expect you?"

"Well," I said, "I've an appointment on Saturday in Bristol. I could come on from there. But not if it's going to inconvenience you any way. I'm not under the illusion that because a man comes home after a spell abroad, he can sponge on his relations all he wants. All the same, I'd be glad to see her."

I hoped I was keeping it nice and casual.

"Naturally," he said. "Blood and water, eh? Then we'll expect you tomorrow or Sunday. Any idea what time? We'd better have a car at Shilstone to meet the train."

"Don't trouble," I said. "I travel light, and I'm quite capable of carrying my baggage a mile or two if there's no taxi."

"I suppose you get that way," he said, "out in the backblocks."

"I wouldn't know," I answered. "I've never been there."

There was a lot of mush on the line. I didn't catch his next remark. So I said through the sputtering:

"My regards to Sheila, then. And I'll be looking forward to seeing you."

The telephone seemed to leer at me as I dropped the handset back.

Next day, Saturday, an envelope postmarked SHILSTONE rattled into the box. It was the promised dossier on the life and works of Harry Cardew. There wasn't a covering note.

I sat down with that dossier for an hour's earnest study, then put in a further hour's work on a street-plan of Sydney as I remembered it. By the time I put away the plan and

23

burned the dossier, I could have believed that instead of going along to Fortes for a sardine-salad I was walking down Castlereagh Street to the Australia. Or maybe Cardew would have favoured Tattersall's.

The same day, about half-past nine in the evening, I went out for a drink. I dropped into the Daggers Drawn, near my two rooms in Fremont Street (the Fremont between Albany and Stanhope; it's handy for the Zoo). Half-way down my modest pot of mixed, I happened to look over the rim of my glass and saw one of the people I'd rung up for information about Fabian.

It was Jensen, the licensed gent who had told me about Fabian's Richmond menage.

"Mind," he said to me, "I was never on intimate terms with him. It was in the days when I kept the Bargee and Maiden, and Fabian seldom did more than pass the time of day and ask for his whisky."

"Alone?" I asked.

"Sometimes. More often not. I used to wonder where he found them."

"Found what?" I said, and Jensen gave me a knowing look.

"He liked them with yellow hair. I used to think he carried a packet of hair-dye just in case he picked up a brunette some dark night. . . . Anyway, that's neither here nor there. But I remembered an odd thing after you rang up."

I pushed Jensen's glass across the counter. And mine. They came back full.

"Nothing to it, maybe. . . . It happened one evening in front of Ham House. On the towpath. I'd had a spot of business on the Middlesex side, stopped on Eel Pie Island for a drink and was walking home. Fabian happened to be walking the same way."

Jensen squinted at his beer. "There was a hedgehog on the path."

24

It was my turn to give Jensen a look. "Useful things to have in the garden," I said. "Or are they?"

"Garden . . . ? Oh, quite! Now it's funny how a thing like that gives you a slant on a man's character. Fabian gave it a kick that would have slammed the ball clean through the goal. Poor little devil plumped into the river half-way between us and Twickenham. Odd thing, but after that I never had much use for Fabian. Only a hedgehog and all that, but you see there wasn't any damned need for it, was there?"

"No," I said.

"I remember thinking, if that's the way he treats his yellow-haired molls, somebody's going to find him one morning with a slit under his ear."

"There's something in that," I said.

I thought about Peter, and Mrs. Crummett's back-yard, and Yeo's Jinkin, what and wherever in hell that might be. And a spot of cold water trickled down my spine.

RHUINE REVEALED

I REACHED Shilstone at four o'clock next day, Sunday, after a fairly quick journey on the one through train. I accosted two taxi-drivers who said no thanks, preferring local jobs, and decided to take a bus. It was cheaper anyway.

The bus left at five, so there was time for a snack at a fly-blown lunch-bar near the station. At twenty past five I was getting off the bus at Shilstone Corner. My week-end case lacked quality but was light to carry, and I began to walk briskly towards Rhuine. The bus had sheered off towards some other coastwise district. Rhuine is not closely approachable by heavy traffic, a circumstance to which it owes a good deal of its charm.

I happened to come in by the north side. Half a mile past Shilstone Corner the road forks. Right, TO THE BEACH by way of South Score; left, TO THE BEACH by way of North Score. I learned later that a Score in those parts is fishermen's English for any sort of a narrow road or alley.

As I walked, I noticed that a stream to my right was sinking deeper and deeper into a little twisting valley till I was trudging along the bank of a ravine. And across that ravine, less than a hundred yards away and roughly at the same level, I could see the South Score road through the trees.

I came on the village like turning on a light in a dark room. One minute I might have been ten miles from a house. Next, there it all was in front of me. I was standing on the high ground five hundred feet above the sea, and below me the stream and the ravine and those two lovely, fantastic streets tumbled down to a harbour the size of a tennis-court, with two stone piers crooking their arms around it.

I walked down North Score. There were crazy lanes leading off here and there, and low walls guarding dizzy drops into the garden of the house next door. I passed a pub on my right, with a sign that said *THE SPANISH GALLEON* hanging over the road. It looked like the visitors' pub, built some time in the sixteenth century but tricked out to make suburban London feel at home.

At the bottom of the hill I plumped my fibre case on the harbor-wall and looked back. It was the most perfect bit of Ye Olde Teashoppe Englande I'd ever struck, even to the

26

carefully-careless disposition of the hydrangeas round the cottage doors. Some of those cottages were built of natural stone, others of brick color-washed in pastel shades. One was thatched, the next tiled. I could see that North and South Score were never more than a few yards apart, but they didn't communicate much, having the ravine between them. Later, I discovered that the ravine was bridged in two places by insecure and terrifying wooden structures that no one used except in broad daylight.

I could also see that the ravine stream was bridged in a third place, just short of where it dashed into the harbour, by a newish-looking stone arch. And just over that bridge a steep lane led towards the church and a big house—Sheila Fabian's house, I supposed—which were accommodated on one of the few areas of flat ground in all that humpy and highly-photogenic paradise.

Close at hand was a cosier-looking pub than the one I had just passed. It was called *THE DOLPHIN*. There was a bench outside, under an open window. I wasn't sure about opening-time, but I sat down. A man with a face like an educated monkey put his head out and asked what? I said half a pint, and he passed it through the window. I'd meant beer, but the stuff he gave me was cider, rough cider, and well-named. It was strong enough to have kept its cylindrical shape if the glass had broken.

"Staying round yur?" he asked.

I said I wasn't sure beyond a day or so, but I might be back for more of the same later. I left my bag on the bench and strolled down the three stone steps to the level of the jetty. It was like every other jetty, with steps at intervals down to the harbour floor and a nasty drop if you omitted to use them.

A man in a blue jersey wanted to know if I would like to take out a boat. I said I was allergic to water, inside or out, fresh or salt. He grinned and nodded. He was a red-faced man, built like a muscular porpoise.

"Ah well, zur, if you change your mind, you come'n arsk for Jonquil. Jonquil's the name, zur. There'll be plenty arsking you, but don't you take no notice of'm. Jonquil's the name, zur."

I said I'd remember, though I wasn't making promises. And I added that I'd never been to Rhuine before.

His eyes were half-lost in a net of wrinkles.

"It's a place that grows on you, Rhuine," he said, and I noticed he pronounced it Reween, as Sheila Fabian had done. He nodded towards the fringe of the ebb. "My boats, zur. All seven of 'em. And I've a share in yon. . . ."

He nodded again. It was a profound nod that brought his chin half-way to his waist. His little eyes were fixed proudly on a small motor-trawler lying off the harbour mouth.

"Looks as if she might have been over to Dunkirk," I said, without a thought in my head but to flatter him.

"Three times, zur," he told me. "Arsked 'em for a gun, but they said thur wasn't half a dozen in the country. So I mounted th'old duck-shooter in the bows, and we had a pot at the barstards even if she didn't do much hexecution."

It occurred to me that Isaiah Jonquil would be a good man or a very bad one according to whether he was a friend or an enemy. He might have said a lot more, but a late coach must have disgorged its crowd of trippers at Shilstone Corner. They were coming down North Score, hobbling on high heels, squealing with delight. Blazers blazed, cameras clicked, and before I reached the end of the jetty, three of Jonquil's boats were bobbing merrily in the harbour. He was spoiling the Egyptians.

Past the jumble of hydrangeas and fuchsia-hung cottages I looked up the steep lane towards the house I suppose was Sheila Fabian's. I looked at it a long time, thinking that she might be somewhere there, and probably Old Horny too. I liked that house on sight. It was built of reddish-brown

28

stone, half-covered with a close creeper that was beginning to turn coppery. It had a lot of gables, and wide low windows with dripstones over them.

Looking at that house, I began to feel depressed. I wasn't sure of my ground. I was here to prevent something happening, that's all. There wasn't going to be much action, I thought. But I'd thought wrong. There'd been a lot already, and another spot was blowing up right under my nose.

Apart from isolated parties like the one that had brought Jonquil his custom, Rhuine quietens down most days after tea. I could almost have counted the parties within sight. Under the lea of the jetty was a family party, having a quiet picnic. Past the harbour, walking away from me across the shingle, was a couple who might have been father and daughter or September and April. Being a natural cynic, I suspected the latter.

He was a well-preserved specimen with white hair, and he wore nothing that hot night but maroon trunks. She wore the feminine equivalent, but three inches briefer, plus, I supposed, a brassiere. I only supposed it because there wasn't anything visible from the back. It was probably a cantilever type that stayed put without struts. Or she might use glue.

She had bleached hair that looked nearly as white as his against shoulders the colour of clover-honey. I suspected September and April because a blonde of that calibre doesn't normally take her father walking across the beach at quarter past six of a Sunday evening.

I strolled back to the Dolphin, noticing on the way that Isaiah Jonquil wasn't anywhere in sight. That struck me as curious, because I should have thought he would have been keeping his eye on the boats that were out or else soliciting more custom. I picked up my bag and went into the pub. It didn't look the sort of place that caters for meals, but you never know. And I badly wanted something to kill the taste of the sausage rolls and twopence-a-cup moisture they had

29

sold me at the Shilstone eatery.

You never know. . . . Within ten minutes I was sitting down to beefsteak pie, with loganberry tart and cream and good coffee to follow. I didn't see anything of Monkeyface. I was tended by a thin, ugly, and efficient waitress who didn't take my mind off the food. Only snack-counters have to trouble about glamour and plunging necklines.

It was quarter past seven when I finished. I didn't know what time they dined at Edward's Bounty, so I thought I'd take a stroll round the lower part of the village and get the lie of the land before presenting myself. And walking towards the stone bridge I saw the blonde and her escort again.

But this time they weren't so close together. Probably father had been giving daughter good advice, or sweetie had been telling daddy where he got off the bus. Well, that happens.

They walked sulkily towards the foot of North Score. Man and girl both wore wraps now, probably parked till required among the boulders. I should say they needed them, for the breeze was getting cooler. They ambled along, stood a minute near the bridge, then parted without enthusiasm. The girl went up the Score and the man in the opposite direction.

Then I saw Isaiah Jonquil, and if the old porpoise wasn't following the girl with intent, my eyes were weakening. He walked twenty yards behind, looking unconcerned the way you do in those circumstances. By all the rules of the game, Sugar Daddy shouldn't have seen what was happening, but he had left a towel on the tubular steel rails protecting the little bridge, came back for it, and caught Jonquil in the act.

It was no affair of mine. It had nothing to do with the reason I was here at Rhuine. But I was willing to make a third party. So I put my bag behind the wall and proceeded to do so.

30

Up the Score we went. . . . The girl first, Jonquil next, Sugar Daddy third, and me bringing up the rear. Or that's what I thought. But I wasn't. Someone was following me, too. I could have sat down among the hydrangeas and laughed when I realised that. I—or we—were being followed by a thin, adolescent-looking man with the pastiest face I had ever seen, dressed in Sunday best and looking as cheerful as a condemned man having to eat his last breakfast-egg with no salt.

I thought quickly. I turned all innocent and stopped to look in the post-office window till the pasty-faced man had passed me by. I wanted everything in front of me.

I saw the girl go down three steps into a tiny garden and unlock the back door of a cottage. She waited there till Jonquil joined her, and they went inside together. At that, Sugar Daddy folded his arms inside his wrap and looked like Jasper Murgatroyd in a barnstorming melodrama. He took twenty seconds to decide. Then he too went down the steps and over the garden. He didn't trouble to knock. He put up his foot and the door-sneck gave way. But he shut the door behind him, which was disappointing from my angle.

I had been so engrossed, watching this development, that I hadn't thought of Pasty Face. When I looked round, he simply wasn't there. By that time the sun had gone behind the headland and that corner of Rhuine was getting murky as well as cool, so it was easy to do a vanishing act. I forgot him and watched the cottage window.

It was approximately three feet square. I was reminded of watching a circus on a television screen. Not one of them was in line with the window at that moment, but I started to hear voices. The girl's, then Jonquil's, then Sugar Daddy's.

It went on for ten minutes. They were now passing the window and re-passing it, and I saw what didn't surprise me at all. The two men were fighting it out. I wouldn't have known which to put my money on, but it seemed Jonquil was getting the worst of it. Any minute, with all that din, I expected the neighbours to come running. But they didn't. And the fight must have been inconclusive, for the verbal battle was starting up again.

It happened so quickly, I didn't realise I was hit. The girl had said something in a sobbing sort of voice, and Sugar Daddy must have objected. He hit her with the flat of his hand and she dropped out of sight. But next second there was a crash and something put an inch-long gash in my wrist. It would have been my face if my reactions had been slower.

I looked down. I had stopped the lower half of a milk bottle in full flight. I judged it was time to make my presence heard if not felt.

So I pushed open the sneckless door. I didn't get into the main battle-ground, however, for Sugar Daddy was on his way out, and we met in the kitchen. There was blood on his face, a lot of it. I surmised that the milk bottle had smashed against the wall, cut him first, crashed through the window, and slit my wrist as an afterthought. Not bad for a pint-size bottle hurled by a pint-size girl. It had probably worked more hexecution than Jonquil's duck-shooter.

The man glared at me, then went on his way to the kitchen sink and washed away the surplus blood. Always polite, I awaited my turn. The inner door was still shut, and whatever way Jonquil and the girl were passing the time, they made no noise about it.

"And who in hell," asked Sugar Daddy, "are you, and what are you doing here?"

"An innocent bystander," I said. "On my way from Evensong I heard ungodly sounds and gave way to curiosity." I looked at my still-bleeding wrist. "Now, I wish I hadn't."

I nodded towards the gash. His, not mine. "It might be an idea," I went on, "to do something about that."

I produced my first-aid kit, always carried in view of the queer things that happen to me, from my hip-pocket. It comprised elastic adhesive and a phial of iodine. Judging that his wound was less than stitchworthy, I applied the iodine and then the adhesive. It was with some satisfaction that I observed his wince.

Next, I started to do the same for myself. But, not to be outdone in gallantry, he applied iodine and adhesive to me, then we stood looking at each other. I wished I dare push open the middle door to see what was happening in the next room, but judged it wiser not. The girl was crying now, and I fancied I could hear Jonquil muttering something.

So I said to Sugar Daddy, "What comes next? Are you going back for the other half of the bottle?"

He glared at me, pushed me aside, and stalked across the little garden. I followed him into North Score. But he didn't speak to me any more, or even turn around. He continued his stalking and turned into the Spanish Galleon.

Which was almost the end of that little episode. But not quite. For coming thoughtfully back towards my own chosen pub, I remembered the white-faced man who had disappeared. I walked down the alleyway to the back of the girl's cottage, wondering if he could have found a way out at the other end. But he hadn't. There was a light burning in the cottage and the curtains were drawn, but they didn't quite meet across the window. And with his white bulbous nose screwed close to the pane, peek-a-booing on whatever was taking place inside, was my lost friend.

And as I watched, he went softly to the door, tapped, and went in. I stood rubbing my chin, remembering that Jonquil was still there.

I'd craved action and it had come dead on time, even if it had nothing to do with the matter in hand. Clearly, Rhuine was a lively little place. A place where old fishermen chase rich men's mistresses and bottles are thrown with all the gay abandon of a Soho Saturday night. I should have kept out of it. All I had to show for my pains was a cut wrist and a

33

lot of jumbled thoughts.

Away from the houses it seemed a little lighter. My watch said it was only twenty past eight. I picked up my bag from behind the wall, went into the Dolphin bar, and had another glass of rough cider. They should have sold it by the pound, not the pint. Then I began to think seriously about showing up at Edward's Bounty and reporting to Sheila Fabian.

When I came out of the pub I saw Jonquil, never showing a sign of his adventure, tying his boots on the high-water mark. He looked up as I passed, but didn't speak beyond a respectful salutation.

I turned up the lane from the harbour mouth. It was labelled Church Staithe. Then I saw a still shorter cut, a steep, narrow track with Yeo's Jinkin painted on a house end. I remembered hearing that name, and for some reason I gave a shiver.

It was then I saw Peter.

I should have thought he would have been in bed by that hour. But he was sitting astride the wall. Yeo's Jinkin was cut into the hillside, with rising ground to the right and a sharp drop over that wall to the left. He was looking over that drop as if he liked it.

"You'll do a Humpty-Dumpty act if you don't cling tight," I said.

He looked up and saw me. I got a queer feeling. I must be crazy, I thought, coming to this place under an assumed name when two brats aged seven and five knew who I was.

"I shall never fall," he said.

I went to the wall and looked over.

"That's Mrs. Crummett's back-yard," he told me. "Down there."

It was all of fifty feet below. The fact that it was a nice wall, with things growing out of the crevices, didn't make me feel any happier. Mrs. Crummett's back-yard looked mostly a chicken-run, with a tiled shed backing up to the

34

house. I had an impulse to pull him off the wall by force, but resisted it.

"I'm looking for a Mrs. Fabian," I said. He lifted his leg over the wall and slid down to the cobbles. "Do you happen to know where she lives?"

"What do you think?" he said. "Mrs. Fabian's my mother. I'll show you."

He trotted along beside me. We climbed the hill to Church Staithe, then along the lane. When we came to a wrought-iron gate in the high garden wall of Edward's Bounty he nodded casually towards it.

"Through there," he said.

"Thanks," I said. "Isn't it time you were in bed?"

"I go to bed when I like."

I looked at him, hard. He had heard me say I was Lee Vaughan. He had stood in my office above Covent Garden and listened to everything that was said.

"I'm your mother's cousin," I told him. "That makes me second cousin to you. I've come from Australia. My name is Harry Cardew."

"Mummy's at home," he volunteered. "I think she's expecting you."

I nodded. "See you later, then. Unless you're coming in with me?"

"Not yet," he said. "I've a 'pointment. With Jonquil."

"Have a good time," I told him.

I lugged my bag up the drive, between an avenue of well-grown trees. The house looked to me as if it were the only place in the world, and as if it had been there half as long as time. To the left of the porch, three windows were lit up. It was a stone-roofed porch, like a lych-gate, with stone benches on each side of it. The main door was in two sections, of oak, with linenfold carving. One half was ajar. I pulled an iron handle beside the jamb, put down my bag and waited.

I was to have a lot of shocks before coming through that door for the last time, but never a bigger one than I had at that moment. For the man who answered the bell was the pale-faced snooper with the bulbous nose whom I had last seen opening the cottage door off North Score.

I kept my poker face. I told him who I was—or who I wasn't—and he picked up my bag and carried it into the stone-flagged hall. He didn't give anything away either. Probably he didn't recognise me.

There was nothing in that hall but rush-matting and two oak chests and an open-hearth fireplace with fire-dogs and a copper log-box. I saw two doors off to the left, but we went past these to a corridor that opened up from the back of the hall. At the end of that corridor was another door leading into the room with the three lighted windows I had seen from the drive.

Paleface opened the door and I went in. It was the biggest inhabited room I had ever entered, carpeted in one piece and with more things in it than I could have catalogued in a month, yet it looked bare.

My eyes went straight to Sheila Fabian. She was sitting by the fire. A Corgi dog looked up, snuffed and wuffed, then put its head flat down again on the carpet. I noticed that Sheila had some kind of embroidery on her knees, and beside her was a box filled with dozens of reels of silks and cottons, all colours of the rainbow.

Then I looked past her to another figure stooped over a radio-console, thirty feet or so away, and if ever I needed my poker face it was then. Something thumped me straight in the kidneys. It was a well-preserved man of fifty or so, with a head of snow-white hair. And on his cheek was a strip of adhesive put there by my own hands less than an hour earlier.

I pulled myself together.

I had to remember that I was acting a part. I couldn't afford a slip-up. The next few minutes might be sticky. I ignored the man and spoke to Sheila.

"Well," I said, "you've altered a lot since last time I saw you, Sheila."

She looked up at me, smiling. Smiling this time with pure pleasure. But not account of seeing me, I reminded myself sharply. Just seeing somebody.

"You've grown up a lot in eight years," I said. I felt I was good. I could almost have believed I was her cousin Harry Cardew.

"You've altered too," she told me, and it gave me a kick to hear that voice again with its husky overtones. "Somehow I thought I'd never see you again."

"Didn't I always say I'd be back?"

"Stuart," she said over her shoulder, "this is Harry."

He came over, walking like a big heavy cat. I put out my hand. He looked at me. He knew how to control himself too, but there was a tic in his cheek.

"We're old friends," I said easily. He must have thought I was going to give him away, and for a second I saw the devil in his eyes. Then I added easily: "It was Stuart I talked to over the phone."

The tic was there again. He had a grip like iron. Iron wrapped in satin. The skin of his hand was so soft and pliable that I thought, till I looked down, that he must be wearing doeskin gloves.

"Hurt your face?" I asked.

"I fell on the shingle," he replied.

"Nasty," I said. "You'll have to be more careful."

He let go my hand. "Glad you've decided to come," he told me. "Had a good journey?"

"I got in an hour or two ago and took a look round. You've chosen a nice place to live."

"Very nice," he agreed. "A shade monotonous at times, perhaps."

"I wouldn't have thought that. I had the impression it was the kind of place where anything might happen." I smiled. I hoped it was a meaning smile.

"Rhuine certainly has its points. . . . I take it this is your first visit?"

"First, and I suppose it'll be my last. For a good many years, anyway."

"When did you last have a meal?" Sheila asked.

"Seven o'clock at the Dolphin."

"Why didn't you come straight here?"

"I saw no reason to upset your domestic arrangements," I said. I turned to Fabian with what I trusted, this time, was a good-humoured grin. "I'm merely a distant relation by marriage. I hadn't actually intended coming down when I rang Sheila. It was just an enquiry. It's good of you to bother with me at all."

"You would have been here at the right time," he said. "We usually dine at seven. . . . I wasn't in, but you'd have been company for Sheila. What about a drink?"

I said I wouldn't say no to that.

"Sheila?" he said, without looking at her.

"No," she said. Then: "Oh well, yes. Sherry."

"Sherry. And Cardew . . . ?"

He had a slight, scarcely-perceptible lisp. I plumped for Scotch. He moved towards a side-table and bent over it. He was so big he seemed to stoop from a great height to perform any normal action.

While he was pouring the drinks I had my first good look at him. The white hair wasn't relevant either to his strength or his age. It was simply white and beautiful, with plenty of it brushed straight back. He looked in the pink of condition. His face was the colour of walnut, and he had deep-set eyes that showed a lot of white around the grey irises, and a big straight nose. I finished up my tour of him with his mouth, which was big and full-lipped and sensuous under a mous-

38

tache three shades darker than his hair.

You could have gone a long way and not met another man as striking.

But it was his movements that fascinated me most. I said he walked like a cat. You seemed to sense the ripple of muscles. I wondered if his body had the same doe-like skin I had felt on his hands, and that started a train of thought, not unconnected with the blonde, that I wouldn't have cared to share with Sheila.

He brought the glasses, carrying them like a practised barman: Sheila's sherry held in the crook of one finger. She took it from him. "Water?" he said to me, "or soda?"

I said neither, thanks. He had been generous with the whisky. There was a good three fingers in my glass. I took half of it at one smooth gurgle. You taste it that way.

He wasn't looking at me as he put away his own drink, and my eyes moved round the room. The light came from a brace of big standard lamps disposed in strategic positions. There was also a centre-spray of bulbs in a cruciform wooden electrolier, besides wall-brackets. A room that size needed some illumination. There was a grand piano on a kind of dais, a tapestry-covered settle that would have held six, and enough deep armchairs to furnish a theatre lounge. Nothing showy—just solid luxury. I found myself wondering if the late Mrs. Charles had made the room that way.

"It seems a long time," Sheila said, "since I heard from you."

"I didn't write because there wasn't anything good to tell you till recently." I hoped I was making a convincing job of it. "The only point in writing would have been to ask for a loan, and I'm not a good hand at that."

"What have you been doing out there?" asked Fabian.

"Most things from house-wiring to book-keeping," I said. "I went out as an electrical engineer. Worked for Stringers at first, but there wasn't much scope."

"Stringers on Park Street?" he said, and I jumped.

39

"You're not so far out." I was thankful I knew my Sydney and still more thankful I'd read up Sheila's dossier. "On Market. Know their place?"

"Only by repute. A firm I was interested in had a contract out there and we employed local people for some of the work. How's Sydney looking these days?"

"It doesn't alter," I said, "aside from getting bigger."

"Where were you living?"

"Am living," I corrected him. "Three months from now I'll be back home, don't forget . . . Up Rockdale way, off Prince's Highway. I'd a spell in Parramatta, but it's too far out."

"You're out of my depth there," he said, and I felt relieved to know it.

"How long have you been here, Harry?" asked Sheila. She hadn't touched the sherry.

"Four weeks or so. I ran up to Glasgow, then put in a few days with Craik and his wife. . . . He's living just out of Bolton now, place called Doffcocker if you can believe it. Then I went back to London by degrees, spent more than I could afford, got drunk a few times, did a few shows, and here I am."

"And when do you go back to Sydney?"

"Six weeks next Saturday. I might have stayed longer, but funds won't run to flying back."

"Still, if you have six weeks, there's no reason why you shouldn't stay a few days with us."

I put on a doubtful expression.

"A few days!" I said. "How long is that? It's nice of you to ask me and it'll be grand to talk over old times. But I had fun and games in mind when I spent all this on a trip home. I wasn't thinking of dumping myself in a place like this. You'd always a taste for the quiet life. I can't say I had."

"Rhuine, of course, is something quite exceptional among dumping-grounds," Fabian said. "You'll find it in every

40

amateur's snapshot album."

"Why?" I asked, all innocence.

"Simply because it's Rhuine, I imagine. Rhuine the unique, the unspoilt, the incomparable, the Artist's Paradise."

"It's certainly a pretty place," I admitted. There was an undertone to his words that I hadn't missed. "But when you talk like that . . ."

Fabian laughed. If it was meant to be a pleasant laugh, it just didn't make the grade.

"Don't think I'm underrating your tastes, Cardew. I suppose one's reaction to Rhuine depends upon one's own mental approach to such phenomena. You may see it as an earthly nirvana or a huddle of insanitary cottages. You may appreciate its isolation; on the other hand you may think a decent bus service, one or two good hotels and a bathing pool might improve it. It's purely a question of personal preference. Either way I wouldn't blame you."

"I'll look it over," I said easily, "then tell you how it strikes me."

Without asking, he took my glass and was going to fill it again when I held up my hand. "Thanks all the same," I said, "but I'm no drinker."

That didn't stop him taking a second helping himself. This time he didn't drink socially, but hurried it down as if it were a business matter.

"I don't know," he said to Sheila, "whether you've made arrangements for Cardew?"

"There's always room," Sheila answered. "I wasn't sure whether he would stay, of course. But I thought the Punch-bowl . . ."

She turned to me. I must have looked puzzled. It sounded as if I were being grassed out to a neighbouring pub.

"We call it the Punchbowl Room because it has rather a lovely bowl in blue fluorspar. One of the largest pieces ever worked, I think. Apart from that it's quite pleasant, with a dressing-room and a bathroom, so you can stay there all day if we don't amuse you."

"I shall appreciate all that," I said. "I'm not used to such palatial luxury."

"Perhaps Cardew would like a bath now to wash away the stains of travel," Fabian suggested, and I got the idea it was less for my benefit than his own. A three-sided conversation with his wife and one of her poor relations might not be his idea of fun. "Later, we'll have another drink and a snack. I don't know what your views are, Cardew, but I don't care to go to bed on an empty stomach. And mine's usually empty after dinner at seven."

I said no doubt I could put something away in honour of the occasion, and moved to the door. Sheila came with me. I fancied there was a half-smile on Fabian's face as we left him.

When we got back to the hall, my bag had vanished. So she must have been sure enough of my staying to instruct the pale-faced manservant to take it to the appropriate room when I arrived. I followed her up a staircase ten feet wide, with an oriel window on the half-landing. I wondered if she would take advantage of the situation to say a kind word, but she didn't. And I reminded myself that after all I was a hired man. I couldn't throw my weight about here as I did in my own office.

At the head of the stairs she indicated a corridor over the one below, and said my room was at the end of it. I thanked her and went on alone. It was a medium-sized room, with a window looking away from Rhuine towards the wooded bluffs. My bag was there, unpacked. I'm not used to that kind of thing. I wondered if Paleface had seen my darned socks. My one decent blue suit was laid out, my two spare shirts neatly folded in the top drawer of a walnut chest. Across the room was a small oval table, and on it, like something floating on a shining lake, the fluorspar punchbowl. I kept looking at

42

it while I was in the room. It was a lovely thing.

I ran the bath full of scalding water and soaked in it. I changed into my blue suit, and gave myself half an hour by my watch before I started to go downstairs. Even then I didn't go down right away, because I heard a sound from beyond the next door. It wasn't quite shut. I gave it a gentle shove.

I saw two cots side by side, a few pieces of miniature furniture on an inlaid floor. There was a big doll sitting in a chair. There were a few lengths of rail-track, part of an electric train set, propped in a corner.

Ninian was in bed, asleep and murmuring as I had heard. The second cot was empty. I wondered about Peter. And as I was wondering, I noticed that a second door out of the room was open, with a chink of light showing through. Not only a self-contained guest-suite, I thought, but a self-contained nursery-block as well. Nice, if you can get it.

Then the communicating door opened a bit further, and Peter came through. He was wearing a bath-robe. I was standing in the shadow and he didn't see me. He must have been cleaning his teeth. He seemed thoughtful and self-possessed. I realised that he must have come back from Jonquil's place, let himself into the house and come to bed without reference to his elders. He took off the bath-robe, turned back the covers and got into the cot, and lay like a full-grown man for a few seconds, hands behind his head, looking at nothing. Then he reached up to the cord of a ceiling-switch and the dim bulb went out.

Something about that, the pitiful adultness of it, touched me as much as all that his mother had said.

I didn't want to startle him. I said quietly, "Good night, Pete."

He reached for the cord again and put on the light.

"Your cousin Harry Cardew," I said. "Remember?"

"That's all right," he said. "Good night, Cousin Harry."

"If Ninian wakes up, you might tell her I've arrived."

43

"Sure," he said. "I'll tell her. She'll be glad."

"Good night," I said again, and closed the door.

I stood outside it a minute, then went slowly downstairs.

From the half-staircase I saw a maid flitting about the hall. I wondered how many domestic staff they had. I supposed that knowledge, along with a good deal else, would come later. The girl glanced at me as I came down the second flight, and said, "Good evening, sir," with a pleasant smile.

I said good-evening and went on to the big room where I had left Fabian and his wife. The door was open. For a moment I thought the room was empty, All but one of the lights were out. Then I saw Sheila standing alone at a single window on the seaward side.

Earlier, I hadn't even noticed that window. Her back was towards me. Two semi-circular steps went up to a little platform in the embrasure. On a ledge running the whole way round were two copper bowls full of early chrysanthemums. She turned and saw me, but didn't speak. I went up the steps and joined her.

"Where's Stuart?" I asked conversationally.

"He went out twenty minutes ago. Usually he isn't home before midnight, but he's coming back earlier in your honour. Or so he says. . . . Do you play snooker?"

"Billiards," I said. "I'm not so good at potting."

I looked past her through the window. I could see all the lower part of Rhuine: the bridge and the Dolphin, lights in the cottage windows, lights at the pier-head, riding-lights on a yacht anchored in the bay. And all the sea and sky between Rhuine and Ireland. There wasn't a breath of wind. It was still as a picture, like something painted on an act-drop.

I came down the steps and she followed me.

"I've just seen Peter," I said. "He's gone to bed."

"Yes?"

"I saw him earlier too. He told me he was going to see

Jonquil. I supposed it would be Luke. Isaiah was at the harbour when I left the Dolphin."

"He spends a lot of time with Luke." She added, after a thoughtful minute: "I hope Peter's knowledge doesn't worry you."

I didn't reply directly to that. "*Heaven lies about us in our infancy,*" I said. "*Shades of the prison-house begin to close upon the growing boy.*"

She looked up quickly. She had long, lovely lashes, and I saw they were wet. "I would never have suspected you of that," she said.

"I once learned to read. The trick stays with you, like cycling and swimming."

I looked at the long-case clock. It was twenty past ten.

"Who plays the piano?" I asked.

"Ghosts," she said without moving.

"Can't you make any reasonable sort of noise?"

I was thinking that up there on the dais, if the music didn't require more than normal concentration, two people could talk.

She sat down at the piano and started to play. She was no genius, but better than average. She fooled around for a while, then started one of Poulenc's *Mouvements Perpetuels.* It was Number One. I knew that much. I had a good education even if it was largely wasted on me.

Over her shoulder she said: "Be careful of Dillon. It was Dillon who took your bag upstairs."

"You mean Paleface," I said.

"He's Stuart's man. He came with us from Richmond. All the others are local. Rose and Phoebe are Rhuine girls, Cook comes from Shilstone."

"So much for Dillon," I said. "Awaiting further orders."

She came to the end of the Poulenc and looked up at me, her hands limp on the keys. "Did I play that very badly?"

"I've heard better," I said, "but I could bear you to go

through it twice more."

But she started playing something else; something warm and lazy that I knew but couldn't place.

"I've no orders to give." She spoke over her shoulder again. "You're my cousin. What you learn from your own observation and what you decide to do about it are your own affairs."

"I see. *Carte blanche.*"

"*Carte blanche.*"

"You don't even answer questions from now on, is that it? I use my own eyes. The other day it was the choosey agent and the beseeching client. Now it's the princess and the jester. Dillon's your husband's man, I'm yours."

"Isn't that a satisfactory arrangement?"

"It might be if we'd started on a footing of mutual understanding. But I've come to the conclusion that you could have told me a lot more."

"About . . . ?"

"Yourself, to begin with. There's something behind all this that I don't understand."

"Perhaps I could tell you more. . . . But it would confuse the issue. Please take my word for that. The issue as far as you are concerned is simply Rhuine and the children."

"Simply!" I repeated. "I rather like that."

"What is it you want to know about me?"

"I can think of six things, but I don't think you'd tell me any one of them. If you did, I should be wondering if you'd given me the right answers, and life's complicated enough without that. I'll find out what I want to know in my own way. There's an extra one you might answer, though. It's about Peter. This prejudice he has against Old Horny. . . . What's at the back of it?"

She hesitated. "I don't know."

"You're his mother, and you say you don't know what he has against your husband?"

46

"Peter and Ninian are both old in the head," she answered obliquely. "They've had the run of the village ever since we came. There's no danger from traffic and they swim like fish. Obviously, they've heard people talking. As you heard, Ninian is quite aware that Phoebe considers Lora a whore."

She looked up from the piano. "Funny what a horrible, filthy sound that word has. . . . But I suppose Lora is. And besides hearing second or third-hand scandal, Peter must have seen a number of things under this roof that have made him think."

"Such as . . . ?"

She stopped playing. "Oh, any number of things!"

She said it enigmatically, and I wondered why. Why had she been so frank in some directions—even letting me read the Charles correspondence, for instance—and yet so cagey in others?

It was a long piano stool. I sat at one end of it, my hands around my knees. She started playing again; the same warm, honey-smooth thing she had broken off a moment ago. It came to me what it was and where I had last heard it.

It was *Liebestraum* by Liszt. Not the da . . da . . da . . . di-da-di-da-di-da . . da one, but a more subtle number in the same series you don't hear so often. And I'd last heard it during a war-time leave when I was sitting one night in the Cornmill Theatre. I'm an emotional type, and that night I was maudlin with whisky. I remember wondering how the hard-worked pianist in that palace of decortication could bear to play that sad and lovely thing when any moment half a ton of T.N.T. might have ripped the braid off his trousers.

Hearing it now made me feel maudlin and emotional again. I tried to cover it by being hard-boiled.

"Every question I have to ask an outsider is going to cost you money," I said.

"That isn't your worry. You can have anything you ask

47

for. I don't want to see any expense-accounts. You should be able to make quite a good thing out of this. I have no check on you."

"That isn't a very nice thing to say."

She flung me a quick look. There was something more warm and impulsive than I had yet heard in her voice as she said: "I'm sorry. I'm truly sorry. It was a beastly thing to say. Please forgive me."

She put her hand on my arm for a moment, then went on playing. I got up. I walked away from her, went to the window and stood there looking out over Rhuine.

I'd struck some queer things in my time, but nothing queerer than this. All of Rhuine, this narrow strip of heaven with the harbour and the ravine and the cottages, belonged to that slender packet of glamour and mystery playing Liszt on the dais yonder. It didn't seem natural.

After a while I began to prowl around the room. I tried one chair and another. I looked at the books in the fall-front cases that flanked the fireplace. There was everything in them from county histories to Sinclair Lewis. I wondered if Stuart or Sheila Fabian had bought any of them or if they had all been inherited.

By the time eleven o'clock struck, I was beginning to doubt Fabian's promise to return early. Either of the local pubs would have turned him out before this. By quarter past, when he still hadn't put in an appearance, Sheila rang the bell and told the maid to bring some food. I said I would just have milk to drink if she didn't mind. Ten minutes later the girl came back with a tray. There were two glasses of hot milk and a silver basket piled with chicken sandwiches. I was hungrier than I thought, and made good use of them.

At quarter to midnight there was still no sign of Fabian, and I said I felt tired and would like to go to bed. So, Sheila told me, would she. Stuart certainly wouldn't expect anyone to wait up longer than this. I said good night and went up to

48

my room. Before I reached the end of the corridor I heard the piano again. She had gone back to the Liszt, and hearing it made me clench my hands, and I noticed they were damp with sweat.

I went past the night nursery and opened my own door. I didn't close it behind me. That was force of habit. In most hotels where I stay, one has to go along the corridor to the bathroom. Then I remembered I was living in unaccustomed style, and went over to pull it shut.

But half-way there I heard a footstep, and next moment Dillon stopped respectfully with one foot just inside the room. He called me sir, and asked if there was anything else I would be requiring.

"No thanks," I said. "Not tonight. But if you're waiting up for Mr. Fabian, you might tell him I've turned in because I'm tired. I'll lose to him at snooker some other time."

"Very well sir," Dillon said. "I'll tell Mr. Fabian."

"Strange to these parts, aren't you?" I asked idly.

"I came with Mr. Fabian from the London district, sir."

"I thought so. You haven't acquired the local tan yet."

He smiled. "I haven't as many opportunities as I might like to bask on the beach, sir." His voice was smooth and silky, like Fabian's skin.

"I suppose you do get out, though? I'd have thought Sunday evening was a good time."

I couldn't see his eyes. "As a matter of fact I do take an occasional stroll, sir. I did tonight. But there isn't much to do in Rhuine."

"No?" I said. "Quiet and peaceful place, eh?"

"Oh, very quiet!" He smiled again. "Good night, sir."

"Good night," I said.

He closed the door. I sat on the bed, listening to the creak of the old boards in the corridor as he padded away. It wasn't till three minutes later that an unpleasant thought struck me. I slipped off my blue jacket, the one Dillon had unpacked, and looked at the tab on the lining.

It was the tab of a not-very-good tailor on the Hampstead Road.

I lit a cigarette and thought that one over. Dillon might not have seen it. Or, having seen it, he might have thought it was a suit I had bought in London since coming from Australia. But it had been worn a lot. . . . And Dominion visitors with money enough for a three-months' stay in the Old Country don't usually seek out obscure tailoring establishments north of Marylebone Road.

Well, there was nothing I could do about it now. If it became necessary later, I might be able to cover myself. And certainly most of my other effects were convincing, even to a copy of the Sydney *Sun*, sent over by a friend, that I'd used for packing.

I got into bed, still smoking, and tried to forget it. Or, rather, I tried to push the doubt to the back of my mind and concentrate on other things.

And there were plenty to concentrate on.

When I started taking my impressions to pieces, I found I wasn't half as much disturbed by facts as by feelings. That was unusual for me. I'm a highly-imaginative man, and for that reason I've schooled myself to keep my imagination and the intuitions rising out of it pretty well in check. You can't go through life with an uncontrolled Plus-X imagination unless you want to finish in the loony-bin. I like to judge and act by facts.

But the facts I tried to grapple with didn't add up to the right total. Nor did the people.

Fabian, the white-haired giant. Sheila, his lovely wife. The frighteningly-adult Peter. The blonde in the strapless swimsuit, who must be Lora. The white-faced Dillon. . . .

I couldn't think of them as real people. They were like characters waiting in the wings for something to happen.

I lay back and thought about Dillon's unnecessary unpacking of my scanty possessions. About Peter going unobserved to bed. About Fabian's trip after dark and his non-return. About Dillon's late-night visit to my room—which, I felt sure, was for some reason quite unconnected with anxiety for my comfort.

I thought about the fracas at Lora's cottage. I'd wondered, during the last hour, whether to tell Sheila about that, but had decided against it.

And last and longest, I thought about Sheila.

In my office, I had outlined her obvious course. It remained just as obvious. Legally, there wasn't a thing Fabian could do within the limits of Rhuine, providing that the place was owned absolutely by his wife and everything was in order regarding entail.

Peter, I told myself, was as far out of Fabian's jurisdiction as Rhuine was. If Fabian's influence was in any way detrimental to the child's character, Sheila could simply send him away to school.

As for Ninian, a strong-minded nurse in the house would do the trick.

While Lora could be taken care of by any divorce lawyer. She was, in fact, the obvious instrument of Sheila's permanent release.

I'd said most of that earlier, to Sheila. I said it again now to myself.

So what? I asked myself.

On the surface, I was here because Sheila had so exhausted herself, combating the forces ranged against her, that she needed someone to think and act on her behalf. And in my office, she had certainly given me that impression.

She might still be exhausted. . . . The Sheila I had just left was as cool and capable and intelligent as any woman I had ever met, but she might have rallied her resources, knowing she wasn't fighting alone any more.

I couldn't be sure of that. But it came to me—and I felt

my skin pricking at the thought of it—that I had been brought to this house for some purpose I wasn't even beginning to understand.

I lay smoking and staring at the fluorspar punchbowl. That thought wasn't a good lullaby. It was a long time before I went to sleep.

WHITE-HEADED BOY

WHEN I came down to breakfast next morning, I found Fabian and his wife in a small room off the hall. I learned as the days passed that breakfast was invariably a sideboard meal at Edward's Bounty, probably because they never showed up at the same time.

By daylight Fabian's hair seemed whiter than ever, and his colour ruddier. As I came into the room he gave me a nod that was meant to be friendly and asked me if I had slept well. I told him I always did, and added the futile crack about having a good conscience.

"Sorry I couldn't get home earlier last night," he said. "I was detained."

"That sounds like the time-honoured late-at-the-office story," I said. "Surely you haven't business activities in a spot like this?"

He laughed insincerely and said he didn't quite mean it

52

that way. But a number of people with interests in London or the north spent their summer months hereabouts, and he made it a habit to keep in touch with them as far as possible.

"You'll have to meet some of them before you leave," he said. "A good contact is always useful."

I said I appreciated that.

"How do you like to spend your leisure hours?" he asked. "There's plenty of swimming and fishing here, and you might get a bit of rough shooting over Shilstone way."

I said that outdoor sports had never appealed to me. "And before I went in the water," I told him, "you'd have to heat it up to the temperature at Bondi."

I helped myself to roes and anchovy. As I was doing so, the Corgi waddled into the room and sniffed at my ankles. I imagine he approved of them. Sheila called him over, and I noticed his name was Atkin. I thought it an odd name for a dog. But then, I once knew a girl called Savina Enfrida.

The coffee, I was glad to see, lived in an earthenware pot. I don't like the percolated stuff, preferring to feel the grounds between my teeth. Sheila poured me out a cup. She didn't look at me as I took it, but remarked absently: "You've a loose button on your jacket, Harry."

I glanced down at the button. Till then I hadn't noticed it. I was on my guard. I had put on the suit I had travelled in yesterday, a Donegal tweed. I saw Fabian look at it. He was probably comparing its age and quality with his own, a careless stroller that must have cost thirty-five guineas in the Arcade. Also, it had probably reminded him of my blue suit upstairs—if, that is, Dillon had confided in him the circumstances of the reach-me-down tailor's tab. I thought there could be no harm in confusing any issue that might have arisen, so I casually remarked that I hadn't brought much over in the way of clothes.

"Thought I'd buy something in London to take back," I said. "Even the suit I was wearing last night was borrowed."

Somebody made polite throat-noises. Probably of interest, probably of sympathy. I went on to talk about the man Craik who lived at Doffcocker near Bolton, who was about my size, and who had said that until I fitted myself out there was a blue suit lying fallow in his wardrobe that I could use.

When I am in form, my lying is powerful and smooth as a new Rolls. Sheila looked rather mystified. I made a mental note that I must tell her, the first time we were alone, exactly what that elaborate slab of deceit had signified. I only hoped the slab was big enough to cover the tailor's tag.

A maid I hadn't seen before came in with the morning papers, and for twenty minutes or so we scanned them over. Then I said that if it was all the same to them, I'd take a turn round the town.

"Drop into the Galleon any time after half-past eleven," Fabian invited. "You'll find me there, and I'll introduce you to a few of the local types."

I said I probably would. I picked up my raincoat from the hall and left the house by the front door. I didn't see a soul till I reached the end of Church Staithe, and then it was one of the local inhabitants. The time of the visiting coaches was not yet.

Deciding to explore South Score, I turned uphill to the left. By now the sun was really hot, and I began to wish I had left my coat at home. Half-way up, I sat on one of the garden walls to cool off. The top of that wall had already been polished by some thousands of bottoms, I decided, before mine had graced it. Rhuine is a place where you frequently stop and sit and look.

Sitting and looking now, I couldn't believe in the place. It was fantastic, with its cobbles and cottages and fuchsias and steps and passages and walls, all packed against one another so steeply that a good shove, it seemed, would send the whole lovely, crazy street tumbling into the harbour. Teashoppe Englande. . . . And for every hydrangea round

54

the door there was maybe a business-like cash-register just inside. Yes, you could safely say that. But it was all done so well, better than I had ever seen in any other place.

I was getting up to resume my walk when I saw Peter, strolling down the Score. I hadn't been thinking about him, and seeing him there gave me a mild shock. I supposed he had got up, bathed and dressed himself, breakfasted alone, and left the house without a by-your-leave from his mother or anyone else. He saw me and stopped, looking at me across the cobbles.

"Taking a morning walk?" I said.

"Sort of."

"Where've you been, Pete?"

"Oh, wandering around."

"Going home now?"

"I'm going to Jonquil's place."

"Where is Jonquil's place?" I asked.

"He lives in the Brickhole, next to his brother, but the garden's up here. He hasn't come yet. Want to see it?"

I thought it might be a good idea. I went with him along the alley. Past the houses it became a narrow path between thorn hedges. We seemed to have reached the outposts of civilisation so far as Rhuine was concerned; beyond us were the woods.

But Peter pushed open a nailed gate, and there in front of us was a clearing among the trees. If Peter spent a lot of time there I couldn't blame him. That garden looked as if it had first been tilled by Old Adam. There was a shed with a tarred roof and little square window-panes. Beside it were heaps of loam and leaf-mould and sand, and down one side of the garden ran a thin trickle of a stream, coming out of the woods and seeping towards the village.

"That's where I get frog-spawn and taddies," Peter told me abstractedly.

"What do you do with them? Take them home?"

"Not now. I keep them in Luke's shed."

"Luke Jonquil must be pretty fond of you," I said. He didn't seem to think that merited a reply. "Do you spend a lot of your time here?"

He nodded. "Sometimes I sleep here."

"What does your mother say about that?"

"She doesn't say anything."

"Doesn't she come looking for you?"

"She doesn't care as long as I keep out of Old Horny's way." He looked past me, a trick his mother had. It wasn't an evasion of the eye; it was as if he—and she—could see something in the distance of brooding interest.

"I keep the taddies till they start growing legs, then I put them back in the stream."

"Sound idea, Pete," I said.

"I did take some home. . . . But when they started growing legs, Old Horny put them down the lavatory."

I scratched the back of my neck. I saw his eyes fill with tears; they spilled over and ran down his brown face. He made no attempt to wipe them away. Maybe he accepted the inevitability of tears in the world he was inheriting.

"Pete—" I began, then shut down. He looked at me out of those wet wide eyes and I turned away.

"Well?" he said to my back.

"I wondered if there was anything else you'd like to tell me about Old Horny's habits?"

He stood with his hands in his pockets, his lower lip stuck out, shuffling his feet on the path.

"Anything about Old Horny and the Jonquil family, for instance," I went on. "I've not forgotten that good advice about the way to break a man's knee-cap, you know."

"You want to ask Isaiah," he said. "You wait till you get talking to Isaiah. Isaiah says Old Horny's a bloody lousy bastard."

I swallowed that. . . . It stuck, but I swallowed it. On

56

top of the anchovy it didn't taste so good.

"And then there's Lora," I said.

"Oh, Lora! She's all right."

"I gathered from what you said the other day that you've a soft spot for Lora."

"She's all right. She buys me ice-cream on the beach. Nearly every morning. They're always down on the beach early."

"You mean Lora and Old Horny?"

"Horny? He's never up that early. Lora and the Poskett. Poskett's an artist. She paints Lora without any clothes on. You ought to see her. Lora, I mean. She's a smasher."

I blinked, and it wasn't the sun in my eyes. "And she buys you ice-cream," I said. "Does she know who you are?"

"Of course. Everybody knows who I am."

"What is Lora's second name?" I asked.

"Don't know." He was silent a moment, jingling coins in his pocket. "She's just Lora. Nobody really likes her but me and the Poskett.

I thought it was time to change the subject, so I asked if he would like to walk up to the village with me, but he shook his head. He was going to wait for Luke. He knew where the shed key was. I nodded, patted him on the shoulder, man-to-man fashion, and returned to the cobbled street.

I walked to the top, where the houses began to thin out as the street grew less steep. By then it was eleven o'clock, and I walked slowly back to the harbour and dropped into the Dolphin for a sun-up. The cider was rougher than ever. I had a second glass, wondering how many more I could have stood without feeling the weight in my head. Not many, I fancied.

Till then, I hadn't made up my mind whether or not to call at the Spanish Galleon. I decided I would. I walked up the Score and went in. It presented a big contrast to the

Dolphin. There were no blue-jersied fishermen spitting into the sawdust. At one time it might have been an ordinary honest pub, but not so long ago it had been rookery-nookeried like a Thames-side cocktail palace. Apparently it catered to the classier tourist fraternity and the top-drawer local residents.

It was well-patronised, too, considering the hour. I've never been one for drinking much before evening, and not too much then, but there were several people in the bar who wouldn't have agreed with me. When my eyes got accustomed to the religious dimness, I saw Fabian with his back to the bar counter, talking into the face of a little fat man who was nodding at every second word. The Corgi, looking bored, was lying with half-shut eyes under Fabian's legs.

I didn't break in. I glanced around, trying to detect possible friends or enemies. It wasn't easy. They were a well-breeched, self-satisfied crowd if appearances were anything to judge by, with the usual percentage of young and not-so-young bleachettes. One woman whose posterior seemed to be screwed down to a red-leatherette stool stared at me haughtily. I thought she was going to ask for my membership card. She had the face of an old horse under television make-up. I stared back and put out my tongue just far enough to pretend at licking my lips. That usually beats down a starer's eyes.

Beyond Fabian and the fat man was a thin, nondescript individual who was also staring at me, but not offensively. It was a tolerant, interested look. I felt drawn to him because his suit was probably the only one in that place older and shabbier than mine, and I half-hoped he would give me an excuse to pass the time of day.

But he didn't, so I went up to the counter and asked for something short. If I had any drinking at all to do, I might as well take something that would loosen up my inhibitions. I have plenty.

58

I swilled the short stuff round in its glass, the way the connoisseurs do. I was listening to Fabian's statements and the fat man's agreements. I heard the name Boldry two or three times, and wondered who Boldry was. Then Fabian saw me out of his eye-corner and stopped breathing into the fat man's face. I pushed my way through the merry throng. Fabian, as soon as I was abreast of him, told me the fat man's name was Mackender, and told him that I was a cousin of his wife's from down under.

"Sheep-farming?" asked Mackender.

"Never saw a sheep except in a butcher's shop," I said.

"Retired?"

"Twenty years ago, when I was eighty," I said. The cider was mixing with the short stuff and taking effect. The little fat man laughed, God knows at what, till tears oozed out of his piggy eyes.

"How long y're staying?" he asked.

"A few days," I said. "Depends on how soon Fabian kicks me out."

"Mackender," said Fabian, "is one of our biggest local landowners."

"Not so big a landowner as your wife," Mackender said, and laughed again. It was an odd sort of laugh; a silent opening of his mouth to a spout-like orifice, then a soundless interval till a series of wheezes came from the back of his throat. "Not so big as your wife by a hell of a distance. Ha-ha—zzz!"

"I'm known locally," said Fabian, "as Mrs. Fabian's husband. If ever I meet Prince Albert in the Elysian fields, I shall shake him by the hand."

Mackender produced another of his unnerving, soundless laughs. "That'll be a meeting worth seeing, my lad." He turned sharply to the counter. "Three doubles."

"Not for me," I said, and he shot me a rheumy glance.

"Not for you?" he repeated. "Ha-ha—zzz! That's good!

59

Three doubles."

I looked around for a palm-pot. There didn't seem to be one.

"How long've you been here?" Mackender asked.

"Since last night," I said.

"Ha-ha—zzz! Got a lot to see yet, eh? Got a lot to learn, eh? T't't't't!" He looked at Fabian and shook his head. "Nice little place, Rhuine. Don't live in it myself. Still, a nice little place."

"Mackender lives just outside the Kingdom," explained Fabian.

"Kingdom!" said Mackender. "Ha-ha—zzz! Good, that. Have to get a passport soon, eh?" He blinked waterily. "Fabian's wife rules with a rod of iron. Don't do this, don't do that. Can't build a bloody hen-house without permission. Bad as ever the Old Woman used to be."

"Old Woman?" I said.

"Old Woman Charles. Queen Mary Louisa, damned old bitch. Took these people ten years arguing before she'd let 'em modernise the place. Ah well! Cheers . . . !"

It was too much to expect, of course, that I should get an up-to-the minute history of Rhuine this early. I wasn't surprised when Mackender steered away from the subject and started discussing horseflesh form.

But I was able to gather, from what was said between then and one o'clock, that the Galleon was the headquarters, not of the local gentry—there weren't any in the village itself, anyway—but of the retired stockbrokers and bankers who had bought up every decent bit of property between there and Shilstone.

Also, I was able to take a good look at the map hanging in the bar. It was contoured, and showed that Rhuine as owned by Sheila Fabian was nowhere more than half a mile wide, and that the rising ground on each side stretched as far as Haldom Head to the north and a cliff called The

60

Downfall to the south. Any development on those slopes would share the natural advantages of Rhuine—beach, harbour, and local shopping facilities—but completely destroy the character of the place. I could see that without telling.

What Rhuine needed was protection for a full mile north and south. Haldom Head was marked *National Trust* on the map. That might be a starting-point. I decided to do some letter-writing that night. And I shouldn't mail the letters in Rhuine.

By now I was seeing everything through a pleasant rosy haze. The man in the shabby suit wandered to the bar and invested in another pint of bitter. He put down a pound note.

"No less, Mr. Smith?" said the man behind the counter.

"Sorry."

"S'all right, Mr. Smith."

He waited till the man scraped the till; nodded thanks, and put the change into his pocket.

"Thanks, Mr. Smith."

So his name was Smith. I wasn't surprised. He went back to the wall and propped himself against it, tilting back his head and looking at me, at Fabian, at Mackender through those tolerant, rather sleepy eyes.

I was still looking for a palm-pot at quarter past one, when Fabian showed signs of breaking up the session. He was carrying a good deal of liquor by then, but didn't seem embarrassed by the fact. Neither did Mackender. The horse-faced woman still had her backside screwed down to the stool. After several pink gins she seemed to be getting melancholy. She must have been even older than she looked. She had walnut elbows and long stringy fingers like bundles of pipe-cleaners.

I didn't much like any of the people in the Galleon that morning, with the possible exception of Smith, who could have been a bus-driver down on holiday from Battersea.

"Met any of the local celebrities yet?" Mackender asked me.

"Are there any?" I said.

"Are there. . . . Ha-ha . . . zzz! What d'you say to that, Fabian?" He turned back to me. "Met the Poskett?"

"Who's the Poskett?" I asked, remembering Peter.

"You'll see, you'll see!" He wagged his head. "You'll meet the Poskett! We've a string of celebrities here, eh, Fabian? Local and imported. S'right, Fabian, isn't it? Fabian imports his own. Eh, Fabian? Ha-ha—zzz!" He drank up. "Met Mrs. Dukas yet?"

"Not to know her," I said. "Who's Mrs. Dukas?"

"One of Fabian's wife's tenants."

"You see," Fabian said mournfully. "Not my bloody tenants. My wife's bloody tenants." He gently fingered the strip of adhesive on his cheek.

"What's the odds, eh? All my worldly goods I thee endow. Sickness and in health, till death us do part, heretofore, as beforesaid, Amen! Mrs. Dukas is going to sue Fabian."

"What for?" I asked.

"Because he treads on her garden-strip every time he goes past. And because he's trained his dog to wet on her hydrangea."

"My wife's dog," Fabian said. "Even the damn dog belongs to my wife."

"Yours or the wife's, it wets on Mrs. Dukas's hydrangea. No getting away from it. Damn plant's turning blue. Damn dog must have an over-acid condition." He winked at me. "Binder?"

"For the child, or for the dog?" I asked, feeling funny for once.

"One for the road, eh?"

"No thanks."

"Well, you know best. Ev'body knows best." He shook hands with Fabian and with me, and waddled towards the

62

door, where he turned as if he had forgotten something. He had.

"Jasmine!" he said. "Jassy, I'm going."

And to my surprise the horse-faced woman slid off the stool and went to him at the door.

Fabian and I followed them out. I looked over my shoulder. The man called Smith was drinking the last of his beer and watching us over the rim of his glass. The grey eyes were sombre and thoughtful.

"Who is he?" I asked Fabian.

"That's Smith," he said, and I felt oddly deflated.

The Mackenders had turned left up the hill. We turned right. Fifty yards down, Fabian turned right again, along one of those alleys in which Rhuine abounds, and we came to the wooden footbridge I had seen earlier that morning from the other side.

"I only come this way when I'm sober," Fabian said. "When I'm drunk I go straight down the Score, over the bridge by the harbour, and up Yeo's Jinkin."

"I should imagine that's safer," I agreed.

He stopped and leaned over the wooden rail. "It wouldn't do for anyone with suicidal tendencies to live at Rhuine. The place has too many lethal drops."

"Suicidal or murderous," I said, and he looked at me sharply.

"No," he said, "that's true."

The Corgi had waddled after us and now sat between Fabian and me, unconcernedly looking down.

"Your turning up has broken the monotony," Fabian said.

"Nice of you to take it that way." I looked at the adhesive strip. The look wasn't lost on him. He smiled, but it didn't make him appear any more genial. He picked up a stone and dropped it into the ravine. It rebounded and splashed into the water. Even on such a sunny day as this, the depths of the ravine were dark, a green darkness of moss and fern. It

63

would be an unpleasant place on a black night.

"You must have seen a good deal of my wife when you were both young," he said.

"Children practically brought up together do."

"Noticed much difference in her?" He dropped another stone.

"Quite a lot," I said.

"That," he told me, "is money. Nothing like a sudden windfall of unearned increment to bring out the high-lights of one's character."

As I leaned over the rail with Fabian I wasn't too clear in the head. It was probably the short stuff. It occurred to me that there was an easy way out of all this, if only the interested people could be induced to see it.

"I think you had something," I said, "when you mentioned Prince Albert the Good to Mackender."

"You do?"

"It must be damned trying to be a prince consort. But he made a pretty good job of it."

"There may be a hell of a difference," he said, "between Victoria and Sheila."

We walked on. It wasn't till we reached the bottom of the Score that I realised, subconsciously, that Fabian hadn't troubled to stride over the little strip of unfenced garden that stood on the corner of South Score and the alley. He'd trodden on it, to the detriment of a cluster of lobelia. Also, Atkin the Corgi had joyfully be-sprinkled a hydrangea that was probably its owner's pride and joy.

We lunched together, the three of us. I was told that the children had their meals in the nursery, and that Ninian spent much time in the kitchen with Cook. Afterwards, Fabian said that he had correspondence to attend to, and Sheila that she was driving into Shilstone. If I had any shopping to do, she told me, I might as well go with her.

I put on a good act of reluctance, indifference, and finally agreement. Edward's Bounty, as I have explained, lay near the bottom of the hill. We had to climb up a narrow path along the fringe of the woods to a garage at the top, where two cars were kept. One of them was the resplendent creature I had seen in London. On this occasion, however, Sheila took out the smaller one.

We didn't talk much during that short journey, but I asked if she knew anyone named Boldry. She said Boldry was one of her few staunch friends; the local Rural District Councillor. He lived at the top of North Score and was in business as an estate agent at Shilstone.

"If I get in touch with him," I said, "is there any chance your husband will hear about it? I don't want any mines springing yet."

She said that as I was unknown in the district, there would be small danger in calling at Boldry's office. I could do that while she was otherwise engaged. Stuart would most likely go out—and here she smiled, a twisted little smile—about half-past four or five and stay out till midnight, so it wouldn't matter what time we got back.

So I arranged to meet her at five. She parked the car in the market-square and I went along the High Street to Boldry's place, where I gave my assumed name to a girl in the ante-room. There was a client with Boldry, but ten minutes later I was taken through.

Boldry was a stocky, square-faced man with a local burr and eyes shrewd as a stoat's. I realised that the policy here was cards on the table, and that's the way I tackled him. I said I wasn't wanting to buy a house. I was Sheila Fabian's cousin, up from down under, and after no more than twenty-four hours I'd come to the conclusion that something was wrong.

The corners of his mouth turned down.

"There's a lot wrong," he said. "Some of it, doubtless, due

65

to circumstances that none but the Almighty knows, for none but He, my friend, can see into the hearts of men."

That startled me. Sheila had omitted to warn me that Boldry was a staunch Methodist and a redoubtable local preacher.

I said I agreed with him, though I was interested in more practical aspects of the case than that.

"I'd no idea that Sheila was married," I said. "Not even a first time, you understand. And I still can't get used to the fact that she's inherited a fortune.

"Mrs. Fabian," he told me, "is a remarkable young woman of strong character and high integrity. And being so, she regards Rhuine as a stewardship for which she will have to answer when the Judge of all the earth calls her to account."

I said I agreed with that too.

"And," he said weightily, "she is married to an ungodly man who is trying to undo in Rhuine what generations of faithful nurture have accomplished."

"That's how it looks to me," I said. "Now, Mr. Boldry, you're on the spot. How far has this campaign of Fabian's gone, and what's the chance of checking it?"

He didn't waste words. He reached two sheets of the Six-Inch Survey from a drawer. I saw that the boundaries of Rhuine were marked in red ink. North and south of those lines were others in black.

"You might call these the marginal lands, Mr. Cardew."

"Under one ownership?"

"Ah no, my friend! Fourteen people own land bordering on Rhuine. And some of them at least would be more than willing to part with their holdings at a good profit."

"What does the acreage amount to?" I asked.

"Something like three thousand."

"And Fabian's trying to buy up those three thousand acres in job lots. . . . Can he afford it?"

"Apparently so. He's already snapped up one of the

66

choicest strips, a twenty-acre piece of land adjoining Edward's Bounty."

I remarked that it wasn't a matter of personal concern to me, because I should probably never see Rhuine again after next month, and never hear of Sheila except at Christmas. But anybody with half an eye could see she was worried, I said, and while I was here I felt I had to do all I could to help.

"Three thousand acres is a lot," I said. "But if the opposition can raise funds, why can't Sheila? What figure would you quote as the overall value?"

He was cautious about that, and pursed his lips a lot. But he thought most of the valley land would fetch fifty pounds an acre.

"A hundred and fifty thousand pounds, eh?"

"If Mrs. Fabian would put that sum at my disposal, I could guarantee the preservation of Rhuine for ever."

"Presumably she hasn't that much," I suggested.

He smiled dryly. "I can tell you in confidence that the late Mrs. Charles had investments in England alone of well over half a million."

"And everything came to Sheila," I thought aloud.

"Everything. And so the problem presents itself: Why does she not enter the market herself?" He looked at me across the table, his mouth turned down. "One is tempted to wonder," he said slowly, "if her hands are in some way tied."

"Do you think they are?" I asked.

Faced with that direct question, he folded up. So I left it alone and asked if any steps were being taken locally to fight Fabian's activities.

"A good deal of quiet work is being done underground, Mr. Cardew."

"I had that idea." I looked at him and waited.

"A man named Isaiah Jonquil is acknowledged leader of the movement."

"What's he done so far?"

"On the surface, little. . . . But he is something of a strategist. I believe his plan is to wait until Fabian and his friends have sunk their money in purchases here and there, and then strike. If Jonquil were successful, Fabian would then have nothing to show for his trouble but some hundreds or thousands of acres for which he had paid four times its market value."

I thought back to last night's episode. The cut on my wrist gave a sympathetic jerk. "So you could say that Fabian and Isaiah Jonquil are sworn enemies?"

"Exactly. And either of them would be a bad man to be up against."

"Do you know Mackender?"

"George Mackender? I do." I was getting the reverse side of Mr. Boldry's medal now. He might preach godly forbearance around the neighbourhood, but he was sharp enough in his replies. "Mackender is one of Fabian's most active associates. A man with little regard for anything but money and strong drink."

"Has he sold any of his land to Fabian?"

"Either sold it or come to some equivalent arrangement. Fabian's tentative plans provide for a luxury hotel to be built on a parcel of land owned by Mackender, immediately adjacent to the village."

"Where would it be, Mr. Boldry?"

He pointed to the plan on the desk. "There you are. Locally known as the Liquorice Gardens, Mr. Cardew. For the last three or four generations it has been let to the Jonquil family. The present tenant is one Luke Jonquil, brother to Isaiah."

All this, I felt, was adding up to something obscure but unpleasant. I was getting facts. But two streams seemed to be moving side by side; a fact stream and something else. Occasionally they seemed nearly to touch. And they were

68

never far apart. But they were separate as oil and water.

"The Jonquil factor seems to crop up pretty often," I said. "Take young Peter. . . . He seems to spend a lot of time with Luke Jonquil and his brother. I don't understand why."

"Probably because Luke Jonquil is a very child-like man," said Boldry. "He has a breadth of mind, a simplicity not often found these days. Those attributes may appeal to little Peter Charles. It is not unusual to find a close understanding between the very old and the very young."

He might have something there. But it was right away from what had brought me to see Boldry, and I didn't pursue the matter further. I asked if there were any people in the district I might approach for support.

"The Rector," he said. "The Jonquils, of course. The landlord of the Dolphin. . . . I am a temperance advocate, Mr. Cardew, but aside from his interests in the liquor traffic, the man is to be depended upon. And Miss Poskett—yes, I think you might profitably get in touch with her."

"I seem to have heard that name before," I said.

"And if your stay in Rhuine is of any length, you will no doubt hear it again. Miss Poskett is one of our most commanding local characters. And any time you wish for such further enlightenment as I can give you, by all means call and see me again."

I said I appreciated that and it was more than likely he would be seeing me.

"Either here on any weekday or in Rhuine. The name of my house there is Abel's Corner."

"Before I go," I said, "is there anything worth knowing about Dillon?"

"There I can't help you."

"Or about a fire in the coach-house at Edward's Bounty?"

He didn't answer that one so quickly.

"I know there was a fire, of course."

"And what started it?"

"In the opinion of authority, the villagers as a demonstration against Fabian. In the opinion of the villagers, Fabian himself."

"For what reason?"

His face set tight. "I prefer not to voice my own opinion, Mr. Cardew. But I have a feeling that there be trouble of a similar nature this week. It is Mischief Night on Wednesday."

"Local feast of all fools?" I said.

"Something like that. An ancient custom that provides excuse for a good deal of horseplay. The general confusion might prove a cover for some unpleasant occurrence, I think."

"Induced by Fabian or the villagers?" I asked.

"I'm not sure," he replied.

I tried to work that out. I could see Rhuine tarring and feathering Fabian. But I couldn't quite see what Fabian could do to Rhuine during the dancing on the green or whatever they did on Mischief Night. I wondered if it tied up, perhaps, with what seemed to be at the back of Boldry's mind that he didn't want to talk about.

I thanked him again, shook hands, and left.

I went down the street, thinking hard but without much success. And half-way back to the market-place I saw a gilt-lettered window that said SHILSTONE ARGUS. On the spur of the moment I went inside. There was a clatter of printing machinery from somewhere at the back. When I told a dusty youth that I'd appreciate a chance to glance through the files, he took me into a cubby-hole and gave me all that year's back-numbers without question.

I turned them over till I came to a picture of Edward's Bounty, obviously taken at night. The retouching department had drawn in some convincing flames and smoke, I imagined. Still, the photograph showed that the coach-house blaze had been serious enough.

Then I read the story. There was a lot about Sheila Fabian. Even the late Mrs. Charles had been dragged in. It seemed that the fire had started shortly before midnight, and was discovered by Stuart Fabian when returning home from the village. He had given the alarm, and Sheila had sent for the Rhuine squad. The Shilstone Fire Service had also set out with portable equipment, which was all they could get down the cobbled street.

But Stuart Fabian himself had put in such good work with the Edward's Bounty apparatus that there wasn't much to do when the regulars arrived. As the story put it, the conflagration was confined to the roof of the coach-house, and due to Mr. Fabian's gallant efforts, was prevented from spreading to the rest of the mansion.

There was a flash-bulb picture of the gallant Mr. Fabian, sweat-grimed but triumphant, a little lower down the column.

I thanked the dusty youth and asked to see the editor. I was taken to an inner office and found him up to his neck in copy. As there were only ten on the staff, including printers, he must have been a busy man. I told him I represented an insurance firm which had been asked to cover certain fire risks in Rhuine, and I was a trifle doubtful about certain suspicious things I'd learned.

He stared at me under his green shade. "You manage your job, I'll manage mine," he said. "I print news, not forecasts."

"Sorry," I said. "I was only asking."

I lit a cigarette and waited.

"You're wasting your time," he said. "That's what I told the police."

I pricked up my ears at that. It was the first mention of the police I'd heard in connection with the Fabians. I looked bang into the editor's eye. He was a thin grey man with a face like crumpled paper.

"Did you know Mary Louisa Charles?" I asked.

"What if I did?"

"Nothing at all. But I think she might have sanctioned my curiosity, that's all."

"So you're not an insurance man?"

I didn't answer that one. He stared at me, pushing his thumb up his left nostril and pinching the skin. "Who are you working for?" he asked.

"Sheila Fabian's my cousin," I said.

"So what do you want to know?"

"No more than your paper could tell me if I'd time to go through all the issues. What were the police asking questions about?"

He pushed back the copy and rested his elbows on the desk. "The coach-house, among other things."

"If you don't want to tell me, I'll go around and see them," I suggested.

"You'd have a long way to go. It was the Yard."

That shook me. "I pass! The Yard came down here to find out who dropped a match in the coach-house."

"They added that to other things. The car-smash, and Fabian's illness."

I nodded. I was evidently supposed to know all about those things. Well, I could find out in time. I wasn't going to confess my ignorance to the editor of the Argus.

"I'll try to add them together as well," I said pleasantly. "Forgive me for interrupting. I only blew in on impulse. The coach-house seems to be a complex with me. It shouldn't mean anything. Just a midnight blaze. And yet when it's mentioned there are meaning looks."

I went towards the door. As I opened it he spoke to me sharply. He said: "You're Mrs. Fabian's cousin?"

I nodded.

"She's a good woman."

"She always was," I said. "That's why I don't feel like going back to Australia before I'm sure there aren't going to be any more fires." I added, though I didn't known what I was talking about: "Or car smashes."

He pushed back the green shade.

"I'll tell you something," he said. "I'll tell you something because I like Sheila Fabian. It's not pleasant. But it's the reason the coach-house blaze wasn't passed off as just one of those things. . . . Stuart Fabian, at ten years of age, set the family dog-kennel alight and burnt two Labradors to death."

I felt my lips dry. "I suppose there's no proof of that?" I asked.

"It happened. And ten years ago he was living in Kent. He left there for Richmond when the house was burnt down and two maids suffocated."

He pulled down the shade. "I wouldn't have told you that, but you could dig it out anyway. And I've been wanting to tell somebody for quite a while."

"Is there such a thing," I said, "as an arson complex?"

"If you'd been a newspaper man as long as I have you'd know there's such a thing as sheer naked wickedness. And Fabian's a personification of it."

I wasn't sure whether to believe that. But I was inclined towards the theory as I left the Argus office and went on my way down the High Street.

There was plenty of time before I had to meet Sheila Fabian, so I wandered round the town and found myself a cup of tea and a bun at a market-stall. Just before five I went over to the car and sat in it till Sheila came. There was a pile of parcels in the back; she must have already made two or three trips.

She drove carefully out of Shilstone. When we were clear of the town and going towards the Corner she said:

"Any progress?"

"I couldn't say that," I told her, "but I've added to my stock of knowledge."

"I thought you'd get on well with Mr. Boldry."

73

I didn't say yes, I didn't say no. I sat there beside her, wondering again whether to tell her about last night. And about what the Argus editor had told me. I wanted to know about the car smash.

But I kept quiet. She'd said it was *carte-blanche*. I had the idea, right or wrong, that she wanted me to play the game my own way without further reference to her.

"Who are you, Harry?" she asked suddenly. "Or, as we're alone, I should call you Mr. Vaughan."

"Lee," I said. "And what do you mean, who am I?"

"Where do you come from? I don't know anything about your background."

"Is there any reason why you should? Born at Tottenham. Elementary school. Errand-boy at fifteen. Then I went to the Academy on a scholarship."

"You don't mean music?"

"What else?" I hugged my knees and stared through the windshield.

"So you play. . . . And you listened to me last night! What instrument do you play, Lee?"

"Piano, cello, bassoon and French horn," I said with a wry mouth. "I studied composition and conducting, you see. So I don't play anything well enough to earn a living."

"But you get a lot of fun out of it?"

"I wouldn't say that. It sometimes saves my soul. If I have one."

"When you get back, will you play for me?"

"I don't know," I said. "I brought one or two miniature scores with me. I'd rather sit and read them."

"I've often wondered about people who do that. Can you really hear the music as you read, Lee?"

"We fool ourselves that we can," I said. "Actually it's as hollow as an old oak. Like most other things in my life. A shadow of what should be."

"Which scores have you brought with you?"

74

"Brahms' Second," I said. "I don't believe in heaven and wouldn't hope to get there anyway. But the Second is a good substitute."

I was feeling sorry for myself again. And again I covered it by being unpleasant. I glanced past her at the drop to our right. "Nasty place," I said, "for a smash."

She didn't speak. But her face went dead white.

It was a minute before she said: "Lee or Harry, which ever I call you, don't try to dislike me too much. Be my cousin, my friend or my employee, but don't dislike me."

"I don't," I said.

"And remind me to stitch on that button. You'll be losing it. You give one the impression that no one's ever troubled to look after you."

I said nothing.

She was looking straight ahead at the narrow road. She fumbled with a cigarette, put it in her mouth, snapped a lighter. It didn't work. I took out a match and struck it.

"Thanks," she said.

It was the nearest I had ever been to her. Her hair brushed against my forehead. I drew back sharply, flicking the spent match through the open window. As she exhaled, a cloud of pungent blue smoke eddied around my face. I closed my eyes, gritted my teeth. I was just a man who read miniature scores instead of hearing a full orchestra. I opened my eyes again to stare through the windshield at the sea and the sky, stretching away to Ireland, to somewhere beyond Ireland, to some place that never was except in dreams.

We came to Shilstone corner and turned right. We lurched down the road towards the private garage, and halfway there we saw Peter. He was standing in the road, doing nothing. Nothing but munch an apple.

Sheila waved to him as she might have waved to a casual acquaintance. But she didn't slow up, and he didn't wave back. He went on munching the apple as we drove past.

75

I looked back at him through the rear light.

"Why didn't you pick him up?" I said to Sheila.

"Why should I?" she asked.

The sun through the open window was hot on my back, and scorched my neck, but I felt a shiver go right through me. As if I had taken a plunge into cold water from the top splash. I felt blue with cold, and I didn't know why.

AROUND THE TOWN

I SPENT that evening drafting my letters, and early next morning, before the rest of the household was up, I walked to the post office at Shilstone and saw them safely away. It was still early when I arrived back in Rhuine by the North Score road.

The harbour was almost deserted. The first person I saw was Isaiah Jonquil. I thought he might have written me off as a casual visitor and be surprised to see me again, but he didn't appear to be. I climbed down the steps to the shingle. There was a stiffish wind blowing, but under the lee of the jetty it was sheltered and the sun was hot.

"Still yur, zur?" he said. "You wouldn't be wantin' to take out a boat?"

I said I wouldn't.

"I hear you're Luke Jonquil's brother," I said. "Luke of

the Liquorice Gardens."

"That's right, zur. Same as I hear you're Mrs. Fabian's cousin from Australia, and you're stayin' awhile to see her through some of her troubles."

"I don't know who's told you that."

"Surprising what you 'ear," he returned modestly. "You might remember that, zur, for yourself. Just go about with your ears pinned back."

"I'll bear that in mind," I said.

I offered him a cigarette, but he shook his head. I leaned my elbows on the wall and squinted across the harbour. They were adding a short stumpy mole to the opposite jetty. Three men were leisurely handling a primitive lifting apparatus comprising four stout wooden uprights with a long T girder lashed between them. A block hung from rollers on the girder. They pulled up a hunk of stone, pushed rollers, block, and stone along the overhead T, and solemnly lowered the stone where they wanted it. It was exciting watching them. Like a wet morning watching cricket at the Oval, something happening every second.

"You should call and have a word with Mr. Boldry, zur."

I didn't tell him I had already done so.

"And the Poskett. Remarkable woman the Poskett is, zur. Half-man, they do say."

"I'd be glad to meet one," I said. "I never have."

"And then there's Lora."

"I've heard a lot about Lora, too," I said.

"Harlot by all accounts, but pretty as a buttercup. There's not a man in Rhuine doesn't look after yur with lustful eyes, except the Rector, and I've seen him giving a sideways glance, zur."

"I shall have to be careful of Lora," I said. "Where does the Poskett live, Mr. Jonquil?"

"Half-way up North Score between here and the Galleon. You can't miss it. And any time you need a helping hand, zur,

77

don't you be afraid to arsk me."

"I won't forget that," I promised.

"You see, zur, there's what you might call a cold war being waged in Rhuine. Everybody polite to everybody else,
but it's fierce—oh, don't you make no mistake about that,
zur! Take Mr. Fabian, now. Very open and affable, but
underneath—oh yes, it's all there underneath! Two or three
mornin's a week I takes him out Haldom way in one of my
boats. Likes a bit o' fishing. Or that's what he says. But there's
more to it than that, zur. Likes to talk, does Mr. Fabian. Likes
to tell me he's the wickedest man that ever lived. Tells me
about the women he's ruined and the tricks he's played."

"There's nothing like being open about things," I said.

"Tells me, half-laughin', he's going to kill me one of these
fine mornings. 'I'll upset the boat, you flat-faced barstard,'
he'll say, 'and there'll only be one of us back for breakfast.' "

"You don't seem to lose much sleep about it," I said, looking at the cheerful grin on his face.

"It's all polite," he said. "Like the way they do talk in a cold
war."

"They've also a habit," I warned him, "of starting hostili-
ties without troubling to break off diplomatic relations."

"I'm all mobilised," he said.

I took my time up the hill, thinking about the various slants
I was getting on Fabian's character. Usually, when I'm making enquiries, I have to get information out of people with
shoe-lift, forceps and stomach-pump. All I needed this time
was a sieve to sort the sand and gravel.

I came to a cottage on the right, narrower than most of the
others, and three stories high. It lent a Mediterranean look to
that corner of Rhuine. True, there were no sun-shutters or
balconies, but hanging from the top windows were half a
dozen canvases and a big notice. It read: EXHIBITION.
STRAIGHT UPSTAIRS.

The front door stood open. The ground floor was evi-

78

dently a cafe in tourist hours, and most of the first seemed to be let off to guests. I surmised that the Poskett ate, slept and painted in the attic range.

I went up the second flight of steps and reached a square landing. I knocked on a door and a voice bawled: "Come in!"

I went in and found the Poskett at work.

She was squatted on a donkey stool, with six easels around her. The same picture was on each easel. It was a lithographic representation of Rhuine harbour, complete with setting sun and lamp-lit cottages.

"Shut the door," she said.

I shut the door.

"Who are you?"

I said who I was. I started to explain but she cut me short. "I know," she said. "I've got you taped, Cardew."

"Getting people taped seems to be a common accomplishment in Rhuine," I said. "Isaiah Jonquil has just been telling me why I'm here."

She whisked up a dab of lemon chrome and transferred it to the six harbour-lights of the six canvases around her. I watched with awe.

"If you've nothing better to do for ten minutes," she said, "you can be painting the Dolphin chimney." She indicated a brownish blob on the palette. "No skill needed. Learn to paint in six easy lessons. Money refunded if not entirely satisfied. Astonish your friends. Widen your social contacts. If Winston Churchill can do it, why can't you?"

I wiped a spare brush in the blob of raw umber and tried my hand on the Dolphin chimney. It didn't look too bad. It pleased me so much, I started casting about for something else. The hydrangea shrub near the bridge seemed promising.

"I like this," I told her. "Application of mass-production principles to art. I could do this for a living, except the first outline. How d'you do that?"

"Stencil," she said. "Equivalent to the factory jig. This is one of my two best-selling lines. *The Harbour from Rhuine.* The other is *Rhuine from the Harbour.* In the season I do six *per diem,* Sundays included."

She had a deep voice. She was a big, heavy woman, with a pink-mottled, greasy face. She wore blue slacks and an indescribable jacket, something like Van Gogh wore in the picture he painted of himself; a kind of half-cloak fastened with an enormous medallion brooch. Surprisingly, her hair was light and fluffy. A redoubtable woman.

"How does Isaiah Jonquil come to know who you are and why you're here?" she asked suddenly.

"I haven't an idea. But Fabian, apparently, pays Jonquil to take him fishing in one of his boats, and boasts of his evils. He may have told him about me. . . . If so, things are going to take an awkward turn pretty soon, because by the rules of the game Fabian himself shouldn't know why I'm here."

I was getting on nicely with the hydrangea.

"Or it may be wishful thinking and inspired guessing," the Poskett said thoughtfully. "Everybody knows, Cardew, that Sheila has been fighting a losing battle with her husband's vices. Then there appears on the scene a relation from abroad —obviously a reinforcement. One who will support her case against Fabian. And, incidentally, Rhuine's case."

"Maybe," I said, hoping she was right.

She opened a box of cigarettes, black ones. I'd never seen a black cigarette at close quarters before, and didn't much care for the sensation when I stuck one in my mouth. Nor was it the only sensation I was disliking this morning. Everything was turning out differently from the way I'd expected. The cousin from Australia seemed unsuspected (unless Dillon and Fabian had drawn conclusions from the tailor's tag), but aside from that, my prejudices in the case seemed taken for granted.

"Do you spend all your time painting these two variations on the Rhuine theme?" I asked.

"Good God, no!"

She got up, the black cigarette in her mouth, and shuffled across the attic. She looked like an animated bundle of old clothes. A dozen canvases were stacked against the far wall. Without ceremony, she skimmed them across the dusty floor. I picked them up and propped them against the model's throne that probably hadn't been used for years. Then I sat back and took a deep breath.

The Poskett was at least half-way to genius, and the collection of canvases she had there were as wicked as one would expect of a woman like that. There was one of Fabian. I knew, looking at that picture, why Peter had called him Old Horny. All the things I'd overlooked in the man's general impressiveness and sheer physical appeal were there—the drooping eye, the sensuous nostrils, the too-thick and too-moist lips.

There was one of Mackender and the woman with the pipe-cleaner fingers. Boldry too was there, coming out of the ruthless operation much better than most, but with all his latent pomposity underlined. And there were others I didn't recognise; harsh, astringent, brutal studies.

"And here's your cousin," said the Poskett from her knees. She threw Sheila over.

"Sheila's one of the few people I like, but that doesn't blind me to her characteristics."

"What are they?" I asked, staring at the picture.

"You knew her as a child."

"Not like this."

"Life's been working on her a long while since then," the Poskett said. "Compare her with this." And she came waddling across the room with the last gem of her collection.

This was a girl younger than Sheila. Under the Poskett's brush, her hair was yellow shot with silver lights.

"A lovely girl, Lora," the Poskett said.

I remembered Jonquil's description. *Pretty as a buttercup.*

"Why so kind to her?" I asked. "Where's the lust and

81

temptation?"

"There isn't any."

"She was a hundred yards from me across the beach, but I should have said there was."

"Then it's unconscious, and I wasn't trying to paint any Freudian complexes."

I put the canvas down and picked up Sheila again. I'm not an artist. I don't know the way an artist gets under the surface and produces something exactly like his subject yet as different from it as pitch from flour.

"Did you know her first husband?" I asked.

"Godfrey Charles? I did. And his mother. I've been here twenty-seven years."

"What was he like?"

"All you'd expect in a boy born in England of good American stock and educated at Winchester and Oxford."

"Then why did Sheila marry Fabian so soon after he died?"

"Why does any woman marry any man? I wouldn't know, Cardew. I've never been married. Perhaps to guarantee her children's future. Perhaps not."

"That's what she gave me to understand," I said, "but I can't feel sure of it. And yet it's such a good and obvious reason that I should do. . . . I don't know why I can't accept it."

"Why not ask her?"

"She wouldn't tell me."

The Poskett returned to her lithographs and contemplated them, her head on one side.

"When a beautiful, charming, penniless widow with two children marries a man of Fabian's virility and amoral tendencies, and then discovers that she has inherited a fortune from her first husband's family, all kinds of queer things are likely to happen. I don't mean in the purely physical sense. An impact of that sort must have quite frightening complications in the mental adjustments of the two people concerned."

"I think it has done," I said.

"That's why Stuart Fabian started this ridiculous campaign to put Rhuine on the map. Purely to spite his wife and enlarge his own self-esteem. To spoil and destroy the thing her first husband gave to her. That is also why he installed Lora. He's no affection for her—not a scrap! Lora's quite amoral too. But in her case it's the amorality of innocence. I'm quite prepared to be told that's a contradiction in terms, but it isn't. Lora's a lovely, submissive, innocent animal."

"I can understand that," I said. "I can even sympathise with Fabian's resentment—"

"Oh, so can I! Up to a point."

"—but I keep on wondering if his resentment came to a head some time before I arrived here. At first, I thought I was just in time to prevent something happening. Now, I've an idea something's happened already. I can't put my finger on anything, but the feeling's there."

"I know. That's what I've put into Sheila's picture."

"And I don't think it only affected Sheila, whatever it was." I was thinking of the car-smash and the police inquiries. "I think the children had something to do with it. Especially Peter."

"I've never been good at understanding children," the Poskett said.

"Why do they never come into a room if Fabian and Sheila are there? Why do they live their own lives, take themselves off to bed when they feel like it, get up the same? Why does Peter spend all his spare time with Luke Jonquil?"

I had asked Boldry that question, and in his own fashion he had answered it. The Poskett didn't try. Instead, with a sort of heavy finality, she said: "I suggest you spend the next few days trying to find out."

"I'm going to do just that," I said, feeling grim.

I dropped Sheila's picture, put Fabian's opposite the window, and stared at it with my arms folded.

"You must have observed him pretty closely to get that resemblance from memory."

"I didn't. He sat for it."

"Then why hasn't he taken it away?"

She smiled crookedly. "Would you have done?"

I was still staring. I wouldn't have done.

"He sat three mornings a week for four weeks. Quite unnecessary, of course. But he enjoyed himself. Fabian's a very complex character, Cardew. There's a streak of sheer wickedness in him and he's diabolically clever. But he oozes self-pity by the bucketful and he loves to dramatise himself. There he sat, pouring out his soul, telling me about his humiliating position. Hour after hour of it. Telling me whom he'd like to kill and who'd like to kill him."

I looked up sharply. "Sheila among them?"

"Oddly enough, I don't think that's entered his head. The arch-enemy is Isaiah Jonquil, of course. He's a sea-lawyer, Isaiah, a man who can stir up a lot of trouble. And I think he's going to do it. Fabian told me quite soberly that he should have to kill Jonquil."

I didn't tell her that Jonquil had already said the same thing.

"In that case," I suggested, "Jonquil's safe enough. A man doesn't announce he's going to kill someone and then do it."

"I wouldn't bet on that," the Poskett said. "Any more than I would bet on Jonquil not killing Fabian. Each of them is a symbol in the eyes of the other. Personally, I don't think it would make the slightest difference one way or the other to Fabian's plans for Rhuine if Jonquil died tomorrow. But Fabian thinks it would."

"I'm trying to think straight," I said. "I don't want bogging down in theories and psychological slants."

"My dear man, I'm not trying to bog you down," the Poskett sniffed. "But when you're considering murder, you can't confine yourself to facts. Murder often ignores facts, doesn't it? No man, for instance, ever need murder his wife.

84

All he has to do is walk out of the front door and forget his name and address. Much less drastic, when you come to think of it, than the blunt instrument with all its attendant risks. But stupid men still go on using the blunt instrument."

She sat astride the donkey stool and began to wash in the skies, working with astonishing speed.

"I'm very glad you called, Cardew. I've been longing to talk to somebody about Sheila and her husband."

I went over to the window.

"You must like Rhuine," I said over my shoulder, "to stay here twenty-seven years."

"Between October and April it's as near paradise as anything you could ask for. I can't even complain about the fools who come to gape at it in summer, because they butter my bread. I sell them my pictures and run a nice side-line in plain teas. . . . Then there's my permanent exhibition of local pottery and brassware. They come from Stoke and Birmingham and show a handsome profit. And my folk-weave fabrics, supplied by the same Bolton firm for many years. You must look round some time, Cardew."

"I'd like to," I said.

"Yes, you're right enough about my being fond of Rhuine. But I wouldn't kill Fabian for it."

"I was wondering if I dare ask that."

"I'm quite capable of killing him for other reasons, of course," she added thoughtfully. "I shouldn't hesitate to do so if I thought he was a serious menace to poor Sheila's future happiness, or the children's. . . ."

"But at the moment you don't think he is?"

"I said, future happiness. The future may be worth murder. The present rarely is. You can bear anything while you count ten, and then another ten. And I'm optimist enough to hope that the future may show a more inviting aspect."

"That's only a hunch," I said.

"So is any feeling you have about Fabian."

85

I looked at my watch. It was half-past eleven. I didn't want to meet Fabian and be dragged into another session at the Galleon. But I did want to see Luke Jonquil, who was so far an unencountered enigma. I told the Poskett I'd be calling again, and she said any time.

"If you'd like to meet Lora," she said, "I'll take you down and introduce you."

"I'm not at all sure that I do," I said cautiously.

"You might do worse than take her away from here, Cardew. Back to Australia. Your days and nights would never lack interest, and you'd be an object of considerable envy wherever you went."

"Fresh from the arms of Fabian?"

"I should not call any man common or unclean," she quoted, her mouth full of brushes.

"I suppose it would be splitting hairs to say that Lora's a woman?"

"Some day I'll paint your picture, Cardew. A portrait, I think, of a conscientious, puzzled, rather puritanical gentleman."

I went downstairs.

On the steps I met a stout mother and her offspring. I guessed they were in search of morning coffee. The offspring was saying as I passed: "Oo Mom, look at that! Isn't it lovely?"

She was pointing to a picture hanging invitingly just within the doorway. It was marked *ORIGINAL OIL-PAINTING,* 25/-. It depicted the *Harbour from Rhuine.* I looked affectionately at the Dolphin chimney.

Art, I told myself, is a damn fine thing.

I crossed the road and turned off the Score again to the bridge over the ravine. I didn't meet Fabian. A minute later I was passing between the high thorn hedges and opening the tumbledown gate of Luke Jonquil's garden.

To my relief, Peter was nowhere to be seen. I didn't feel equal to another conversation watched by those grave, adult eyes. I went into the potting-shed and found Luke Jonquil there. He reminded me of his brother, but he was of a gentler kind, a little hesitant, a man who had spent his life for the most part in solitude. He took off a pair of steel-rimmed spectacles as I came in, and picked up from the bench a blackened cherry-wood pipe.

I told him the name I went by. His expression didn't change. I told him Peter had brought me in yesterday, and I thought I would like to take another look.

"You wouldn't think," I said, "that a garden this size was tucked away between the houses and the woods. How much land have you, Mr. Jonquil?"

" 'Bout—let me see—two acres or thereabouts."

"And it keeps you?"

"Well . . ." He seemed to consider. "Yes, it keeps me."

"Why do they call it the Liquorice Gardens?"

"Well zur . . ." He knocked the pipe against the bench-end. "You might say because there's been liquorice grown in this yur garden for a good many years."

"And is that something out of the ordinary?"

"Oh, 'tis indeed, zur! Not many places where she'll grow."

That was news to me. I'm always keen to pick up any bits of useless information, and I spent the next ten minutes pumping the old boy. At the end of those ten minutes I'd learned that liquorice roots go down to such extravagant depths that the soil's depth has to be equally extravagant to accommodate them.

"No clay, no water-logged subsoil, no rock, understand," said Luke. "Just good soft loam, ten or twelve foot of it."

I nodded wisely. He went on to tell me there are only three or four places in all England where liquorice thrives.

"Only where there's sand and rotting limestone, zur. Not enough places in England to grow what we need, and

87

it's a powerful good thing for the bowels, zur. Most of it comes from Hasherminer."

"Oh, Hasherminer!" I said.

"Turkey and such-like, zur."

He took me into the garden and showed me the liquorice plants growing. They looked just plants to me. But in late autumn, he said, he would dig deep trenches down the side of each row.

"Then I picks her out without damagine her, zur."

It wasn't time wasted. The next case I had, if I survived this one, might for all I knew call for professional knowledge of liquorice culture. Also, I was getting very close to something elemental. I was beginning to realise the appalling revulsion that people like the Jonquils must feel for a man of Fabian's type. That one of the few places in England where liquorice grew should become a palace of cocktails and red leatherette stools and light love was blasphemy to them.

And there was something to be said for it.

"Mebbe next year," he told me sadly, "will be the last."

"You're giving up?"

"It's not my land, zur. You're not in Rhuine now, in a manner of speaking. Only as far as the stream." He pointed to the ditch where Peter gathered his frog-spawn and tadpoles. "This side, you're on Mackender's part, and it's likely he'll be wanting it for building."

"A pity," I said. "I suppose you've looked after this garden all your life?"

"And my father and grandfather before me, zur."

"You should have had a lease," I said.

He walked slowly in front of me along the path.

"There was never no need for leases and agreements between a Mackender and a Jonquil zur, till the old people died and young Mr. George took over. The Liquorice Gardens has always been owned by the Mackenders and let to the Jonquils. That's been so for a hundred years, zur."

88

"Now the old order changes, eh?"

"And not for the better, zur. I'm not one to stand in the way of progress, but when progress means that money's your god and your spoken word isn't your bond, then it's not for the better, I say."

"And I agree with you," I said.

We were back at the shed.

"There's been a lot in the papers, one time and another, about Jonquil's Liquorice Gardens. Maybe you'd like to see the clippings, zur?"

I said I would, and he took a box from a drawer under the bench. I glanced through them, but I was using my eyes in other directions too. It was a biggish shed, with the tools of Jonquil's trade hanging neat and clean along one side. There was an iron stove in the middle, with a rusty kettle sitting on it. In front of the window was a broken-backed chair. And near the bench was another chair, a smaller one . . .

Jonquil must have seen the direction my eyes were taking.

"I brought it up for my little grandson," he said. "Five, mebbe six years ago."

I nodded, looking at the chair.

"The diphtheria took him off, zur."

There was no sound but the gentle rasping of his rough hands as he rubbed up a flake of tobacco.

I went over to the chair. Someone had sat in it more recently than that. A wooden box stood in the corner beside it. In that box was a toy drum, a ball, a little ship. On top of the box, cheek by jowl with seed catalogues and a few old newspapers, was a stack of boys' annuals, all new fifty years ago. New in the days when desert islands and the North West Frontier was the latest thing to hold a child from play.

I went to the bench and leaned my elbows on it, staring out of the window. I knew he was looking at me. After a while I turned round.

"Mr. Jonquil," I said, "I'm Mrs. Fabian's cousin."

"Yes, zur." He nodded respectfully. "Most people in Rhuine know that by now."

"And I'm very fond of my cousin." I waited half a minute. "Is there anything you'd like to tell me?"

"Tell you zur? Well, no, I don't think there is."

He wasn't looking at me now.

I nodded towards the chair.

"That little grandson . . . I suppose Peter's taken his place to some extent?"

"Nobody ever takes the place of one you've lost, zur."

"I know that. And I'm sorry if I'm opening up old wounds." I felt something hot, like pepper at the back of my eyes. "But I think you know what I'm getting at and you're trying to evade it. In one way, Peter has taken that lost child's place, hasn't he? But is that the only reason he comes here?"

"What do you mean, zur?"

"I'm trying to get behind this curious relationship between you and Peter. Between a man of—seventy, shall we say, and a seven-year-old child. Is it just the affection an old man feels for a boy who resembles his dead grandson, or is it something else?"

I watched him closely. It was the best part of a minute before he answered.

"That's something I can't tell you, zur."

But he had already told me, after a fashion.

I took to staring through the window again. It was like being in a padded room. The more you batter, the less impression you make.

I could see the backs of the Rhuine houses, the little stream that marked the boundary. I looked at the liquorice plants, at the trees hung with apples turning red. I thought that if I were Peter, seven years old and suffering some appalling inward torment, this was the place I should want to be.

"I don't blame you," I said without turning round. "I'm

not trying to force your hand, Mr. Jonquil. But if you want any help, or feel you'd like to help me, remember what I said. I'm very fond of my cousin."

And as I said that, I had a queer feeling inside.

"Can anyone stop him coming here, zur?"

"His mother, probably. But I shouldn't worry about that. She doesn't seem disposed to do."

I went to the door. Another thought struck me there. I stopped and said:

"I'm in the dark about a lot of things, Mr. Jonquil. There's one you might be able to clear up for me. Is Peter in any danger?"

"Who should he be in danger from, zur?"

"I wasn't thinking of any specific person. But as we're talking about that, shall we say—Fabian?"

An odd expression crossed his face, so quickly that I couldn't make up my mind what it signified. As I remembered it afterwards, I fancied it could have been relief. The relief we feel when we've been expecting something, keyed ourselves up for it, then it doesn't come.

"Peter hates Fabian," Luke Jonquil said, "but he's not afraid of him."

I sorted that out. If Peter wasn't afraid of Fabian, then of whom? Or what? I felt those cold shivers again.

I nodded and thanked Jonquil and walked away. Going past the liquorice plants I saw they had pods like pea-pods. I pulled off a couple and put them in my pocket. I might try them in the window-box at Fremont Street.

Ten minutes later I was back again at Edward's Bounty. It was just past noon. The first person I saw as I crossed the lawn was Sheila.

And seeing her started off the most fantastic episode of the case so far. Something that seemed nightmarish and quite detached from everything else that had happened. Till later, of course, when I realised it wasn't detached at all.

"You must have been out early this morning," she said. "Have you seen Peter anywhere?"

I was surprised at that. Peter's whereabouts weren't usually regarded as cause for anxiety. I said no, I hadn't.

"He wasn't in all last night."

"You take that pretty coolly for a young mother," I said. "Most parents with a seven-year-old son would have been telephoning the police before this."

She looked at me, her head on one side. She didn't appear even to resent what I'd said. "I'll walk up to Luke Jonquil's garden," she murmured.

"I wouldn't trouble. I've just come from there."

She was still looking at me, in a helpless sort of way.

"Then I suppose we'd better have lunch," she said.

"That's right. We have to eat even if the heir to Rhuine is missing."

"I suppose he'll be all right."

We went in. Fabian wasn't home for lunch today. We ate it alone, one at each side of the oval table in the little room off the hall. Little, that is, compared with the living-room. It was only about five times the size of my office.

"What have you been doing this morning?" she asked, making polite conversation.

"Furthering your interests. Writing letters, mailing them. Interviewing certain people."

"If you'd rather not talk about it . . ."

"I'll talk," I said, "when I've finished the job you gave me. In case you've forgotten, that was preserving Rhuine from further defilement and doing something about the influence he has on the children. Those two things add up to quite a lot."

"I appreciate what you're doing," she told me stiffly.

"Thanks for the bouquet. They add up to a lot because they're two entirely different things. It's like asking a man to make an inventory of the furniture and cement the kitchen floor."

"If you'd rather give up—"

"I wouldn't. If you paid me off now, I still shouldn't give up. If you turned me out of here I should take a room at the Dolphin. Everything's working out different from the way I thought, and working out in a way I don't like, but I'm going to get to the bottom of it."

"I don't think," she said slowly, "that I quite understand what you mean."

I took a minute to straighten out my own thoughts.

"I think the trouble between you and your husband has a slant I've not yet accustomed my eyes to," I said. "And I'm pretty sure the children are mixed up in it. Or Peter anyway. It's not all covered by what you told me last week."

She sat quite still, looking at me across the table. That strange, waiting stillness I'd noticed before.

"I think Fabian's a borderline psychopathic, if that's the right term," I went on. "I think you're touched with the same brush, though you haven't got it so badly. I think all the things I've been shown and told and all I'm digging up are just symptoms of a disease I don't understand. But I'm going to understand it before I'm through."

"Whom, besides Boldry, have you been talking to?" she asked.

"Luke Jonquil of the Liquorice Gardens. Isaiah, his brother. A Miss Poskett who paints pictures . . . And that brings me to something I don't like. Your husband may not know who I am, but I think he knows why I'm here. He's accepted me as your cousin, but I think he suspects that you contacted your cousin and asked him down here to help."

"And how does that make him react to you?"

"He hasn't reacted yet. Not openly. But I've a feeling that he's amused. He's twice my size, as Peter said. He's rather more intelligent than I am. And, of course, he has the ad-

93

vantage of seeing this thing whole. He knows the basic plan and the working drawings. . . . He sees himself as God. He pities himself the way I suppose God must pity himself when he realises the trouble he made for himself, creating the human race. But he's still God."

She didn't answer, so I went on: "If I'm right about all this, I think he's playing with me, Sheila. Waiting till it seems good and proper to him to rub me out or beat me up. He's playing with Lora and Isaiah Jonquil the same way. In fact, he's playing with Rhuine. He doesn't stand to gain a thing by the urbanisation of Rhuine. It's a game to him, a form of sublimation. A game he has to win for the sake of his own ego. That's the conclusion I've reached."

I think that shook her. I think she might have opened up on the spot if Rose, the girl looking after us, hadn't entered at that moment. She stood half-way between table and door as if she didn't know what to say, then blurted out:

"Excuse me, madam, but we're very worried about Master Peter."

"I'm worried too, Rose," said Sheila, "but I don't know what we can do about it. Master Peter is quite well able to look after himself. It wouldn't be the first time he had spent a night and a day away from home."

"No," Rose said flatly, "but Dillon's gone too."

Sheila dropped her knife. Rose took a knife from Fabian's unoccupied place and gave it to her. "When did that happen?" Sheila asked.

"Early this morning, Mrs. Fabian. I—I think he went looking for Master Peter."

"Why should he do that," Sheila asked, "instead of telling me?"

Rose didn't speak. She was a dark, good-looking girl, apparently very fond of Sheila. She suddenly burst into tears.

"Rose," Sheila said. "What on earth is all this about?"

"I don't like telling. But early this morning, soon after Mr.

Cardew had gone out, Master Peter came into the house. Into the kitchen. Cook asked where he had been all night, but he wouldn't say. He went up to the nursery. And Dillon—Dillon followed him."

"Why should he do that?"

"I don't know, Mrs. Fabian. But next thing, we heard a scuffle. I'm surprised it didn't disturb you, but the nursery is over the kitchen, so perhaps that's why we heard it so plain. And then Dillon came down moaning and holding his face."

The atmosphere was taut. I broke it by laughing. There was probably nothing to laugh for, but the notion of the pale-faced Dillon retreating before a seven-year-old child did something to me.

The two girls, mistress and maid, looked at me as if I had done something unpardonable. Maybe so.

"There was blood on Dillon's face," went on Rose. "He said Master Peter had thrown a Scout knife at him."

"Good for Master Peter," I said.

"And then, Mrs. Fabian, we saw Master Peter running across the lawn. He must have come down the main staircase and let himself out by the front door. As soon as Dillon saw him through the kitchen window, he went off after him. Towards the garage. And we haven't seen either of them since."

"Thank you, Rose," Sheila said, and with a pitying glance the girl left the room.

Sheila got up from the table. She went to the mantelpiece and leaned her arms on it. I couldn't see her face. I could only see that her whole body was shaking.

I went over to her. "Sheila," I said, "why don't you tell me what's behind all this?"

She shook her head. From the door I said: "I'm going out. I'll find him. Unless you want to telephone the police?"

"No," she told me.

I went across the lawn at the double. The scent was six hours old and chilly by now, but I had to do what I could.

I panted to the top of the steep track to the little plateau where the garage was built. But there was nothing to be seen. There wouldn't be. What was I looking for, anyway?

Was there even anything to look for? Shouldn't I admit to myself that Peter was most likely at the foot of the cliff, and Dillon either with him or twenty miles away and still running?

All around the garage plateau were the Rhuine woods. I started looking for other paths towards the sea. I found one eventually, leading obliquely down the hill. I spent an hour going down it and searching among the rocks. But Peter wasn't there. Not unless the tide had got him.

I went back to the garage, with half a mind to ring the police on my own initiative. I thought it was about time I had some official assistance. With the proper people taking care of Peter's whereabouts, I might be able to concentrate on the angle I was getting paid for. A blood-feud between Sheila's child and Dillon seemed slightly off my beat.

The garage wasn't far from the Liquorice Gardens. Nowhere was far from anywhere else in Rhuine; all the ways out of the place led steeply uphill and were roughly parallel with one another. I wondered if there was a path linking the two points. Probably not. Jonquil could have no reason for going to the Fabians' top-of-the-hill garage, nor were the Fabians on such terms with Jonquil that they would want a path from their property to his.

But there was a path. Just a scuffing-aside of the brambles and a faintly-trodden line between the trees. Such a track as one pair of feet might have made, walking that way once or twice a day. Peter's feet.

I turned down that path. And then, out of nowhere, I got the idea I was being watched.

So instead of going down the track I sauntered back a little way, and sat down on a log as if I didn't quite know

96

what to do next. But my nerves were keyed up and all my senses alert.

Within five minutes I was hearing sounds I wouldn't have heard otherwise. Faint rustles in the undergrowth, the whip of a branch as it came back against a tree-trunk. Someone was there all right, and trying to put a little more distance between us. I waited another three minutes, then moved quietly back towards the garage.

And at the garage door was Dillon.

He was opening it. He went inside. I heard an engine start up, and next minute the back wheels of the smaller car showed behind the opened door.

He was getting out to shut the door when I moved over. If possible, he turned a shade paler.

"What are you doing?" I asked.

"Doing?" He stared at me. "Nothing."

"Where are you taking that car?"

"To—to Shilstone. An errand for Mrs. Fabian."

He was forgetting, I thought, the respect due to an upper-class visitor. "Dillon," I said, "you're a damned liar." I reached into the car and switched off the ignition. "Where's Peter?"

He was licking his lips and shaking his head. "Peter? I don't know."

"He hasn't been seen since early morning," I said. "Not since he left the house with you haring after him. Now, come out of your coma! Where is he?"

He didn't speak. I could see a lot of little red spots in front of my eyes. I grabbed the lapels of his jacket and pushed him back against the car. I cracked his head against the door, and he gave a sort of surprised grunt. Then I manoeuvred the back of his head against the sharp edge of the door-frame, and told him where the door-frame was.

"Dillon," I said, "I'm going to crack your head again after I've counted five. Harder this time. Against the sharp edge

97

this time. It'll go straight through your skull into whatever brain you've got. I mean it. Now, open up."

He gibbered into my face, and saliva ran down his chin. If ever I saw a man frightened, Dillon was frightened then.

"I don't know," he whimpered. "For Christ's sake . . . I haven't seen him. He dived into the woods."

I gave another gentle crack.

"Into the woods," he gasped again. "I've been looking for him all morning."

I stared down at him. I thought he was telling the truth. Or partly. Men in the shoes Dillon was wearing then don't lie unless they're made of sterner stuff than ever he was. I let go his jacket.

"Looking for him, why?" I asked. "Out of love?"

He must have known that his moment of danger was over. I have to work myself up to murder-pitch, and it isn't a thing you can do oftener than once or twice a day. He was sullen and frightened still, but obstinate too.

"If you haven't seen Peter all morning, haven't done anything to him," I said, "why are you trying to make a getaway in Mrs. Fabian's car?"

"I've had enough of Rhuine," he said. "So would you have if you knew as much about it as I do."

I looked him over.

"You'd better get back to Edward's Bounty. And stay there. If you're going to skip Rhuine, it'll cost you trainfares. If you're not in the house when I get back, I'll put the police on your trail and you'll be picked up wherever you go. You can't dodge the column this time, my lad. . . . Now get out of my sight before I cut your heart out and throw it to the crows."

I gave him a kick on the seat for luck, and he went staggering down the path. I didn't much care whether he intended going back to the house or not. I didn't think Dillon was capable of much further damage that afternoon. It was unlikely that he would do anything but cut his own throat, and that wouldn't have caused me any worry.

I pushed the car into the garage, locked the door, and went thoughtfully once again along that little one-man track towards the Liquorice Gardens. I kept wondering if I was halfway through a nasty dream. Or if the whole thing had got out of proportion in my mind.

Suppose Dillon had merely got on the wrong side of Peter, and Peter had thrown his Scout knife and disappeared, and Dillon, realising he would be held responsible for the lad if anything happened to him, had spent the morning looking for him as he claimed and was now afraid to go back and face Sheila's wrath?

It could be as simple as that, I thought.

And Peter, by now, might be safe with Luke Jonquil.

Hoping my soft-pedalling was justified, I pushed on through the undergrowth. The strong sunlight ahead showed where I was coming to the edge of the wood. Twenty yards ahead of me was an unkempt thorn hedge. There was a hole in it such as Peter might have made. I squeezed through, and found myself in Jonquil's garden.

There didn't seem to be anybody about. There was a spade pushed into the ground at the end of a bean-row. There was a wisp of smoke coming from the tin chimney of the hut.

I walked down the path and pushed open the door. The light was dim, and at first I didn't see anybody. I was turning to come out again when I noticed that the pile of boys' books in the corner was upset. I stepped over, and then saw what the bulk of the iron stove had so far hidden from me.

Luke Jonquil was lying in the dark corner, propped against the wall. It was presumably one of his flailing arms that had knocked over the books.

I dropped on my knees. Even then, one thought was scream-

99

ing through my mind. It shouldn't have been Jonquil. It should have been Peter. Where was the sense in a thing like this happening to Jonquil?

I didn't touch him. A lot of blood had run down his face and neck. There was a nasty gash on the old man's temple, and a great dark patch further back. He had been struck more than one blow.

But he wasn't dead. That came as a shock to me. He had been left for dead. If I had struck an old man like that and seen the blood streaming over his collar, I should have left him for dead.

I still didn't touch him. I picked up the kettle and found it was half-full of water. I yanked the lid off the stove, pushed in a handful more wood, and set the kettle on top of it. I was remembering that I had seen a doctor's plate on a house near to Boldry's, over on North Score.

I doubled out of the shed and down the garden, into the narrow path between the thorn hedges. I ran faster than I had ever thought I could, across the road, over the crazy wooden bridge, into North Score and up the cobbled street.

I pushed past the tourists, still clattering down on their high heels and gaping at the loveliness of Rhuine. I jammed my thumb on the doctor's door-bell and kept it there.

A bald, middle-aged man opened the door.

"Jonquil's shed at the Liquorice Gardens," I said. "There's been an accident. He's probably dead by now. I wouldn't waste time."

He didn't. He reached back into the hall for a bag and started off with me, jog-trotting by my side.

I wasn't paying much attention to the scenery. But as we passed the Galleon, I caught sight of a man standing against the wall, eyeing us with interest. He was an ordinary-looking man dressed in an old suit not quite as smart as mine.

When we got past him, he stepped off the cobbled footway and I thought he was going to follow us. But he didn't do that. He just stood there, looking after us, rubbing his chin thoughtfully. For some reason, the way he did that got under my skin.

It was Smith, of course.

ENTER MR. SMITH

I STOOD at the door of the shed and watched the doctor. I watched his fingers move over Luke Jonquil like an insect's antennae.

"Now take his legs," he said. "Over and on to the floor. Easy. . . . Is that stove burning? Got some water heated."

"I looked after that before I came for you," I said.

He gave me a hard straight look.

"Think quickly, don't you? Steady now . . . !"

We got Luke Jonquil over. We got a folded coat under his head. I fancied I saw his eyelids move.

I took the water from the stove, and the doctor bent down again. He worked efficiently for ten minutes, never speaking a word. Then he stood up and pulled his mouth into a grimace.

"Difficult to say. No fracture, apparently. Some slight concussion, and he's lost a lot of blood. Can't be sure with a man of his age. We'll know better when we've got him to Shilstone."

Then we heard Luke Jonquil's voice, like something scrabbling at the bottom of a barrel.

"Not Shilstone. . . . Not there."

The doctor looked down abstractedly. Luke was just a hunk of flesh to him. It was an impersonal matter. His objection wasn't even worth answering. The doctor, in fact, seemed slightly put out that Luke had recovered sufficiently to make it.

"They're tough," he said, "the older generation. You're not in any hurry?"

"I've all the autumn," I said.

"Then you might go over to the post office telephone. Get Shilstone four-five-o. Ask for an ambulance to the top of South Score. We'll have to get him there on a stretcher."

There was more scrabbling at the bottom of the barrel. It was Luke saying no again. The doctor passed his fingers across the old man's forehead and gave me an understanding nod.

But I didn't leave. I could see Luke Jonquil's eyes.

"It's your pigeon," I said to the doctor, "but you know what these people are. If it's going to upset him. . . ."

"Take me home," said Luke.

The doctor looked puzzled and slightly outraged.

"Shilstone's the place for him," he said. He bent nearer to Luke. "You ought to go to Shilstone," he said in that loud, patient voice which the medical profession uses to all senile patients above the age of fifty. "You've had what would kill many a man. You'll get every attention at Shilstone."

But he glanced over his shoulder at me and added: "Wonder if there's anybody capable of looking after him here?"

"I wouldn't know," I said. "I'm a visitor."

"He lives next door to his brother. And his brother's married. I think I'd better stay with him while you go down and see how the land lies. Isaiah Jonquil's the name. Bit of a beachcomber. You'll find him somewhere around the harbour or else in the Dolphin. If he thinks Luke can be taken care of at home, tell him to get some of the boys up here with a stretcher."

I found Isaiah with his boats. He gave me a shrewd, sharp look when I told him Luke had had an accident. Were there any facilities, I asked, for nursing him at home?

"My wife'll look after him zur," he said.

I told him about the stretcher and went back without waiting for him. Isaiah, apparently, could move quickly enough when he felt the need, and in less than ten minutes he came rolling up the garden path with four men and the stretcher. They eased Luke on to it and carried him down the Score. The Brickhole, a group of cottages on the site of an old brick-yard, was just off North Score, not fifty yards from the Dolphin. Luke lived at seven, his brother at eight.

We squeezed the stretcher through the front door, but there was no question of getting it upstairs. Two of the men went up, dismantled the bed, and fixed it in the sitting-room. Then the stretcher-party retired with gruff murmurs of condolence and hope. And Luke, his thin hands blue on the coverlet, was left alone with his brother and the doctor and me.

Or that's what I thought. . . . But before anybody had opened his mouth to say the obvious thing, the kitchen door opened a crack and I saw a solemn blue eye watching us.

It was Peter.

I hadn't thought of Peter for the past hour. Now, the fact came rocketing back at me that Peter was actually the hinge of the whole episode. To indulge in a satisfying mixture of metaphors, what had happened to Luke Jonquil was only a by-product of the hinge.

I looked at the door and said: "What are you doing here, Pete?"

He came into the room without answering and went to the bed, standing there with his back towards us.

"Luke's going to be all right," I said. "You don't have to

worry about that, Pete."

"I live here now," he said, not turning round.

Isaiah and the doctor were flummoxed by that. I wasn't. I was finding out by this time how to handle Peter.

"If that's the way things are," I said, "you'd better do something about taking care of him. Any milk in the house?"

"Plenty."

"Then heat some over the stove . . . If there is a stove?"

"An electric."

That took him out of the room. The doctor looked at me uneasily.

"Is it safe to let a child that age handle an electric stove?"

"You could trust Peter to handle a fully-loaded automatic," I said. "Or a fully-loaded London bus."

"What happened up at the Liquorice Gardens, zur?" put in Isaiah.

"Your guess is as good as mine. Peter's been missing since morning. I came into the woods to look for him, found myself near the Gardens and thought I'd glance in. And I found your brother unconscious. That's all I can tell you."

"Missing since morning," the doctor said curiously. "Now he tells us he's living here with Luke. Sort that out."

I was doing, by private mental processes I didn't intend sharing with anyone at the moment. I saw no reason to tell them about the Dillon angle, for instance.

While we had been talking, Luke Jonquil's eyes had flickered wider open.

"It was an accident," he said in a stronger voice. "I fell against the stove."

The doctor nodded. "You're in good hands now. We'll have you walking about in a couple of days."

"An accident, that's all . . . Against the stove."

His eyes closed again. He started to breathe more deeply, more regularly, and the doctor looked at Isaiah with a wry grin.

104

"Tough as a bit of tarred rope, but you're lucky there isn't a funeral in the family. I'm still not too sure about him. If we'd been able to get him to Shilstone I should have liked a pint of blood in him. Ah well . . . !"

"Luke was never one for doctors and hospitals," Isaiah said, and the doctor glanced at me as one educated man to another.

"Queer," he said, "the prejudices you find in these rural backwaters. They think you're taken to hospital to die."

"Maybe there's something in that," I said.

"I'll call again this evening," he told Isaiah. "If there's any change, send for me right away, of course."

When he had gone, I sat by the bed until Peter came back with the milk. I had only suggested hot milk to get him out of the room, and anyway, Luke was asleep. I told him how it was, and he nodded as if he understood. There was a footstep outside, and Mrs. Isaiah Jonquil came into the room. She looked a capable woman, handsome as a side of fat bacon and displaying just about as much warm human emotion.

Judging that Luke was in safe custody, I got up to go.

"What about coming home with me?" I said to Peter.

"I'm staying with Luke," he said. And he pulled up a chair to the bed and crooked his legs round the chair spindles.

I didn't argue. I went into the Brickhole. I felt I'd earned a drink since jumping up from Sheila's table, and made a beeline for the Dolphin. The landlord, I fancied, would respect the licensing laws with the elasticity they deserve. And the first person I saw when I got inside was the doctor, whose ideas had probably been the same as mine.

There was the usual what's yours and chins up, then he said into his beer that it was a queer business.

"Rhuine's a queer place," I said into mine.

"You know, he's an old liar. He was attacked."

"Oddly," I said, spicing the words with what I hoped was

rich sarcasm, "I had the same thought."

"I even know what with. I've bought my plants for years from old Luke. I go into that shed regularly. I could tell you the position of every tool on that wall. While you were summoning the stretcher-party I took a good look round. There's a dibbler missing."

"What's a dibbler?" I asked.

"An instrument for the making of holes. Saw eighteen inches off the haft of an old spade, sharpen the end, and you have something like Luke's dibbler. If you looked long enough in the woods I think you'd find it, liberally crusted with blood and hair."

"I might even look," I said. "But he says—"

"He can say what he likes. It couldn't have been an accident."

"I thought we were agreed on that? I'm merely wondering why Luke chooses to say so."

"I'm also wondering," the doctor said, "why Peter was at the cottage when we got there. I don't know whether you noticed, but the place was locked up when we took the old man back. I got the key out of his jacket pocket. Peter was in the kitchen. And in those primitive establishments there isn't a back door out of the kitchen. Am I making myself clear? . . . Peter must have been in the house since before Luke went up to the Liquorice Gardens."

"In other words," I said, "locked in. And not against his will. Peter doesn't do anything against his will."

"Curious! But that hasn't anything to do with me."

"No," I agreed. "The dibbler's your worry. And the dibbler's consequences. What are you going to do—tell the police?"

"I'm not sure," he said cautiously. "If Jonquil refuses to prefer a charge, where would we stand?"

"In cases of murder or attempted murder, I suppose it isn't necessary to have the victim's consent?"

"I suppose it isn't."

"On the other hand," I said, "it might be as well to wait on events. For a day or so at any rate. I've an idea this ties up with something else."

Not for the first time, he gave me a searching look.

"I don't think you told me your name?" he said.

I thought quickly. That was one of the reasons I didn't want him to go to the police. I couldn't give the police any name but Lee Vaughan. The police are funny that way.

"My name's Cardew," I said. "My father and Mrs. Fabian's were brothers."

"Oh!" he said, and whistled softly. "Well, that throws a different light on the matter!"

"It doesn't," I said, "but it's probably a relevant factor."

The landlord seemed anxious to be rid of us, and I didn't want to waste any more time. So I went out with the doctor, thanked him for his prompt action, and left him at the foot of the Score.

I hadn't the faintest idea what I was going to do next, but I was damn sure I had to do something. My blood was up.

It was nearly four o'clock. If I hurried, I might catch Fabian at home. And I wanted to do that. Badly. While the mood lasted.

This time I didn't enter by the front door. I went round to the servants' quarters. The first person I met was Cook, who seemed to recognise me though I hadn't met her before. She was alone in the kitchen.

"Where's Dillon?" I asked.

She was badly flustered. "He came—he came back about an hour ago, sir. I think he's gone up to his room. He said he wasn't feeling well."

"I can believe that," I said. "Do you happen to know if he's had any private conversation with Mr. Fabian?"

"I'm sure I couldn't tell you, sir."

It would have been interesting to know that, I thought, pushing open the baize door. But Dillon was back in the house, and that was something.

As I was crossing the hall I heard a movement above. It was Sheila, standing on the half-landing and looking over the balustrade. I knew what she wanted to ask, and spared her the trouble.

"Safe," I said. "At Luke Jonquil's cottage in the Brickhole."

I saw her eyes close and slowly open again, but didn't wait for further reactions. I went along the corridor to the big living-room. My timing was just about right. But I hadn't expected to see Fabian sprawled across two chairs, wearing a bath-robe with a pattern of peacock's tails.

"Oh," he said, "it's Cardew! Come and help yourself to a drink. Don't meet so often considering we occupy the same quarters, do we?"

I went in, without closing the door behind me. I thought if Sheila heard anything that interested her, she would maybe make a third party. I didn't help myself to a drink either. I needed a clear head.

He had a glossy magazine opened across his knees, and pretended to keep on reading it. But I knew better. When I sat down on the other side the fireplace he gave up the pretence and looked across at me and made some fatuous remark about hoping I was having a good time.

"I might have had," I said, "if Rhuine had been allowed to give me one. Certainly I've met a lot of highly interesting human specimens."

"I said you would. . . . So you've been cultivating the local characters."

"*En masse*," I said. "Boldry. The local sawbones. The Poskett woman Mackender mentioned." I looked for somewhere to drop my cigarette-stub. "And the brothers Jonquil."

He took that on the chin. The half-bored smile didn't leave his face. "You didn't meet Lora by any chance?"

He was fishing. If I'd heard nothing about Lora, I should have asked who she was. But I said: "No, that's a pleasure to come."

"Pity! Lora's the most seductive little bitch west of Bristol."

He leaned over to get a cigarette from the box on the table. I did the same. Our heads were close together. He looked at me, and I had that faint sense of repugnance and unwanted intimacy you get when you're very close to a person you dislike.

I noticed the unnatural clearness of his eyes. I noticed something else too. His bath-robe was tied only loosely, and I saw that his chest was as much like the barrel certain chests are said to be like as any I ever came across. And it was covered, literally covered from the base of his throat to as low as I could see with hair. Strong, wiry black hair.

I pulled back sharply and lit my cigarette.

"Fabian," I said, "why the hell do you trouble to be civil with me?"

He seemed faintly surprised. "My dear fellow, why shouldn't I be? It's my policy to be civil to everybody. Even to people I dislike. For that matter, even to people who might jeopardise the things I want to do."

"Why?"

"It makes life easier. And occasionally it has amusing results. Consider your own reactions, for example. Yesterday, I was most touched by your allegorical allusions to Prince Albert the Good. You were appealing to my better nature and trying to reinforce your own belief in it. You were trying to assure me—and yourself—that if only I were content to be a good prince consort in this delightful kingdom, all would be well, all auspicious."

"Do you think," I asked, "that I jeopardise your plans?"

He took half a minute to answer that.

"Frankly, no!" he said at last. "I think you might like to do. After all, isn't that natural? You're related to my wife.

You've been alone together. She must have told you quite a lot about her private grievances. It isn't to be expected that you should side with me rather than with her. You must be feeling considerably frustrated. No doubt you wish you could do this or that. . . . But I don't feel disturbed by your animosity, Cardew, any more than I do by Jonquil's, or by Boldry's."

He smoked a while in silence.

"Frankly," he went on, "I haven't too high an opinion of your intelligence. And I don't think your physical prowess would cause me much concern."

I kept my hands clenched in my pocket.

"In those circumstances," he said pleasantly, "I don't see why I shouldn't tolerate you until such time as you see fit to leave us. And you mustn't hurry yourself, Cardew. After all you're one of my wife's few relatives. I've no wish to deprive her of your genial company. . . . Shall we go up to the Galleon tonight and drown all unkindness in their cups?"

"Gladly," I said, "if you feel like going anywhere by the time I've said what I have to say."

I saw a sharp flicker in his eye. He was probably wondering what I meant by that. So I let him wonder.

"It's just as much fun for me to pull the wool over your eyes as it is for you to do the same with me. If you can be civil, so can I. That wasn't my intention when I came in. But if that's the way you feel, it suits me fine."

"That is known," he said, "as urbanity. My opinion of you is going up. If your good progress continues, I shall bid you goodbye with genuine regret."

I kept him on toast another minute. He could banter all he liked, but I knew he wasn't sure of me. Then I said, as urbanely as ever he could have wished:

"Have you seen Dillon since you came in?"

He hadn't been expecting that. His surprise gave me a slight advantage over him. "I half-expected," I went on, playing that advantage for all it was worth, "he would have come straight to you with the story."

"Story?" he said. "I haven't seen Dillon since last night."

"No," said Sheila's voice behind me. "He went out before you were up this morning, Stuart."

So she had heard. And come down, as I'd hoped she would.

"That's unusual for Dillon," Fabian said. "You mean he's taken the day off?"

He wasn't sure where all this was leading. And Sheila's sudden appearance hadn't increased his composure. It gave me a lot of pleasure to note that he wasn't being facetious any more. Only watchful and suspicious.

"He may have intended to take the day off," I said, "but he's back in the house now. He came back this afternoon."

Fabian looked from me to Sheila, then back again to me. "If you're quite incapable of making a direct statement," he said, "we'd better have Dillon in. I don't see what possible connection he can have with your affairs or mine, but if there's anything about his movements that needs to be cleared up—"

"Dillon's movements won't be cleared up for quite a while," I cut in. "So we can discuss him in absence."

He flung the glossy magazine on the table.

"In that case, go ahead."

"His movements are important to me. They are to Sheila. More so to me than to her, perhaps, because they throw a lot of light on something I don't understand. Or something I'm only just starting to understand."

That brought him to the edge of the chair, staring at me. It made me grin, and I didn't get many grins out of the Fabian case. It's good to be a little man and know for once that you've got Goliath by the short hairs.

"You'd better sit back and listen," I said. "Because in spite of being low both on wits and guts, I've got something to say that you're not going to like."

He didn't sit back. He stayed staring at me.

"It begins with Peter," I said. "He doesn't behave the way any normal child should. Something's happened to him that twists his affections and his actions. The same with Ninian, though you don't notice it so much in her case because she's younger."

I didn't take my eyes off Fabian.

"So my dim wits tell me that there's something wrong with his environment. That conclusion is supported by every damn thing I've seen and heard since I came to this house."

I glanced round at Sheila to see how she took that. It was hard to tell. So I went on to Fabian:

"He spent last night out. I know where, and if I don't know why I can make a guess. Whatever happens to be wrong is moving up to a crisis. Both in itself and in Peter's mind. He's afraid of something. That isn't to be wondered at. But the fantastic thing is that somebody's also afraid of him. Now, laugh that off."

"I'm not laughing at all," Fabian said. "It's a very interesting theory. I've often tried myself to formulate some reason for Peter's sub-normality."

I let that pass.

"When he didn't come home last night, one person was worried. Dillon! And Dillon was waiting for him this morning. Dillon followed him up to the nursery—"

"How do you know that?" Fabian asked sharply.

"The servants told us," Sheila said.

"What happened in the nursery I don't know," I went on. "But Peter must have resented Dillon's presence there, because he threw a knife at him. Then he fled the house with Dillon in hot pursuit."

Fabian took another cigarette from the box. So did I. Sheila had most likely paid for them, anyway.

"Dillon, however, didn't pursue in the right direction. Peter went to Luke Jonquil's cottage in the Brickhole.

Whether he merely asked Luke for sanctuary and Luke unquestioningly granted it, or gave him reasons, I don't know. And don't smirk every time I use that phrase, Fabian. Because I know things in certain other directions that make up for my ignorance in that. I know, for instance that when Luke left the house, he turned the key in the lock. Now why? Not to lock Peter in, because he was a willing guest. So for what else but to keep somebody else out, till Luke came back?"

"Came back!" said Fabian thoughtfully, and I fancied he was working something out in his mind.

"If you're wondering why Luke went out," I said, "I can make a guess. The garden has to be looked after. But I think there was something else as well. I think he wanted to see somebody. Probably me."

"In forty-eight hours," Fabian said, "you've become quite a prominent local figure, haven't you?"

"Meanwhile, Dillon had been hunting for Peter in the woods," I said. "I think he went to the edge of the Liquorice Gardens to spy out the land and see if Peter was there with Luke. When he satisfied himself that he wasn't, he went right in and asked Luke if he'd seen the boy. Luke told him one of three things. I'm not intelligent enough to decide which.

"One, that he hadn't seen Peter this morning at all. Two, that he knew where Peter was but didn't know why Peter had come to him. Three, that the boy was in the cottage at the Brickhole and had told him, Luke, exactly what dirty work had brought him there. And that he, Luke, was going to see Mrs. Fabian's cousin, who happens to be me, and pass on the story Peter had told him."

"I follow you," said Fabian carefully. "Very closely reasoned, Cardew."

"I'm glad you think so. There's a lot of conjecture about what I've just said. But that's no conjecture about what happened next. Whatever Jonquil said, Dillon was so mad with panic or anger that he picked up a dibbler from Jonquil's bench and struck the old man over the head. He left him for dead and was trying to make a get-away in Sheila's car when he was seen and ordered back here."

"Ordered back by whom?" Fabian asked.

"By me."

"And Jonquil?"

"Jonquil is alive," I told him, "by the grace of God and a thick skull. I'd like to tell you that he's in Shilstone Hospital with a policeman sitting by the bed, waiting for a statement. But Jonquil, for some reason of his own, prefers to say it was accident."

I gave him fifteen seconds to fret about that. And he was fretting. There wasn't any fancy-work about what I'd just said. Attempted murder of a harmless old man is something you can't be funny about however hard you try.

Then I said with as much nasty emphasis as I could:

"You can be sure of one thing, though. Luke Jonquil still intends telling me what Peter's told him. I don't know when, but the day will dawn—oh yes, it'll dawn! I'd keep that in mind when you're tempted to be unpleasant with me, Fabian. I'm a dangerous man to you."

He looked me up and down. Then, as if he had reached a decision, he leaned over and rang the bell.

"Send Dillon in," he said to Rose.

Nobody spoke till Dillon came. Sheila had moved closer to us, near the fire. Dillon stood midway between our little group and the door. His unhealthy pallor wasn't improved by the long strip of adhesive on his chin.

Fabian's chair creaked as he leaned back.

"I've been hearing things about you, Dillon. What's happened to your face, by the way?"

"I—I'm afraid I had an accident while shaving, sir," Dillon said.

"Well, that happens to all of us."

"What about the knife Peter threw?" I asked, and Dillon

licked his lips.

"What's this about a knife?" Fabian said, as if he were hearing it for the first time.

"I don't—I don't like making complaints about the children, sir," Dillon replied.

"You'd better out with it."

"Master Peter was out all night, sir." Dillon gulped out the words. "So when he arrived this morning, I followed him upstairs to see if he required anything."

"And did he?"

"Unfortunately, Master Peter was in one of his trouble-some moods, and he threw a knife at me." Dillon glanced in my direction and went on with slightly more confidence: "He then ran out of the house, sir, and I went after him. In fact, I spent most of the morning looking for him."

"Very thoughtful of you," Sheila said. "I've never known you to be so thoughtful before, Dillon."

He kept his eyes on Fabian. He was probably unwilling to face her.

"What about Mrs. Fabian's car?" I shot at him.

"I am very sorry about that, sir." It was still Fabian he addressed. "But I was so upset that I wanted to get away. I only intended taking the car as far as Shilstone, sir, and leaving it in the station yard." He added lamely: "I'm afraid I haven't been very happy here, sir."

"No? We must go into that, Dillon. Nothing to do with your wages, I hope?"

"No sir. Not at all."

"You don't happen to know . . ." Fabian toyed with the cigarette-box. "You don't happen to know anything about an alleged attack on Luke Jonquil?"

"At his shed in the Liquorice Gardens?" I put in.

That made him look at me. If there was anything but stark terror in his eyes, I'm a baboon.

"No sir, I don't," he said in a low voice.

"Naturally, you didn't go anywhere near the Liquorice Gardens when you were looking for Peter?"

"No sir."

"Then it will surprise you to know," I said, sticking out my jaw, "that Luke Jonquil was battered to death within a hundred yards of where you must have been at just about that time?"

His face couldn't turn whiter. So it assumed a delicate green tinge.

"Or it wouldn't surprise you," I went on, drawling the words in the best Ealing Studio style, "to know that he survived the attack and should be capable of describing his assailant in a few hours?"

He pulled in his breath and held it.

"I—I don't quite see how that affects me, sir," he said.

"Apparently it doesn't," Fabian told him. "It's merely a question of your proximity. . . . But then, whenever a murder is committed, someone must of necessity be in close proximity to it. The innocent as well as the guilty."

"Yes sir. That is so."

"We can take it, then, that if Mr. Cardew or some other person were to accuse you of committing this crime, you would have a perfect answer?"

"I—I believe I should, sir."

"I hope so. I wouldn't like to harbour a murderer in my house, Dillon. Or even, shall we say, a would-be-murderer in my wife's house."

There had been other silences during the duel between us. Why was it, then, that the silence following Fabian's words had such a deathly quality? For I was certain it had.

"I think you can go now, Dillon. And be careful, very careful, of what you say. Till we know more or less where you stand, the less you voice your opinion or protest your innocence, the better it will be."

I waited till the door closed behind Dillon. Then I said to Fabian in a voice that sounded tired and flat to me:

"You handled that very well."

"I usually do handle things very well."

"But you haven't altered the facts."

"Facts don't matter in this imperfect world, Cardew. It's their interpretation that makes them comforting or dangerous. Your interpretation of our little array of facts may be quite different from mine. And Dillon's, different from either of ours." He looked past me at Sheila. "You must be deriving a lot of amusement from all this."

"I wouldn't call it that," she returned coldly. "Suppose Dillon did attack Jonquil? What do you suppose will happen when it becomes known?"

"What can happen? Dillon's merely a servant who is presumably responsible for his own actions."

"It may upset the elaborate game you're playing," I pointed out.

"Why should it? Any game I am playing is perfectly open and above-board."

"I wasn't thinking about your proposals for Rhuine," I shot at him, "though I think you're due for some hard knocks in that direction. I'm more interested in personal relationships. In the tie-up between you and Sheila and Dillon and the children and Luke Jonquil."

Fabian took a deep breath. He had made a pretty good recovery from the shaking I'd given him. He was resilient all right.

"You've several noisy bees in your bonnet, Cardew, and the noisiest of them all is your idea that Peter holds the key to some dark mystery that your intelligence can't penetrate. The actual facts are quite simple. Peter is a highly-strung child. He and Ninian have a complex where I'm concerned. I can understand that up to a point. I'm not their father, of course. . . . It's a complex they might have outgrown in time. Unfortunately, Sheila has gone out of her way to foster it. Now, she's reaping the consequences. Peter's uncontrollable and Ninian's rapidly developing into a half-wit."

"How dare you say that!" Sheila gasped.

"The way you flare up whenever I make that suggestion, my dear, shows you're perfectly well aware how true it is. You'll find that out in due course, Cardew. Peter, the young brat, needs a few years at an approved school. If the authorities hear of his knife-throwing activities he'll probably get them. As for Dillon, I'm not greatly troubled about what happens to him. But I imagine that his story is substantially true. He must have realised that if Peter fell over the cliff or down the ravine, he wouldn't come out of it too well after quarrelling with a child that age. So he was clearing out. I'm quite prepared to believe that he was going to steal my car—I beg your pardon, my wife's car—but I refuse to believe that he tried to kill Jonquil merely because Peter had told Jonquil of some fantastic episode hidden in the recent past. I think you're letting your imagination run away with you."

"In the meantime," I said, "Jonquil may recover sufficiently to tell his story."

"Exactly! Well, we can only wait and see."

He smiled mockingly. He was almost his old self again. Smooth, courteous, urbane.

"What we have to consider now, Cardew, is your own position here. It's my wife's affair, of course. As I pointed out a few minutes ago, I expect you to take her side. I expect you to believe any fantastic lies she chooses to tell you. But I don't see why I should have to suffer more than need be. I suggest that we leave all this to find its own level and preserve the courtesies when we happen to be thrown together. . . . Either here or in the village."

"That suits me," I said. "But I warn you, Fabian. You're playing a dangerous game. In your shoes I'd go steady."

"In my shoes," he said, "you'd do precisely what I am

doing, because you'd have my mental make-up. Also, you'd have my motives."

I got up and went out. From the door I looked back at him. He had put his feet on the next chair and reached for the magazine again.

I left the door open. Before I reached the end of the corridor, I heard Sheila following me out. I stood in the hall till she caught up with me.

"Sheila," I said, "send Ninian away."

"I'd like to," she said. "Where to?"

"The Morrises. Or some other place equally sane and uninhibited. Telephone tonight. Arrange for her to go first thing in the morning."

"I'll do that now," she said.

I walked to the Dolphin, where I had a meal. I'd only eaten half my lunch, and it seemed ten years since then.

In the Dolphin I was told, naturally, of Luke Jonquil's accident. Nobody seemed to connect me with it. The general opinion seemed to be that he was getting too old to work at the Liquorice Gardens alone. A man could easily have a fall in a lonely place like that and lie there all day without being found.

I agreed with that.

When I felt full, I left the Dolphin and walked along by the harbour. But I saw nothing of Isaiah. I supposed he would still be with his brother.

I walked back along Yeo's Jinkin and Church Staithe. But when I came to the drive of Edward's Bounty I went past it towards the church. I hadn't been that far before. It looked old to me, but I'm no authority on churches. I saw a notice-board level with the wall near the churchyard, and crossed over to look at it. The notice-board was standing in a little square enclosure of grass with a five-foot wall around it. There wasn't any way into that enclosure except through a

119

two-and-a-half foot gap between massive stone posts. It looked as if there had been a gate there at one time, but now you could walk right in. I walked in. The notice-board was a piece of cast metal that said:

RHUINE POUND

NOTICE IS HEREBY GIVEN THAT
UNDER THE PROVISIONS OF THE
ANCIENT MONUMENTS
PROTECTION ACTS
THE COMMISSIONERS OF
HIS MAJESTY'S WORKS AND
PUBLIC BUILDINGS
HAVE BEEN CONSTITUTED BY
THE OWNERS THE GUARDIANS
OF THIS MONUMENT AND THAT
ANY PERSON WILFULLY INJURING
OR DEFACING THE SAME WILL BE
PROSECUTED ACCORDING TO LAW

His Majesty's Office of Works,
Westminster S.W.1.

That seemed a lot of fuss to make about four walls and a bit of turf. I knew what a village pound was, of course. I knew that back in the good old days they used to put any cattle or horses there that had strayed out of the fields, and there they stayed till the owners claimed them.

What I didn't know about this particular pound till Sheila told me later was that the Maldwyche of his day made a last stand there with a handful of men when Rhuine was held for the King during the Civil Wars. There were still bullet-marks on the walls. Which made it something special in its line.

The road past Rhuine Pound continued towards the cliffs, but soon deteriorated into a narrow lane. It seemed the forestry people had been busy there. Tree-trunks were piled up on both sides the lane. There might have been well over fifty of them. It might have been a regular avenue along there, I thought, till the felling was done.

I sat down on one of the tree-stumps and stayed for an hour, looking over Rhuine and thinking. I stayed till the sun went down and the breeze off the water grew chilly and lights began to twinkle in the village. If Fabian carried out his normal programme tonight, he should be away from the house by this. I gave him another quarter of an hour, then started back.

But near the church, I saw a figure coming towards me in the gloom. I leaned against the churchyard wall, pretending to look over. I didn't feel like casual conversation with a stranger.

He got abreast of me, peered in my direction, and hesitated. Maybe he thought I was waiting my chance to lift the church plate. Then he said good-evening.

I said good-evening too. You have to be polite. He stopped, and said it looked like another fine day tomorrow. I said it did.

I looked at him over my shoulder. He was dressed in a shabby old suit. A nondescript sort of man.

"Peaceful round here," he said.

I said it was very peaceful. I felt in a sarcastic mood, and added that the whole village seemed peaceful, too.

"Yes," he said in a soft burring voice. "It takes a lot to upset us."

"Nice kindly people," I said. "Go out of their way to make a stranger feel at home."

He nodded.

"Disturbances like we've had today seem out of place, don't they?" He smiled at me. "I was thinking of the old man who nearly lost his life. You may have heard about that?"

I said I didn't think so. I was just holiday-making.

He peered closer.

"Then I'm mistaken. . . . I thought I saw you with the

doctor. . . . And earlier this week with Mr. Fabian in the Galleon."

I flicked a bit of moss off the wall on to the grave of someone called Elizabeth Cholleston, Relict of the Above.

"Odd, very!" the soft voice went on. "I had an idea you were staying with the Fabians."

Grin and bear it, I thought. . . . Grin and bear it.

"Mrs. Fabian is my cousin," I said.

"Really? How surprising!"

"We're not much alike. We never were."

"And yet, I think there's some slight resemblance."

I must tell Sheila that, I thought.

"My name," he said, "is Smith."

"One of the Shilstone Smiths?" I asked.

"Well, yes, you might almost say that. I live about half-way between here and Shilstone, in point of fact."

He didn't ruffle easily. "Mrs. Fabian," he said, "is a very charming woman."

"Very," I said. "They're a charming couple. The children are charming too. Everybody's charming. You're charming. I'm charming. With a hey no-ni-no and a hi-de-ho."

His eyebrows rose. He knocked his pipe against the wall. He fished an oilskin pouch out of his pocket and began the ritual that Raleigh started. I felt suddenly ashamed of myself.

"Sorry," I said. "But I wasn't in a talking mood. I thought it was more polite to be funny than to tell you to go to hell."

He nodded. "You know," he said, "I sometimes think the Levite was trying to be polite when he passed by on the other side."

"I'm not so good at riddles," I said.

"No? . . . I beg your pardon. I shouldn't have interrupted your session of quiet thought. I often feel in need of one myself." He took three steps into the gloaming. "Good night," he said with another smile.

I didn't move from the wall.

"I'm no Levite," I said. "I'm trying to be a Good Samaritan, but I'd no idea it was so damn difficult."

That halted him. He came back.

"In a small place like this," he said, "news travels fast. I knew that you were Mrs. Fabian's cousin. I also know you've discovered that she's at odds with her husband."

I didn't understand why I had thought Smith nondescript. At close quarters, a yard from him in the darkening lane, I thought I had never seen more intelligent eyes.

"I don't know whether you have any influence with Mr. Fabian. . . . If you have, it would be wise to warn him of the feeling he's stirring up against himself. I've thought this way for a long time. But I was inclined to watch and hope until this latest indiscretion."

"You mean Lora?" I said.

"Lora? Oh no! His affairs with women are in a different category. No, I mean the trees."

"I know nothing about any trees," I said.

"You probably know he's been acquiring property on the outskirts of Rhuine with a view to commercial development?"

"So I was told."

Smith had finished the Raleigh ritual. He lit his pipe. It needed three matches to do that.

"One of his purchases was a field beyond the church, owned by the Cowdrays. It was crossed by a continuation of this lane, known as Maldwyche Avenue. Trees planted, it is said, by the Maldwyche family more than two hundred years ago. When it became known that Mr. Fabian proposed to fell the trees and dispose of them as timber, there was a deal of local opposition. You see, we felt that Maldwyche Avenue was among the amenities of Rhuine, though strictly speaking it was beyond the parish boundary. Protests were made to the authorities, and an inquiry was pending. But I regret to say . . ."

He struck another match. It flickered between us, a little globe of yellow in the darkness, and I saw the strong line of his jaw, the set of his good-humoured mouth.

". . . I regret to say that Mr. Fabian hasn't waited for a decision. The trees have been felled."

"I'm not surprised," I said. "That's Fabian all over."

"I'm afraid it is. He would have lost nothing by waiting. If the decision had gone against him, he would have been reimbursed financially. If he had won his case, the timber would have been in better condition for felling two months hence than now. It seems to me that he has deliberately flouted local opinion for some obscure reason of his own."

"Or maybe it isn't so obscure," I said. "Maybe he did it to humiliate his wife."

He nodded. "You're possibly right. But tomorrow night is Mischief Night. Traditionally, it is the night to pay off old scores. I don't think Mr. Fabian realises the depth of local abhorrence he has aroused. If it could be pointed out to him that his attitude might result in a breach of the peace, it might weigh with him. Especially coming from one of his wife's relations."

"And it might not," I said. "I've spent a long time this afternoon pointing out things to Fabian that should have made him shiver in his shoes. The only difference is that he's more cocky than ever.

Smith was silent for a while.

"And tomorrow night," he said again, "is Mischief Night. Keep him indoors if you can."

"I'll think about it," I said. I looked at him curiously. "I suppose you wouldn't like to tell me why you're so interested?"

"I was born in Rhuine," he said. "I still like to watch over it in a sort of—well, fatherly way. If you feel you'd like to talk things over while you're here, come over and have a chat. Everybody in Shilstone knows me."

He struck yet another match. His eyes were twinkling. "Smith's the name," he said in that soft, slurred voice. "One of the Shilstone Smiths."

CHAPTER SIX

MISCHIEF NIGHT

NINIAN left next morning.

It was easy for things to happen in the early morning at Edward's Bounty. Fabian was either unarrived after a night on the tiles, or sleeping off his previous evening's activities. Sheila had made all arrangements over the phone. There was a through coach to Paddington attached to the local train that left Shilstone at 8.15 A. M., and the Morrises were to meet Ninian at Reading. So Sheila drove her to the station and put her in the care of the guard.

Meanwhile, I played the piano. I didn't care whether Fabian was in bed or out. I played Beethoven and Bach. You can make a big noise with either, and I got a lot of fun out of it. But I quietened down after half an hour and began to feel maudlin again. So I played *Sheep may Safely Graze*. I often feel like that when someone's kicked me in the teeth or I want to kick likewise. It's like standing under a warm shower. It soothes.

Sheila came in when I was letting the sheep graze for the third time. I could see that she had been crying. I banged

125

down the piano lid and lit a cigarette.

"It's the best thing you could have done," I said, deliberately unsympathetic. "The only definite thing you've done so far."

It was, but I could understand the way she felt.

After breakfast I went up the Score to the post-office. I wanted an extra newspaper and a book of stamps. Thinking always comes easier to me when I'm walking, and I had plenty to think about as I climbed that hill. I was wondering about the way Fabian would react to Ninian's departure. I even wondered if I had exaggerated the importance of Dillon's behavior yesterday.

It was nearly eleven by the time I had stood in the queue among women waiting for rations, children for sweets, and early tourists for picture post-cards. My next port of call was the Brickhole, for news of Luke and Peter. The first person I saw when I got through the door was the doctor, going over Luke with his rubber headphones. I waited with due respect till he was through. I could see that Luke's eyes were shut, but whether he was asleep or unconscious I couldn't be sure.

I was soon to know.

"Not too bad," the doctor said, pushing the ear-plugs round the back of his neck the way they do. "Running a temperature last night, though. Always the risk of pneumonia in a man his age. I think he's feeling pretty sick this morning. I've put him on sulfa and he doesn't react so well."

"No chance of a little private talk with him?"

"Probably tomorrow. I don't want him disturbed before then. Unless he wakens up and asks for you, of course. If he's got anything on his mind and wants to talk, all well and good."

He went into the kitchen and I followed him.

"I've another patient," he said in a low voice. "Your

cousin's boy. Young Peter. He's upstairs. I haven't told his mother yet."

"What's wrong with him?" I asked sharply.

"Stupid thing to say, but I don't know." The doctor rubbed his nose. "Probably delayed shock. . . . I've given him a sedative and told them to keep him quiet. If he doesn't improve, I'll bring Redfern over from Shilstone."

"Specialist?" I guessed.

"Overworked term," he replied. "He knows more about children than I do. Not their organs. Their minds."

I looked at him squarely. "You don't mean to say there's anything wrong with Peter's mind?"

"Not in the sense you're meaning. And I said mind, not brain. . . . I'm sufficiently old-fashioned to suspect some slight difference, you know."

He nodded and took himself off. As he went through the door, Isaiah's wife came down. She gazed at me with understanding solemnity, as if this were a tragic occasion and she was determined to make the most of it.

I sat down and started thinking again. It still didn't get me anywhere. It was time I had some intelligent cooperation. I was out of my depth. It might be a good idea to go up and see the Poskett.

But I didn't have to. As I was sitting there, staring at my shoe-toes, there came a sharp rap on the front door and the Poskett walked in.

Her outdoor dress consisted of the same shapeless garment she wore in the studio, plus a flat-topped blue straw hat and flat-heeled sandals with the straps unfastened, probably to accommodate the bunions that stuck out like a ballerina's breasts from the sides of her big feet. I was surprised that Rhuine allowed her out of doors when tourists were liable to come down the Score.

"Well!" she said loudly, seeing me. "Everything's pretty

127

now, don't you think?"

"Quite a lot's happened since I was talking to you," I admitted.

"How's Luke?"

"Asleep," I said, "unless you've wakened him up."

"And the boy?"

"I haven't been up yet. The doctor says it's delayed shock."

"Delayed from when and what?"

"If I could tell you that, I should have something better to do than sit here turning things over in what's left of a once-brilliant mind."

"Has his mother been told?"

"Not unless the doctor's told her over the phone in the last ten minutes."

She took out one of her black cigarettes and held another towards me. I shook my head and fished for a Woodbine, which I lit with the best air I could muster.

"If anything happens to him," she muttered, blowing stinking fumes into my face, "there's going to be some pretty material for the Sunday papers. Child wandering about the village, going where he likes, sleeping where he likes. And he's put to bed in a villager's house and under the doctor's orders before even his mother knows a thing about it."

"By the way," I asked curiously, "who told you?"

"The Rhuine grape-vine. It's all over the place. Fabian should know about it by now. I saw him going into the Galleon."

She went to Luke's bed and stared down at him.

"Who did it?" she asked.

"It was an accident," I said, bland as a melon.

"What sort of a bloody fool do you take me for?" she demanded with some heat.

"The name of the accident," I said, still bland, "could be Dillon. But that's off the record."

She turned round heavily. "But why Dillon, in the name

of common-sense?"

"You can't invoke common-sense in this business," I told her. "Obviously, because Jonquil knew something."

"What could Jonquil know that was dangerous to Dillon?"

"Maybe something the boy told him."

She pulled the shapeless blue thing closer around her shoulders, as if she felt the cold. The cold that certainly wasn't in the air that morning at Rhuine. I'd felt that way.

"I wonder what we're up against," she said.

"I keep wondering the same."

"I'll go up and see the boy."

I went up with her. They had put Peter in the front bed-room. It was small and spotless. There was a wash-hand-stand in the corner, a recess curtained off, matting on the floor, a couple of illuminated texts on the walls. The one opposite the bed said, in flower-embowered letters: *Safe in the Arms of Jesus*, which struck me as being somewhat pointed in the circumstances. There was a silvery-grey wallpaper with a Morris pattern embossed upon it. The blind was half-way down, and rattled slightly in the breeze. And into the quietness came the sounds of Rhuine; the mutter of feet on cobblestones, the chatter of the tourists, the ever-hungry cries of seagulls as they swooped around the harbour.

Peter lay straight in the middle of the bed. He was looking at the ceiling. He didn't turn his head as we came into the room. He looked very childish and thin under the covers.

The Poskett went up to him. She had a good way with her. Good, that is, for a child like Peter. Not quite brisk, not at all hearty or sympathetic.

"What's wrong this time, Peter," she asked. "Mumps or scarlet?"

He didn't speak.

"You sick in one room and Luke in the other!" she went on. "We can't have this."

His lips moved. "I'm all right," he said. "Why's everyone making a fuss?"

"Anything hurt, Peter? Tummy?"

"Only my head. My head burns."

"Nothing you'd like me to bring for you?"

He didn't answer.

Face like something struck white with spring frost, I thought. No movement. Eyes wide open. He might have been dead. I wondered how long he would go without blinking. It seemed an eternity. I could have prayed for his eyes to close and open again.

"There's nothing I want," he said at last. Then: "Where's Dillon?"

"At home, I suppose," I told him.

"He couldn't catch me."

I waited. A ghost of a smile. . . . Less than a ghost.

"Where's Old Horny?"

"I don't know, Pete. Don't worry about Old Horny," I said. "I'm taking care of him."

"He's a lousy bastard. Isaiah says so. Old Horny's a bloody lousy bastard."

The Poskett caught her breath. She probably hadn't heard that one before. After a minute she bent down and said: "Would you like to see your mummy, Peter?"

Now his eyes moved. "No."

"I'll bring her if you like."

"No. I want Lora."

The Poskett looked at me. She hadn't heard that one either. She was getting the paint shaken out of her hair.

"Lora's a smasher!" came in a faint, valiant whisper from the bed.

We stood there ten more minutes. He didn't speak again. His eyes were closed.

"I think he's asleep," I said.

We went quietly out of the room. Half-way down the

narrow stairs the Poskett stopped. She was cramming the blue abomination into her mouth, she was shaking with tears. Feeling embarrassed, I put my hand on her shoulder.

"I know," I said. "It gets me the same way. Makes you feel helpless when you come up against a thing like this and don't know what's behind it."

"But we know who's behind it!" she said. "And I've something to say to him before I'm much older."

I was afraid she would waken Luke, or the child who had only just dropped off to sleep in the room above. She strode on her short legs through the kitchen and into the Brickhole. "Now don't do anything rash!" I said to that blue back. "There's no sense in rushing fences."

"Rash be damned!" she said over her shoulder, and I followed meekly without further protest. I didn't know what she planned to do. But I thought it wise to be on the spot when she did it.

Growling to herself like an angry dog, she hurried up the Score, me trailing behind and feeling a fool. "I'll be down in a minute!" she snapped at me when we reached the steps leading up to her house, and I dutifully waited.

But I shouldn't have waited if I'd known what was coming. Neither should I have followed her into the Galleon. I was three paces behind when she pushed open the door. I caught it on the rebound, and stood just inside. I felt sorry to be there, but there seemed a chance I should be needed.

She had made enough noise to acquaint everyone with her presence. She handed me the flat brown-paper parcel she had brought from the studio, then, under the blue garment, put her hands on her hips. She looked like a bell-tent on legs. Mackender was gaping at her. So was Mackender's wife, screwed to her stool once again. The doctor was in, too, for a refresher after finishing his rounds, I surmised.

And with Mackender, as before, stood Fabian. I saw the soft skin of his hand whiten as he gripped his glass more

131

tightly, and there was a wary look in his clear eyes.

The Poskett stalked to the counter.

"I don't want a drink, sonny," she said to the barman. "I only wish to use this vulgar and effete establishment as a rostrum. I want to tell Fabian what I think about him."

"You needn't trouble," Fabian said, not turning a hair. "Fabian knows. And returns the compliment."

There was a gust of laughter at this sally. The Poskett ignored it. She took the flat parcel from me, ripped off the paper, pulled up a stool to the wall, and hung the canvas on a convenient nail.

"That's Fabian as I see him," she said. "Stuart Durward Fabian, the blackest-hearted pig that ever rooted in this palatial, chromium-plated trough."

Nobody laughed this time. Looking at the Poskett's picture of Fabian, laughter didn't come easily.

"He posed for me in the nude," said the Poskett.

"You lying bitch!" said Fabian pleasantly.

"You flatter me, sir! Everybody I paint sits for me in the nude, however well-dressed they are. Now, pig, tell them all what I know. Tell 'em how you offered me fifty guineas to paint you. Patronised me, conferred your gracious custom on a local hack! Tell them, you white-haired wart-hog! Tell them you wouldn't take the picture away when you saw what I'd put in your eyes."

The barman tried to make himself heard above the uproar. "We don't want any brawling here," he shouted. "No brawling please, ladies and gentlemen. If this goes on, I'll telephone for the police."

"Brawling?" retorted the Poskett. "I'm not brawling, sonny. I'm pointing out that if you want to keep this pub a decent house for decent people, you'll close your doors to this hulk of sin. You're doing yourself no good in Rhuine by encouraging him." She addressed the company at large. "I've just come from the Brickhole. From Luke Jonquil's cottage. Fabian's stepson is there. Ill, in Luke's bed. The heir to Rhuine, you dim-witted oafs, and he's lying there in that cottage."

"Thanks for the information," Fabian said. "I'll call for him on my way home. If I'd known he was there, I'd have had him out earlier. And when I get him home"—Fabian laughed gently—"I don't think he'll feel like another trip for quite a while."

"If I were you, Fabian," a new voice said, "I wouldn't make foolish threats."

"And who the hell are you to tell me what to do?" Fabian asked, twisting round.

"My name's Warren, in case you're losing your grip. I'm your step-son's self-appointed medical advisor. He's in bed by my orders. And he stays there by my orders."

Regardless of the mixed company, Fabian retorted with one short and ancient word.

"I leave that to you," Dr. Warren replied, and the Poskett howled with glee. "If you attempt to move him and any harm results, I shall take considerable pleasure in having you tarred and feathered by the natives, quite apart from what the law may do with you later."

"And besides that," the Poskett said happily, "you've no legal right to move him. He's not your son. You couldn't breed a boy like that if you tried for a thousand years."

She turned to the barman. "I think it calls for a drink after all. Give me a pint, sonny."

He pulled the pint of beer and gave it to her. It happened so quickly that no one quite knew how. Fabian had no time to duck or dodge. He received it full in the face. He stood in the middle of the floor, shaking himself, while everybody in the place except the barman, the doctor, the Poskett and I guffawed with laughter.

"And I could wish," said the Poskett, "that both the pot and its contents were more appropriate to the occasion."

Fabian didn't speak. But he slowly raised his head and looked at me. I held his eyes for a good quarter-minute before I turned and followed the Poskett into the Score. By that time the reaction had set in and she was wildly crying.

"Was I good?" she sobbed. "Was I really good?"

"You were magnificent," I told her. "From now on, if Fabian's what I think he is, your life's worth about threepence an hour. Now go and have your cry out in comfort."

"Aren't you coming in with me?" she asked.

"I'm going to the Dolphin for a brandy. I need one. Then, if it settles my stomach, I'm going to have a meal. But I don't think it will."

I went to the Dolphin and had the brandy. But my stomach still played arpeggios. I sat on the bench outside and stared across the harbour. I didn't think. I was short of material.

I sat there because it was a good strategic position. I could see if Fabian came out of the Galleon. I could also see if he came down the Score towards Lora's cottage or went towards Edward's Bounty. If he went home, I thought, I ought to follow him, though rather than that I would have walked to Land's End and back. Nothing but an urgent sense of duty sends a smallish and rather timid man in pursuit of another built like a battleship.

I sat there for half an hour. I supposed he would be cleaning himself up. Then I saw him come out of the pub. He didn't turn off towards the ravine. That meant he was going to Lora.

So much the worse for Lora, I thought.

But neither did he turn that way. He's going to cross the harbour bridge, I thought, and go home by Church Staithe. Maybe he feels like a breath of fresh air. I leaned back and watched, telling my knees to keep still. *I am not afraid*, I said to myself in that low, affirmative voice recommended by the psychologists, *of any man on earth large or small. I am full of courage and determination.*

I watched him come nearer. I would give him time to get over the bridge, then up and after him. *Courage and determination*, I repeated to my shaking knees.

But my courage, Dutch or otherwise, wasn't needed just then. He didn't cross the bridge. He came towards the jetty and passed within twenty yards without seeing me. He went down the first run of stone steps and walked over the shingle towards Jonquil's boats. He was pushing the nearest one into the water when Isaiah Jonquil came at a shuffling run from the entrance to the Brickhole.

"You leave my boats alone, damn and blast your bloody eyes, zur!" he shouted.

Fabian straightened up. I could almost have felt sorry for him. If a woman had thrown a pint of beer in my face, I too might have felt like a quiet pull round the bay to get my feathers straight again.

"I'm going to row round Haldom," he shouted back.

"Not in one o' my boats. You leave 'er alone or I'll have the police on you. I will that zur, blast you."

"I've taken one of your boats often enough before," Fabian bawled.

"What you did before and what you're going to do now happens to be two different things, zur. I don't want no suicides and my boat driftin' out to sea. If you're wantin' to row round Haldom I'll take you, but you leave them bleedin' oars alone."

A little knot of people had gathered on the jetty. There was some laughter and plenty of interest.

"You daren't come out with me," Fabian said. "You haven't the guts. You know you daren't."

"Daren't?" roared Jonquil. "I'd row the Devil round hell if he paid me to do it. I'll take your money, zur, even if you're lowest louse that ever crawled."

"I'll take you up on that," Fabian said.

I could see the Poskett's beer-stains on his jacket. He waited contemptuously till Jonquil pushed the boat out, then jumped after him. The last thing I saw, he was sitting in the bow with knees hunched under his chin, glaring at Isaiah's back as he pulled out of the harbour.

I still sat on the bench. I wondered how long Luke Jonquil would stay befuddled by Dr. Warren's pills. There didn't seem any way over the blank wall facing me except by foot-holds Luke could provide. So what? Didn't I do anything till then but sit and stare?

Mostly to prevent myself going into the Dolphin for more brandy, which I didn't really want, I mooched up the Score, hands in pockets, and turned over the ravine.

I kept my head well down. Walking about Rhuine was embarrassing now. Everybody knew I was Mrs. Fabian's cousin, and they looked at me with a sort of dull hopefulness, as if I could probably save them from the fate Fabian was planning.

As I approached Mrs. Dukas's cottage, I saw out of my eye-corner that she was at the window. She opened the door and asked me to go inside. I didn't care to refuse. It was a toy, polished place, like most of the Rhuine cottages, full of rush mats and chintz and old furniture, and Mrs. Dukas was a little starched old lady with the manner of a one-time hospital nurse.

"I do hope you won't mind if I ask a question, sir," she said breathlessly, "but is it true Mr. Fabian's threatening to burn down Rhuine?"

I jumped. I remembered Sheila's story of the coach-house, and the Argus editor's hints at Fabian's arson complex. I also remembered Boldry's reluctance to discuss the matter, and the feeling he had given me that he could have said a lot more.

"If he intended doing that," I said to Mrs. Dukas, "he wouldn't tell everybody beforehand, surely? He'd want it to look like an accident."

"But he's a wicked man, sir!" She shook her head. "Oh, such a wicked, wicked man."

"Any Salvation Army captain will tell you the world's full of wicked men," I said. "You've a personal grudge against him, haven't you?"

"You mean the dog, sir? And the way he treads on my garden? I know they're only little things—"

"Very little," I agreed. "So little that perhaps only a really wicked man would trouble to do them."

She nodded but didn't speak. "How long has this rumour been going around?" I asked.

"Oh, for weeks and weeks, sir! You see, Mr. Fabian says things when he's drunk."

"Which is pretty frequently, eh?"

"Oh yes, sir! And Rhuine was burned down once. They say it was the Spaniards who did it. My brother happened to be in the public-house, sir—he drops in for an occasional glass—when Mr. Fabian and the other gentlemen were talking about it. Mr. Fabian said that what had happened once could happen again, and that more than one problem might be solved if it did happen."

"Most of us say things like that off the top," I said without much conviction. "I know a man who told me he'd pay any bus-driver ten pounds to run over his mother-in-law, but next night he hared down for the doctor because she cut her thumb on a sardine-can."

"But Rhuine could be burnt down very easily," she persisted. "The fire-engine can't get down, sir."

"Surely you've a local squad?" I asked.

"Yes. But if anyone started a really big fire, what chance would there be?"

The constant repetition of the word fire was getting on my nerves. I reassured her as well as I could. The best way to kill rumour, I said, was ignore it.

"In any case," I told her, "you'd probably survive, Mrs. Dukas. Your cottage is detached."

"But if Mr. Fabian's making these threats, sir, why don't they lock him up?"

She had me there. I tried to explain that in our happy country, people are locked up because of what they have done, not what they may do. That happens to be one of the main points of difference between our side of the Iron Curtain and the other. . . . And when you come up against men like Fabian, it makes you wonder if the other side doesn't know a thing or two after all.

When I got away from Mrs. Dukas, I went back to Edward's Bounty. That hadn't been on my programme earlier. But Mrs. Dukas had given me an idea. I wanted to look at, that coach-house. So far I hadn't even given it a glance.

It adjoined the eastern part of the house, at an angle to the kitchen. When I pushed aside the charred door and went inside, the place was open to the sky. There was a stone floor. The walls too were of stone. And judging by the thickness of the roof-timbers, whose ends were still sticking out of the wall above my head, there hadn't been much ply-wood used when the building was constructed. Sheila had told me there had been no inflammable rubbish stored there. And you can drop lighted matches and cigarette-stubs on eight-inch oak beams for several centuries without anything happening.

I leaned against the wall. I was thinking of Fabian and the dog-kennel. Of the house with the two suffocated maids. I was thinking about Smith and his idea that something might happen on Mischief Night. (I must find out who Smith was, I thought.) Maybe I'd put the wrong interpretation on Smith's fears. Had he meant that someone might try to burn down Edward's Bounty, or that Fabian might try to burn down Rhuine?

One thing was pretty certain. If the coach-house, the juvenile prank with the dog-kennel, the suffocated maids, Smith's hint, Boldry's reticence, and the Dukas rumour added up to the right total, Fabian was something more than a smart business man or even the high-power lecher the Poskett had just baptised with barley-wine. He was well on the way to criminal lunacy.

But I couldn't be sure, yet, that it all did add up to that total.

I went into the house. Sheila was alone in the living-room. The big box of coloured silks and cottons was open again, and I instinctively fingered my loose button. But I didn't mention it. A button more or less seemed trivial in the circumstances. She asked if I'd eaten lunch, and I admitted that I hadn't. She rang for Rose, and presently I left her to feast alone in the smaller room. I took my time over that meal. It was three o'clock when I came back to Sheila.

I told her what Dr. Warren had said about Peter.

"I know," she said. "He rang up just before you came." She went on with the embroidery. It was something heraldic that I didn't understand. "Has anyone said," she asked, "that I should have gone down to see him?"

"Not to me."

Then I told her about the episode in the Galleon, and Fabian's trip across the bay with Jonquil.

"And it's Mischief Night tonight," she said.

"So I've been told," I said dryly, and went on to impart what Mrs. Dukas had said.

"Since then, I've been looking over the coach-house. I asked Boldry for information the other day, but he didn't unbutton himself much. Now, unless there's some vital reason why I shouldn't be told, I'd like your frank opinion. Was some Rhuine desperado trying to spite Fabian by burning the place down, or did Fabian do the burning to spite you?"

"It was Stuart," she said.

"Any proof?"

"Not a shred. But I know it was. And I don't think it was to spite me."

"But nothing else," I said, "makes sense."

"Stuart isn't a fool," Sheila said. "The wind came from the west that night. It would have taken a long time for the fire to creep against the wind, and the whole kitchen wing would have had to burn before the main part of the house was in danger. Besides, he must have known that the fire could easily be fought. Rhuine's literally terrified of fire. Every house has its own chemical extinguishers, and we have a fire department of our own, equipped with foam apparatus and all that. . . . The Shilstone engines wouldn't be able to get down either of the Scores, you see."

Mrs. Dukas, I remembered, had already made that point.

"And I have quite an elaborate installation here," Sheila went on. "There's a tank in the false roof, and in an emergency we could pump water from the sea."

I thought that over.

"And Stuart gave the alarm himself," she said with finality. "He was fighting the fire before anybody else could get here."

"Gave the alarm himself . . . Was he in the habit of going to the coach-house?"

"He scarcely ever went. There was nothing to go for. I've told you, the place was absolutely empty."

"You see what I'm getting at? Wasn't it odd that Fabian just happened to pay a visit to a place he normally never entered, and just at that moment a fire broke out? I think that's proof enough, though you said you hadn't any. It's good enough for me, anyway. But why did he do it?"

"Mr. Boldry might have told you if you'd played him more skilfully. I know what he thinks. It was because Stuart is morbidly fascinated by fire. He wanted to see a big fire. He wanted to know how easy it would be to start one here. He knew he could have a gorgeous blaze in the coach-house without any serious danger to the rest of the house. It was a dress-rehearsal."

"I'm beginning to understand why Peter said tell me about the coach-house."

"I wasn't frightened of being burnt to death," Sheila said. "But after that episode, I realised the kind of man I was living with."

"Do sudden storms spring up in the bay?" I wondered aloud.

"Things like that don't just happen. . . . Anyway, we shouldn't be thinking or talking about it, no matter what he is. But I hope he doesn't come home afterwards. Perhaps he won't. He may go to Lora. He keeps a spare suit there and a change of linen."

She said it without bitterness. No doubt she had got past that stage.

I decided I would take a walk, as I had intended doing before Mrs. Dukas came into the picture. There wasn't anything more I could do at the moment. It was too early yet to expect answers to my letters.

I walked along the cliffs to Haldom Head, and sat among the furze for half an hour. I fancied I could see a small boat a mile or so offshore, but couldn't even guess at that distance whether it might be Jonquil and Fabian. I found a cottage up there with a catering sign outside, and had a tea of fresh eggs, toasted scones and plum jam. It was seven o'clock when I came back to Edward's Bounty, and still Fabian hadn't shown up. And still Sheila sat with her embroidery. She might never have moved. I knew she was eating her heart out for Ninian and must be racked with suspense about Peter. I knew she was waiting, as I was, for something to happen. Some blow to fall. And neither of us knew what it would be or when we should feel it.

"When this is over," I said, "go away."

"I think I will. Perhaps to the Morrises. Did I tell you they rang through this afternoon? Ninian's arrived safely and they say she's quite cheerful. . . . I'd like to take the

141

children to America, too. To Carolina. But I should want to be back for spring."

"Back to Rhuine," I said, half-bitterly. "You're the Dame of Rhuine all right, Sheila. You'll always be that."

I asked her to play the piano for me again, and she did. She played for an hour, while I wandered about the room, sometimes watching her, sometimes going to the window and looking across the harbour. There were more lights than usual tonight. A string of coloured bulbs was festooned across the Dolphin, and somewhere in the distance I could hear a brass band playing.

"Mischief Night must have been rather wonderful at one time," Sheila said from the piano. "Now, I'm afraid, it's rather forced and self-conscious. Something like the Helston dancing."

"Do they dance here?" I asked.

"I believe the Poskett organised some folk-dancing a few years ago, but it didn't last. Mischief Night now is just an excuse for eating and drinking more than usual. And the young men can kiss any girl they like. . . . All that sort of thing."

"Useful custom," I said. "I suppose it doesn't extend to these patrician surroundings?"

She didn't answer, and I was sorry I'd said it.

Beyond the Dolphin, on the slopes of the Downfall, a bonfire had been lit. I realise how my nerves must be on edge, because though it was well away from the street, it struck me that Fabian might have carried out his threats and Rhuine was burning.

But nothing like that happened. What did happen, however, was just as terrifying in its own way.

About ten o'clock, Rose came in to say that a crowd of people—all Rhuine, she said—was coming up Church Staithe towards Edward's Bounty. We went to the front windows to look. Rose was right about it being a crowd. Twenty or more of them seemed to be carrying torches—the traditional kind, wood and cloth soaked in oil. It was an eerie sight. I didn't like it at all.

"You've seen those pictures of witch-hunts?" Sheila said.

"And of Ku Klux Klan lynchings," I muttered. "What do you suppose they want?"

I half-expected her to say they wanted Fabian. That's what I imagined. But I was wrong. Edward's Bounty wasn't their objective. They marched past the gates, shouting and singing.

"Where can they be going?" Sheila said with a puzzled frown. "There's nothing past here but the church and the rectory."

"I think we ought to go and see."

We crossed the lawn. Looking back, I saw that Rose and two other maids were following us, with Cook and Dillon a few yards behind. I was interested to see Dillon there. He hadn't been much in evidence recently.

The crowd was making more noise than ever. They went past the churchyard, torches swinging and sending foul black smoke billowing into the air. They didn't stop till they reached the ruined trees of Maldwyche Avenue. We climbed a rhododendron bank at the edge of Sheila's property and had a grand-stand view of everything that happened.

They were mostly young men and girls. They were standing around a timber-wagon that had been loaded up with the newly-felled trees. That wagon was hitched to a powerful tractor, the only thing that could have hauled it up the rough woodland track to the level ground above. The contractors must have intended an early start tomorrow morning. But they were not the only people with ideas about that.

One of the boys started the tractor. The crowd began to cheer, and I soon understood why. He backed those tons of timber as near as was safe to the edge of the cliff. Before I realised what their game was, the tractor was uncoupled and fifty pairs of hands were pushing that wagon towards the brink. There was another rousing cheer as it disappeared.

Smashing something up gives most people a kick. These people were getting it all right. I put my arm round Sheila's shoulders. She was trembling. There wasn't a thing we could have done, even if we had wished. And I don't think we did.

And now, with crow-bars and improvised rollers, they were tackling the rest of the trunks. Those trees had taken two hundred years to grow. They had been cut down in a day by Fabian's orders. Now they went over the cliff in twenty minutes. I could have cheered with the rest. Nothing could restore what he had destroyed. But the profit he had planned to make was swashing about in the Channel, and there was some comfort in that.

But they weren't through yet.

What they had done was sheer mob-violence. The old Rhuine custom had only been its excuse. What they did now was in keeping with the ironical medieval humour of Mischief Night at its best.

They drove the tractor back to the Pound, that rectangle of walled turf I had noticed the previous night. Any other time of the year, the glare of those torches would have been remarked upon, and the Shilstone police might have come bouncing down. But this was Mischief Night and no one troubled.

These boys had come prepared. They wanted the tractor in the Pound. It wouldn't pass through the narrow gap that sheep and cows used in the old days. . . . If it could have passed through, they wouldn't have bothered anyway. They wanted that tractor inside so that Fabian couldn't get it out again.

Above the Pound, straddling it with spidery legs, were three scaffold-poles firmly lashed together at their apex. Outside the Pound, between the wall and the edge of the road, were three similar poles. Firmly secured beneath these two triangles, and joining them together, was a strong steel girder. . . .

I'd seen that girder before.

"The lifting tackle they're using in the harbour," I said to Sheila. "What's their idea?"

The chains rattled in the pulley-block. Five minutes' tricky work and the tractor was gently swinging six feet above their heads. They pushed the rollers along the girder. The tractor moved slowly over the enclosing wall and was lowered into the Pound.

Now they went wild with joy. The crowd was swollen by dozens of other village revellers who had heard the glad tidings and hurried up Church Staithe to see the fun. They were singing again. It should have been something medieval and diabolical. But they couldn't rise to that. It was *Who's Afraid of the Big Bad Wolf?*

Meanwhile the boys were dismantling the lifting tackle. They didn't take long over it. Before the crowd had finished the second rousing stanza, six poles lying on the grass and a thin steel girder beside them was all there was to show how the trick had been done. The tractor was snug in the Pound, and there was no way out. The only access to that bit of old England was a gap just big enough for a horse. How to get that tractor on to the road would be Fabian's headache.

We had moved from the rhododendron bank and were now standing inside the drive gate. All of us, servants included. Nobody took any notice of us. It was Fabian they were up against. They crowded up to the walls of the Pound for a last look. They cheered and laughed. . . . And then, as if a conductor had waved his stick, they stopped.

A man was coming up the road from Church Staithe. It was Fabian. Behind him, panting and blowing, came Mackender and his wife. There were others too—all those, I supposed, who had been in the Galleon bar when the news was brought. But it was only Fabian I had eyes for.

I was frightened of Fabian then, and I admit it. He looked like a prophet out of the Bible. His white hair gleamed in the torch-light and his ruddy face looked ruddier than ever as he marched towards the Pound. He looked over the wall. He went through the gap and stared at the tractor.

Then he came out and faced them, arrogant as a lion at bay. He pushed his way past the crowd and walked into the darkness beyond the Pound. His cronies from the Galleon stayed where they were, so he must have been alone when he saw the Avenue bare of trees, the wheel-marks to the edge of the cliff, and realised what the people of Rhuine had done to him.

It was ten minutes before he came back. He wasn't walking so quickly now. He saw us standing at the gate, but didn't give us a second glance. He flung out his arms, clearing a passage for himself, and stalked again through that narrow gap into the Pound.

He started up the tractor and climbed into the seat. Before anybody could stop him—before most of us realized what was in his mind—he backed to the far wall and then charged full tilt at the gap. The tractor shuddered, the stones bellied outwards. A girl in the crowd screamed as he charged the wall a second time and smashed through, lurching on to the road. The neat board announcing that Rhuine Pound was an Ancient Monument lay on its side, broken in three pieces.

That was the end of Mischief Night.

The crowd roared angrily. . . . Some of them moved forward. I knew then how lynch-law works. Not half a dozen among that punch-drunk mob had anything against Fabian. Most of them were young, belonging to a new generation that might have welcomed his schemes for Rhuine. And whatever grievances they had were already revenged. All that was left of Maldwyche Avenue was down the cliff.

But he was a scapegoat. This was the man who had said

he would burn Rhuine. Now, he had destroyed the Pound. They surged around him. I thought they were going to kill him, pull him to pieces. But when he fell off the tractor they saw he was bleeding about the face. It was only a slight cut, but they didn't know that. The blood saved him. They let him stagger across the road and through the gate of Edward's Bounty, his wife's house. They contented themselves with that low, animal roar.

Dillon had disappeared. Sheila and I stood aside as Fabian opened the gate. He went past us towards the house.

"Don't sleep here tonight," I warned Sheila. "Go to the Dolphin. Or to Jonquil's place. It isn't safe for you here."

"I'll be all right. I'll have Rose with me." She was shivering, but tried to smile. "I'll be quite safe. Don't worry about me. What are you going to do?"

"I don't know," I said.

"I think you're the one who should go to the Dolphin."

"I may do that. But I want to know how you're going to be fixed before I decide."

Behind us, the crowd was dispersing. We stood by the gate till the last group had gone down the road, then I took Sheila into the house.

I don't know what I expected to happen. Fabian, probably, to rush out with a gun. The police to come. . . .

What I didn't expect was to see Fabian standing with a glass of whisky in his hand, dabbing at his cut face with a handkerchief but otherwise practically normal.

Did I say he was resilient?

It was a shock. At least, I'd thought, it would be separate camps from now on. There wouldn't even be a pretence of civility. But there he was. Atkin, the Corgi, nuzzled round his ankles, and he pushed the dog away with his foot.

"I hope you enjoyed the show," he said, still dabbing.

I jammed my knees against the table so they couldn't knock together so easily. But I managed a sour look.

147

"I hope you did," I said. "And the Poskett's show. And your trip with Jonquil. Things seem to be adding up, don't they?"

Holding the handkerchief to his face, he went to the side-table. "Whisky?" he said.

I didn't even shake my head.

"Poskett," he said, "is a demented old bastard."

"You should have told her so."

"Jonquil," he went on softly, "doesn't swim."

I didn't get that for a moment. Not till he added, with an exaggerated drawl: "I do. I'm an excellent swimmer. Isn't that right, Sheila?"

The dog nuzzled again, and again he jerked out his foot. Dogs are poor judges of character.

"You should be careful what you say," I told him.

"One of these days I shall have to deal with the Poskett. And with Jonquil. With you, too. And with the oafs who caused the trouble tonight."

He smiled. The fool of a dog nuzzled again, and still smiling, Fabian kicked it full in the belly. It hit the wall and dropped in a heap, screaming. And Fabian still smiled.

I could have killed him then. Given a knife or a gun, I should have killed him where he stood. But I managed to control myself. All I could have done was hit him. And he wanted that, so he could hit me back. So I listened to the dog yelping and did nothing.

"You didn't like that, did you Cardew? So why didn't you do something about it?"

I stood looking at him. Sheila went to the wall and picked up the dog. She was very white. I opened the door. He said to her: "Take your little hero upstairs and tuck him into bed."

She carried the dog into the corridor. Rose was there. She had been listening, and I didn't blame her.

"Oh Mr. Cardew!" she said. "Has he gone mad?"

148

"Very near it," I said.

I took the dog from Sheila. It licked my face. I felt over it carefully, then put it on the floor and made sure it could walk, if painfully.

"I'll take him to my room," Sheila said. "He can sleep on my bed tonight."

"I want you to stay with Mrs. Fabian, too," I said to Rose. My own voice sounded to me as if it were coming from the end of a cave. I was feeling light-headed. "Lock the door and keep it locked, understand? And if there's any trouble, come to the window and make a loud noise. I shan't be far away."

I left them at the foot of the stairs. I hung about the hall for a minute or so, wondering if Fabian would come out and start trouble again. Then I let myself out and walked down the drive.

There was still no sign of the police. I wondered if there would be, that night. I leaned over the gate, looking at the trampled grass, the tractor tilted towards the ditch. Somewhere in Rhuine the band still played, or maybe it was a radio. I couldn't be sure which.

The church clock struck midnight. I wandered round the shrubbery and across the lawn. There was a light in Fabian's room. Sheila's faced the harbour, so I couldn't tell about that from where I stood. I couldn't hear a sound, upstairs or down.

I didn't feel afraid of Fabian any more, but I felt I couldn't sleep in the house that night. I had to be outside it; outside the pattern of events that seemed to be arranging themselves towards some sort of fantastic climax. If I went into the house I should be caught up in them. Or that's how I felt.

I walked twice round the house. Still no sound. I went to the summer-house and swung it round with its back to the sea and what little breeze there was. I dropped back among the cushions and stared at Fabian's lighted window.

There was only one thing I could be certain of. I wasn't

149

going to sleep that night. I wasn't going to think either, because thinking hadn't got me anywhere at all.

I was going to sit there, relaxed and waiting, in case Rose came to the window and made a loud noise. I wasn't going to think about anything till I'd seen Luke in the morning.

Relax. . . . Mind a blank. *I am quite calm and confident.*

I was a liar. My nerves were like fiddle-strings. As for staying awake. . . .

Next thing I knew there was a grey light everywhere and I was chattering with cold.

OLD, OLD STORY

I UNFOLDED my limbs and looked around. The lawn was a lake of mist and dew. My clothes and the cushions were dripping wet. There wasn't a sound or a breath of wind. I could have thought it was the morning before the world was made.

I looked at my watch. It was five o'clock.

I sprinted half a dozen times on my toes round the lawn. Then I lit a cigarette and sat down again. I stayed there till the sky in the east began to turn red, then got up and went down the drive to the road.

And then I saw the first bill.

It was pasted in triplicate on the harbour bridge. It was

a sheet forty inches by thirty, printed in bold blue-and-red letters:

RHUINE PROTECTION SOCIETY.

PROTEST MEETING

Friday Next
at Seven o'clock in
the

METHODIST SCHOOLROOM.

Speaker, T. H. Bridgeover, M.P.
Chairman, Isaiah Jonquil.
(Hon. Pres., Rhuine Protection
Society.)

THIS MEETING is called as a MASS
PROTEST against recent acts of
Vandalism on the outskirts of
Rhuine, and the danger of commercial
development calculated to destroy
the amenities of Rhuine and deprive
its inhabitants of their livelihood.

COME AND RAISE YOUR VOICE!

It was a striking bill. It must have cost a lot to print.

And the harbour was plastered with them. One was hanging in every cottage window. There must have been twenty on the front of the Poskett's house. The only building conspicuously without one was the Galleon.

So the gloves were off!

I could understand now why Fabian had gone berserk last night. It must be a hell of a thing to realise after a long run of luck that the balls have started rolling against you.

The first man up in Rhuine that morning seemed to be Isaiah Jonquil. I saw him coming out of the Brickhole and followed him down the Score. He heard my shoes on the cobbles and turned to look at me with his slow, knowing smile.

"Had a bit of trouble up your way last night, hadn't you, zur?"

"More than I fancied," I said. "I haven't been to bed yet."

He chuckled and began to pare a cake of tobacco.

"Ah well, it'll all be sorted out! Inspector'll be here soon, zur."

"What Inspector?"

"Police Inspector from Shilstone, zur."

"And tomorrow," I said, "your protest meeting will be covered by every newspaper in the country."

"That's what I thought. I'm having a big table with a card in the middle saying PRESS."

He was placid this morning; placid and content. I had never seen a man more self-satisfied. And it occurred to me that all this build-up hadn't been accidental. It had been planned. The show of mob-violence last night had been strategically timed.

"You're playing a dangerous game," I said. "All in a good cause, Jonquil . . . But damned dangerous all the same."

"You don't have to tell me that, zur. I was thinking the same thing when I was sitting by my brother last night. And we'd a sleep-walking do with young Peter. I've a lot of scores to settle."

We had reached the jetty. "You wouldn't like to be taking out a boat this morning, zur?" he asked slyly.

"I wouldn't. And take my advice, Jonquil. Don't go out with Fabian again."

"I'm taking him tomorrow morning, zur."

I looked at him.

"Mr. Fabian likes his bit of fishing, zur."

"When did you fix that up?"

152

"Yesterday, zur, when I brought him back from Haldom way."

"Had Fabian seen this bill of yours then?"

"It was before I plastered the town, as you might say. But I'd sent him an advance copy, zur."

"And how did he react to it?"

"Well, zur, very reasonable, everything considered. Talked a lot. Said it was a pity, me being the brains of the proletariat in Rhuine, that we couldn't get together and do a deal. Harped on that a lot, did Mr. Fabian. He did mention, too, how easy a boat upsets if you don't handle her right. No threats, you understand. . . . What you might call a war of nerves, zur."

"And you're taking him again tomorrow!" I said. "Jonquil, you're a fool."

"Now don't you go making that mistake, zur! The way I look at it, Mr. Fabian's champion of one cause and I'm champion of the other. What he's doing is challenging me. I reckon it has to be fought out somehow."

"Then fight it out on the platform tomorrow night."

"That wouldn't satisfy me, zur."

I could understand that. But it seemed unnecessary for Jonquil to stick out his neck when there was no need for it. I knew more about Fabian's mental processes than he did, and I was more afraid than he had any cause to be.

"Fabian's being beaten all along the line," I said to Jonquil. "He's a dangerous man." I waited a minute, then added: "And I've been told you don't swim."

I thought that shook him slightly. But his jaw set like iron again as he turned to me and said: "Mr. Cardew, zur, I dessay what you're telling me is true. But no Jonquil ever turned his back on a bloody foreigner."

I walked down the steps with him to the boats. On impulse, I slid one down the slope of wet shingle, unshipped the oars,

153

and pottered about the harbour for ten minutes. I have an instinctive mistrust of boats. Earth is man's natural element, and it seems to me he's cheating when he expects to bear up with air or water underneath him. As I shifted from one side to the other, I saw how the gunwale sank practically to water-level. I didn't like it. But there was nothing I could do about it.

When I returned to Jonquil, he was chuckling over my antics. I was feeling like food. I told him I would be down again later, after the doctor had called to see his brother. Then I strolled past the Dolphin and up the Score.

Early as it was, there were signs of life at the Poskett's studio. Someone was sweeping and dusting the cafe and the knick-knack rooms. I went in and pottered around for a while, looking at the Birmingham brassware and the Bolton folk-weave. A woman came out of the rear quarters and looked at me suspiciously. I explained that I was a friend of the Poskett, and I hadn't breakfasted yet. She said there would be coffee ready in a few minutes.

I told her I wanted more than coffee. I wanted a meal. My eating recently had been very sketchy. She was a good woman. Twenty minutes later I was sitting in front of ham and eggs. By the time the Poskett came down, I was smoking a cigarette and reading yesterday's newspaper. It told me about what was happening in the world outside Rhuine. I was beginning to forget there was one.

"What are you doing here," she asked, "and what's been happening, Cardew?"

I told her nothing had, to me. What had happened was of general interest and she would be hearing about it as the day wore on. What I needed, I said, was some place to sleep for a few hours.

She said if I waited a while, I could use her room. I thanked her and went back to the paper. Then I sat near the window

154

and watched Rhuine waken up. I listened to the clatter of boots on the cobbles, watched doors open and women come out with mats, watched steps being washed and whitened as Rhuine was cleaned up and polished all ready for another profitable day. I half-expected to see them giving the fuchsias and hydrangeas another coat of paint. But the farthest I saw in that direction was a woman arranging the words: *HEAD-ACHE DRAUGHTS SIXPENCE,* in white shells on her front garden strip. I thought that was cute.

It would be about nine when I went up to the Poskett's room. I dropped on to the bed just as I was and slept. I thought I must have slept only for an hour or so, but when the Poskett knocked on the door and I looked at my watch it was three o'clock.

"I'm having a meal," she announced. "Late lunch. You'd better come into the studio."

I was feeling like a dirty scrub-brush. Besides needing a bath and shave, I had a splitting head, a head that rocked me every time I moved. I wondered if the woman over the way had any *HEADACHE DRAUGHTS* left or the tourists had bagged the lot.

I took my head between my hands to steady it, carried it into the studio, and poured two cups of coffee down its dry mouth before tackling any food.

"You've missed a lot," the Poskett said. "But I thought it wasn't worth waking you. Rhuine's been full of police and reporters all day. I've been photographed three times and sold four pictures and the cafe's done rousing business. There's hell's delight in store for the ringleaders of last night's performance."

"What about Fabian?" I asked.

"Can't tell you much. He came to the village half an hour ago and went to Lora's place. Probably needs comfort in his tribulation. And he's plenty. The Inspector from Shilstone was at Edward's Bounty for an hour this morning, and there's a policeman guarding what's left of the Pound. They say the timber wagon's smashed to bits at the bottom of the cliffs and the tree-trunks are somewhere between here and Ireland."

I nodded. If Fabian was now with Lora, it wasn't likely he would be home much before midnight. That left me a clear field. I wasn't sure what for. Still, a clear field is always useful.

I ate what I could, thanked the Poskett for all she had done, and walked to the telephone booth at the top of the Score. From there I got through to the Morrises. It's always useful to keep on good terms with former clients. Some of them have a gratitude-complex. I had an idea the Morrises were still grateful to me.

Linda answered the phone, and seemed surprised to hear who was at my end.

"Just what is happening at Rhuine?" she asked. "We know all about Fabian, of course. But Sheila must be in pretty desperate trouble if she's called you in to clear it up."

"I haven't cleared it up," I told her. "It's getting worse. That's why I told Sheila she'd better let you have charge of Ninian. How's the child settling down?"

Linda Morris said Ninian was fine.

"I thought she would be," I said, "once she was out of Fabian's reach. Now, take a deep breath! I'm playing this my own way. I want Sheila away from here. I want you to write or give her a ring and insist she comes to you. Soon as you like. Certainly no later than the week-end."

"You don't have to wait for that," Linda said. "Tell her to come right away."

"That cat won't jump," I said. "I want the idea to come from you."

She promised she would do as I said, and I rang off feeling

slightly relieved. I'm a great believer in running away when things get really unpleasant. Half the world's troubles are caused by people trying to stick things out when there's nothing to be gained by it.

I wasn't sure why I had taken that line, or specified the week-end. I was just as much in the dark about what was going to happen as I was when Sheila came into my office. But I felt that the fuse was lit and getting short. I knew that, even before Isaiah Jonquil met me at the foot of the Score and said Luke was getting spry again and wanted to see me.

I couldn't get to the Brickhole quickly enough. If there had been time, I should have called at the Dolphin for a brandy. I was feeling giddy. I wasn't at all sure whether it was yesterday or today. All the people around me had had a night in bed after the episode outside Edward's Bounty. I hadn't. In spite of my snoozes in the summer-house and on the Poskett's bed, I was still in the same day that the Poskett had flung that beer into Fabian's handsome face.

"Been asking for you all day, Luke has," said Isaiah as we hurried down the slope. "Top and bottom of it is, zur, he's got something on his mind."

"And when he's transferred it to my mind," I said, "we might be getting somewhere. Or not. As another great man said of another important occasion, it may not be the beginning of the end, but there's a chance it's the end of the beginning."

I added, near the Brickhole: "How's the boy today?"

"Practically normal, zur. Picking up nicely. Wonderful what sleep'll do for the young."

"Sleep and a sense of security," I said. "Must be nice for a child to know the Devil isn't the other side the door."

Isaiah had the sense to leave me on his brother's front step. I went in with a thumping heart as well as a thumping head. Whatever was coming, I wanted to get it over with. I wanted

157

to be finished with it, and catch a train to London. I wanted to smell Covent Garden again. Nice, clean, safe, sane Covent Garden.

Luke's eyes were brighter. His voice was stronger when he told me to sit down.

"I've something to tell you, zur. Something I didn't want the doctor to know.

I pulled up a chair and waited. It was a big moment for me.

He opened and shut his mouth several times as if the words wouldn't come. "Don't excite yourself," I said. "I've been waiting to ask you about this. I was coming in any case, but I'm glad you've made up your mind without prodding. It was Dillon, wasn't it?"

His hands plucked at the coverlet. "You're right, zur. It was Dillon."

"He won't repeat the performance," I said. "He's being well taken care of."

I waited. If that was all he had to say I wasn't much forrarder. But I didn't think it was. And I was right.

"There's something else, zur. About the boy. The things you wus asking me before, when you came up to the Gardens. I wouldn't tell you then. I didn't reckon it would do any good to tell you. But I'd better. If something happens to me . . ."

"Nothing's going to happen to you, Luke," I said. "Don't get that idea in your mind."

"You never know, zur. What I want to tell you is that the boy's got delusions."

"I could have told you that. Dr. Warren's treating him for delusions right now."

"Is he, zur? I don't know about that." He shifted on the pillows. "But I'm not talking about what's wrong with Peter now. I mean the things he's been telling me all these months.

158

The things he won't go home at night for, zur. That's what I mean."

My heart started thumping again. I'd been waiting a long time for this. I would have given a shilling a drop for that brandy I'd missed.

"It's about the safe, zur. The safe in Mr. Fabian's study, or li-brai-ree, or whatever he calls it."

"I didn't even know he had a safe," I said, licking my lips.

"Peter says, zur, there's a body in it."

I didn't think I'd heard properly. I stared down at him.

"A body, zur, in Mr. Fabian's safe," he repeated.

Well, I'd had no idea what was coming, had I? Why shouldn't it as easily be that as Fabian dressing up in tails and horns and staging the Black Mass, or any other of the fantastic possibilities I'd toyed with? Still, it shook me.

"Yes," I said stupidly. Then I added, getting second wind: "That's impossible, of course."

"Is it, zur?" Jonquil asked. "Well zur, you know best. But I thought I ought to tell you, because if anything happens to me . . ."

I forced a grin. "Forget it! Who else knows about all this?"

"My brother, zur. I told him because I'm a man who thinks a lot. Thinks and broods. But he's what you might call a man of action. I thought mebbe he'd do something about it."

"And did he?"

"He tried, zur. You know the woman Fabian brought?"

"You mean Lora? Does she know too?"

"Isaiah told her, zur. You see, she's fond of the little boy. Buys no end of things for him, she does. And Isaiah thought she might be able to help."

"I hope he was sure of the way she'd react," I said uneasily. "I'd have thought she'd be more likely to spill the beans to Fabian than take any risk to help Fabian's step-son. . . . And how could she have helped, anyway?"

"We thought, zur, if we could have got Fabian's keys . . ."

Luke Jonquil broke off, looking at me sadly. I didn't say anything for a while. Things were beginning to tie up. I could see now why Jonquil, during my first hours in Rhuine, had followed Lora to her cottage. It was a conspirators' meeting, apparently. But then, Dillon had followed, too. And where did Dillon come into all this?

I asked Luke.

"Dillon hates Fabian, zur. It's a well-known fact, that. It was Lora said that Dillon could do a lot to settle things up."

But Dillon hadn't, apparently. Dillon had been playing some game of his own. He still didn't fit into any pattern I could think of.

But there were plenty of other things to worry about at the moment. I told Luke that he'd got things off his mind now, so he could go to sleep in peace.

"And if there's anything in Fabian's safe," I said, "I'll have it out."

I patted his shoulder and eased away. I didn't feel like facing Peter just now. Isaiah's wife was at the door. She looked like one of the Knitting Women waiting to count heads as they fell on the guillotine. I felt relieved to see her. Women like that have their uses.

"I want you or your husband to stay here till I tell you it's safe to leave," I said to her in a low voice. "You're not to desert the house for a moment, understand? If Mr. Fabian shows up, he's not to be allowed in. You can use force to keep him out if necessary."

"If he tries," she said unemotionally, "I'll claw his bleeding eyes out."

That wasn't a nice sentiment, even from a Knitting Woman, but it was the sort of reaction I appreciated just then.

On to the Dolphin, I thought.

I got my brandy, and took half an hour over the most substantial dinner they could lay on. Then, like last night, I went out and propped my back against the Dolphin wall. But this time I had more to think about than then. I was working out what I was going to do.

I could see Edward's Bounty from where I sat. Two of the chimneys were smoking. I could see the Brickhole. Further up the Score, I could see the attic floor of the Poskett's house. If I'd been a bit higher on my haunches instead of hulking there like a Rhuine fisherman, I could have seen Mrs. Dukas's cottage, with the strip of garden Fabian always trod on and the hydrangea the Corgi always sprinkled.

I felt like a spider sitting in the middle of the web. A decent, benevolent sort of spider, waiting to catch a handsome, poisonous wasp. I got the feeling again that all these people—the Poskett and Jonquils and Sheila and Mrs. Dukas and Peter—were watching me with hope in their eyes.

And what they had to hope for, through me, I didn't know yet. But, I thought, lighting a cigarette, I'm not going to let them down.

I flicked the spent match into the harbour and started walking towards Church Staithe.

I didn't meet anyone on the way. I don't think I should have recognised them if I had. I went through the gate and across the lawn. Sheila was in the corner of the garden past the coach-house. She wasn't doing anything but stare out to sea.

She smiled as she saw me coming over, an uncertain sort of smile, and asked where I'd been all night and all day.

"You didn't have breakfast before you went out," she said. "You didn't come back for lunch. And there are some letters for you. I put them in your room."

"Peter wasn't home all night or for lunch either," I said. "Worry about him, not me. I'm just the hired hand."

She winced. "Dr. Warren rang up. He tells me Peter's much better than he was."

"Then it's too late for me to give you the same glad news.

I've just come from the Brickhole now."

I started walking towards the patch of lawn near the cliff, where the summer-house was. I thought it was a good place to say what had to be said. I swivelled the summer-house with its back to the wind, like last night. The sun was strong and bright. We could see the bay, and the harbour, and the little boats bobbing on the blue water.

I asked Sheila to sit down. I sat down too, as far away from her as I could get.

"There's something I want to tell you," I said. "Let's set the stage first. I've cleared certain things up. I've uncovered certain mutual relationships I hadn't expected to find. I'm not sure about Dillon yet, but he'll come later. It's another matter I want to talk to you about now. I think it's the thing you've sheered away from all the time. Even when you were in my office. If you'd told me, it might have saved a lot of trouble. But you'll have to tell me now."

"What is it?" she asked.

I waited a minute. Then I said, very slowly. "Peter's told Jonquil there's a body hidden in your husband's safe. And that's the sort of statement you have to do something about."

She sat so quiet and still, so absolutely colourless, that I thought of the Snow Maiden. . . . I had the idea that if I reached out to touch her she would be frozen and brittle and break into little pieces. And I wanted to touch her. . . . Oh God, how much I did want that!

I blinked and swallowed hard. I brought my mind back to the matter in hand.

"It must be a pretty big safe," I went on. "Or else a small body."

We hadn't reached the end of the road, but I felt we'd come to an important turning. For the first time, I could see out of the valley. As I watched, Sheila thawed out. She thawed and went limp and shaking.

"That means," she said at last, "I shall have to tell **you**."
"I think you'd better," I said.

The trouble started, she said, a month or two after Mrs. Charles' legal representatives finished their work on the conveyance and Sheila came into full possession of Rhuine.

She was already seeing certain dark streaks in Stuart Fabian's character. She hadn't thought he drank so much, for one thing. But she made allowances for that, and for his dirty temper. What she couldn't make allowances for was his striking Ninian.

And his behaviour when they had to call in the doctor opened her eyes even wider than the actual striking.

Because Fabian, with all the charm in the world, had explained to the doctor that Ninian had fallen against a chair. A chair he had repeatedly asked his wife not to leave where Ninian might stumble against it.

She realised then that there was something in Fabian's make-up she had never suspected. The man had been cast in a warped mould. That incident put her on guard. . . . She saw he was one of those rare people with a love of evil for its own sake rather than a mere indifference to good.

When Sheila told me that, she asked if I could understand just what she meant. Remembering the story of the hedgehog on the Twickenham towpath, I said I could.

The lawyers had made it clear to Sheila that she would never be able to dispose of her interests in Rhuine, which at her death would pass to Peter. Fabian, of course, had money and plenty of it in his own right. But it was obvious from the beginning that he resented his wife's independence, and her complete control of an estate he could not touch in any shape or form.

He insisted upon selling the Richmond House, on the grounds that it would reduce expense. The sale brought in about fourteen thousand pounds, which he invested without

163

reference to Sheila. She hadn't any kick coming there, of course. But shortly afterwards he began to worry her about certain alterations and improvements which, he said, should be made in Rhuine. She tried to see all this in the most generous light. If he had any genuine interest in the place, she was prepared to consider any suggestions he made.

But when Elias Harkaway, landlord of the Dolphin, came to her one day and said that Fabian was openly talking about pulling down the inn and building a bigger place, to be run on a profit-sharing basis between Harkaway as tenant and Sheila as owner, she thought it was time to protest. And she did protest.

As a result, Fabian left for London. For three months she never heard of him or from him.

Then she had a letter from her lawyers, telling her that Fabian, operating from a London office, had persuaded a number of people whom he styled the progressives of the village to form a Rhuine and District Development Association. This, they pointed out, was a misleading title, implying in effect that she, as owner of Rhuine, was contemplating developments there. They asked her if this was so.

She went up to see them. They reminded her that the Charles family had acted very reasonably. They might well have contested the will, seeing that an estate worth many thousands of pounds had passed to an unknown English girl who had been married only a short time to Godfrey Charles, and had never seen Rhuine until she went there as its owner.

The terms under which she had inherited were elastic, they admitted, and there was nothing to prevent her from carrying out reasonable alterations and modifications. But any drastic development calculated to alter the character of the village might have unpleasant repercussions. They asked her to use her influence with Fabian to curb his activities, or take steps publicly to disassociate herself from them.

To that end, she found out where he was living, and told

him what had happened. He refused to give her the under-taking she asked for. Finally, she applied for an injunction restraining him from using the name Rhuine on any publicity material or letter heading. And the application was granted.

She imagined she might not see Fabian again. But within a week he turned up, full of charming apologies and good intentions for the future. He had only one request to make—that the cottage vacant by reason of Mrs. Ruddan's death should be let to a friend of his and her family, who wished to escape from London to a quiet, healthy place on the coast.

She agreed, in spite of protests from several of the villagers who had married children awaiting accommodation. And shortly afterwards she learned that his friend was Lora, and that Lora's family existed only in his imagination.

From that point, Fabian increased his hold.

Foiled in his schemes for Rhuine itself, he began to acquire properties all around it, in the way she had already explained. He openly flaunted Lora before Sheila and the whole of Rhuine. And he began a subtle campaign against the children. Especially against Peter. Peter, said Sheila, was as well acquainted with the facts of life at six as he should have been at sixteen.

He never struck Peter as he had struck Ninian. He preferred to undermine his character. There was nothing Sheila could do. Nothing, that is, short of taking a firm stand, taking legal action against her husband, and sending the children beyond his reach. But by this time her will to resist had been weakened. Fabian had an overbearing personality, and had used it to make her completely a slave to his wishes. In that he had failed, but certainly she lacked the moral stamina to make any definite decisions.

As the winter went by, Sheila told me, she was driven nearer and nearer the edge of despair. She had failed to pre-serve Rhuine from Fabian. She had even failed to protect her own and Godfrey Charles' children from him. And from that despair came an active, scheming hatred. She was prepared to kill him, even if it meant killing herself at the same time.

And she tried.

One night, coming back from Shilstone after seeing friends off by train, she had tried to drive the car off the road and into the ravine. But Fabian had wrenched at the wheel and brought up the bonnet against a tree. He had known for a long time, he told her, that she had been waiting to do something like that. He had been waiting for her to try. He should be waiting for her to try again. Meanwhile, he should consult a doctor as to the state of her mind and post a full account of the incident, under seal, to his own lawyers in London.

That, of course, tightened his grip on her and pushed her right back where she had been before. It took her a month, she told me, to get her wits back. And during that month, Fabian was completing his conquest of Peter. When visitors came, Peter could not be allowed in the room. The only consolation she had was that Peter and Ninian both hated Fabian and were inwardly loyal to her. Peter began to go about on his own, even to stay out all night. But she knew he was with Jonquil, and encouraged him to do so.

Then there came a second chance to kill Fabian. This time, an almost foolproof one.

Dr. Warren had been attending him for a violent attack of lumbago. He had found it difficult to sleep, and Warren had supplied him with the usual box of small white tablets that have ushered many an unsuspecting invalid through the Pearly Gates. For several nights, Fabian hadn't troubled to use them. Then he thought he would give them a trial, and it was Sheila who put one of them with a glass of water by his bed and left the box within his reach. He hadn't noticed that she had taken half of the remaining tablets from the box and left the room with them.

She found a use for those tablets a little later. Rose was

taking up Fabian's nightcap, a glass of milk, and Sheila found an opportunity to empty the tablets into the milk before it was taken upstairs.

She spent the night horrified by what she had done and yet feeling she was justified. She expected Dillon to find him dead next morning. She had already written a letter to the Charles family in Carolina, explaining what she had done and why she had done it, and asking them to take care of the children until Peter came of age and assumed control of Rhuine. After that, she intended to kill herself.

But Fabian wasn't dead.

He should have been, because he had drunk three parts of the milk and enjoyed the full effects of Warren's lullaby drops. But Fabian's constitution was stronger than most men's. At eight o'clock next morning. Dillon found him asleep, and left him. At ten, he came again, and began to suspect that Fabian's sleep was coma. But by the time Sheila was called, her husband was showing signs of recovery. And he was realising, even before his brain had any right to be clear, just what had caused it.

Sheila said it was a day of howling wind and rain. She spent most of it looking through the window and waiting. At four o'clock, Fabian sent Dillon for her and asked her to bring the children to his room. By then he was sitting in his dressing-gown on the edge of the bed.

Fabian came straight to the point. He said that the previous night he had taken one of Warren's tablets in water. Later, Rose had brought up the milk, and he had drunk most of it before noticing an odd taste. Also, he was beginning to feel drowsy. But he had reached out to the bedside table and opened the box of tablets from which his wife had taken one for his dose. Or should have taken one . . .

But half of them were missing. He realised that his wife must have taken them and put them in the milk Rose had brought. He was too drowsy by then even to ring for help.

But for his excellent condition, and probably Warren's caution in supplying him with a dosage smaller than was usual, he would certainly have been dead by now.

Dillon, by Fabian's orders, was still in the room listening to this. Most of it had gone over the children's heads, but now Fabian told them to come closer and listen carefully to him. He told them that their mother had twice tried to kill him—once, a month ago, and again last night. Their mother was a wicked woman. If he had died, she would have been a murderess. If he had died, they would have taken their mother away and tied a rope around her neck and choked her to death because she had killed him. He wanted them to understand that.

At this, Sheila said, Ninian began to scream, and screamed so hard that the servants came running from the kitchen to see what was wrong. But Fabian told Dillon to lock the door and keep them out.

He went on to explain to the children that even though he hadn't died, if he told a policeman what had happened, their mother would be put in prison for years and they might never see her again. Then he produced a statement, in which he had written down everything that had happened, and asked Dillon to sign it, after examining the half-empty box. The milk that remained in the glass, he said, would be sent to a chemist for analysis. The chemist's report would then be attached to the statement Dillon had just witnessed and would be locked in Fabian's safe.

Whenever they saw the safe in the study, he told the children, or even passed the study door, they must remember that a part of their mother was locked in there, and that one day the safe might be opened and that part of their mother would be seen. When that happened, they must say goodbye to her, because she would be going away for a long time. Till they had grown into a man and a woman.

Then with Dillon's help he had hobbled downstairs, and

made them watch while he locked the statement in the safe. An hour later, Dillon left for London, taking with him the milk for analysis. He came back next evening, and again in the presence of them all the safe was opened and the chemist's report clipped to the statement.

And since that evening, Stuart Fabian had had a free hand with Sheila, and with Rhuine up to a point.

You don't hear a story like that then start firing questions right away. You sit till you get over it. You sit and think. That's what I did, for a long time. The sun wasn't shining into the summer-house now.

"There's something you haven't mentioned," I said. "Why did the police come making enquiries?"

She looked at me blankly for a moment.

"Oh. . . . Do you know, I'd forgotten. I suppose because the servants spread rumours about the scene in the bedroom. The police thought it followed too closely on the other affair to be quite separate from it."

"The other affair!" I said. "You mean the time you tried to kill Fabian in the car. The police came then, didn't they? The Yard. Why? The Yard don't bother with motor-crashes."

Her face was twisted with pain.

"The morning after," she said, "Stuart filed through one of the steering-rods. Then he told the police we'd had the accident because some one must have tampered with the car."

I looked at her.

"You see why? There wasn't anything he could pin on me. But he knew the police being here, making enquiries, taking statements . . ."

She broke off.

"And the Yard too," I said, understanding. "It was just his way of adding to the agony you were in."

"Why did you marry a man like that?" I asked.

"Does it matter why I married him?"

"It does to me," I said.

She twisted her fingers. She looked away from me. At the house, the sea, anywhere.

"Because I wanted what he was," she told me. "Because I wanted what Lora finds in him. That's why I can't forgive myself. His—his virility, his sheer animal vigour. I sacrificed the children to that. And Rhuine too. There, now you've got it."

I stared down at my feet. "It was a passing fancy," I said. "You don't have to blame yourself too much. We all go through those phases. For a man it's easier. He can get over the feeling or satisfy it without a lot of trouble."

I waited a minute, then asked: "Who's Dillon?"

"I don't know. Someone told me he's Stuart's son."

I considered that. It could be. But I wasn't sure. And I had to be sure. I didn't want any more loose ends than were necessary.

"Wait here a few minutes," I said. "I'll be back. Then we'll walk along the cliff and try to shake off the dust."

I went back to the house. I found Dillon in the kitchen and told him I wanted to talk to him. He followed me into the hall.

When we got there I shut the baize door and looked at him. He stood waiting.

"Jonquil's told me," I said flatly.

He didn't answer.

"And I know about the safe." He lifted his head at that. The pale lips opened and shut. "I know what's in the safe," I said in a louder voice. "Dillon, just what sort of a man are you?"

"What's Jonquil going to do?" he muttered.

"I wouldn't know and I don't care. It's entirely in Jonquil's hands whether you go free or spend the next five years on Dartmoor. I don't mind either way. But you might as well

170

get it straight through your head that Fabian isn't going to save your skin now. All that's finished for good. From this point onward, Fabian's going to have all his work cut out looking after himself."

He started running his hands down his trouser-legs. He was probably trying to think of something he could say. There wasn't much.

"Dillon," I said, "there's many a murderer wouldn't have soiled his hands with what you've done. Don't you realise the effect it's had on the minds of those two kids? Don't you realise they're probably warped and twisted for life?"

"I didn't do it," Dillon said. "He did it."

"You helped. I'm not saying your conscience didn't trouble you. I suppose that's why you ran after Peter when you saw he'd reached breaking-point. Then when he beat you to it and spilled the whole bean-bag to Luke, you tried to kill Luke so he wouldn't talk and let the whole wide world know what a crawling reptile you are."

"It wasn't that," he said desperately. "Luke Jonquil knew already. I knew Peter had told him. Weeks ago."

I stared at him. That was true, of course. I'd crossed the wires somehow. "Then what was it?" I asked.

He shook his head and moaned and gulped. I remembered the hint Sheila had given me about Dillon being Fabian's son. I remembered Luke saying how Dillon had hated Fabian.

"Dillon," I said quietly, "who are you?"

He went on gibbering and mouthing, but still shaking his head. He hadn't reached talking-point yet.

"Lora or Isaiah Jonquil, or both of them, took you partly into their confidence and asked you to help them release Peter from the nightmare he's in," I said. "Did you spill the news to Fabian?"

"No," he said.

"You genuinely tried to help them. Is that it?"

"I did, Mr. Cardew. I swear I did."

"And that's why you joined in the general pilgrimage to Lora's cottage last Sunday night! Oh yes, I was there! When Fabian had gone, you went in and joined Lora and Isaiah Jonquil. To report progress or failure?"

"Failure," he mumbled.

"I wonder what you'd failed to do?" I said. "I'll make three guesses, and they're all the same. They wanted you to get Fabian's keys to the safe so they could find out what was behind Peter's story."

He nodded.

"Well, that's what I want. Where does he keep the key?"

"On his ring," he stuttered. "And he always wears it."

"Then get it. I don't care if you have to cut Fabian's throat. Get the key and bring it to me."

"But I've tried!" he said, beginning to sweat. "I've been trying for a month. For Christ's sake don't ask me any more."

"I'm not asking you to do it," I said. "I'm telling you. And if you let Fabian know a word of this, I'll strangle you with my own delicate fingers. It's something I'd enjoy. Now, get cracking! I want that stuff out of the safe by tomorrow morning."

I didn't wait to see the effect that had. I walked out and left him.

But in the coat-room off the hall I stood and thought. There was something still worrying me. I believed Dillon when he said he had tried to get those keys for a month. But why? Because Jonquil and Lora had asked him to help salvage a child's mind? Was his conscience troubling him?

I didn't think so. But I couldn't think what else.

I picked up a fleecy coat and went back to Sheila.

I told her what I'd said to Dillon.

"From now on," I said, "I'm playing this my own way. I'm going to bring Peter back. I'm going to show him the empty safe. I'm going to try my own brand of psychological treatment. Tell him what Fabian is and what he nearly made of you. Peter's old enough to understand. I'm going to tell him the truth, standing there in front of that empty safe."

"And then," Sheila said unexpectedly, "go away."

"And then," I told her, "I'm going to deal with Fabian."

"No. Please go away."

There were tears in her eyes. "I'm a murderess. I didn't succeed, but that makes no difference. I'm still a murderess at heart."

"Most of us are a lot of funny things in our hearts," I said. "And I'm not so sure about you. I don't give a damn for the first time you tried. It's what anybody would have done in those circumstances. Anybody with enough guts, that is, to kill themselves at the same time. As for the second try, have you thought about what Fabian said? That he'd be waiting for it?"

"Well?" she said.

"Well? Doesn't it strike you that he talked Warren into giving him those tablets just so he could leave them where you could lay your hands on them? That he knew you'd doped the milk? That he poured it out and faked his coma?"

I looked into her staring eyes.

"I don't know, of course. But I wouldn't put it past him. And it's not in character for a man expecting to be murdered to leave a handy weapon lurking around. He's smart enough not to have done that. Maybe you tried to murder him. Maybe you were tricked into it. Either way doesn't worry me."

I found out from Rose that Fabian was still absent, then went to the room he called his study. I stared at the safe. It was a big safe, smooth and black, fire-proof and burglar-proof according to the name-plate.

I wondered how many times Peter must have crept in here and looked at that smooth, shining door with fear and horror in his heart. I wondered what torments his little mind had endured to translate Fabian's words into the idea that some-

173

one's body was hidden in that safe. I wondered what night-mares he must have had; how often he must have wakened up, nerves taut and body sweating, in the darkness of that little room next to mine.

I wanted that safe open.

I wasn't under any illusion that Dillon would get Fabian's keys. That had been a counsel of desperation. In any event, Fabian wasn't here and probably wouldn't come home till morning, so Dillon couldn't operate on his pockets however willing he might be.

And morning was a long way off.

Wild schemes began running through my brain. The least fantastic seemed to be to contact certain gentry of my London acquaintance with experience in opening even tougher safes than this one, and pay them liberally on a basis of No Questions Asked.

Another alternative was brute force.

I pondered that idea and liked it. Usually, the opening of a safe under illicit conditions has to be done quickly and quietly. But given time, and Fabian's guaranteed absence, I could maybe knock it open. No steel door can stand up to continuous battering with a fourteen-pound hammer. Swung over the shoulder, I calculated, fourteen pounds should weigh considerably more than that at the point of impact.

I went up to my room and collected the letters Sheila had put there. None of them was definite, all were hopeful. They assured me that the proposed developments on the fringes of Rhuine had been reported and discussed, and that before any serious encroachments were made, some action would doubtless be taken. One of them—from the Ministry—said that the Member for the Shilstone Division had already taken up the matter with the Parliamentary Secretary, and it was probable that in the near future a local Committee would be set up and its report studied.

That was good enough for me. It was another spoke in

Fabian's wheel. I felt I'd earned Sheila's retainer, whatever else.

I left the house and went to the jetty. You seldom had to look far for Isaiah Jonquil. He was usually visible from the white harbour rails outside the Dolphin. When he saw me, he lurched up the steps from the shingle.

"They'll be open soon," I said.

"They're open now, zur, for them as knows," said Isaiah with a wink.

We sat on the bench outside the window. Isaiah tapped on the pane. He said something out of the corner of his mouth. A disembodied hand slid two pints through the aperture and we leaned back, tolerably content.

"I wonder," I said to Isaiah, "if you've such a thing as a fourteen-pound hammer?"

"No zur," he replied. He wouldn't have turned a hair if I had asked for a Bofors gun. "But my brother has. It'll be up at the shed."

"I'll walk round that way," I said, "and collect it."

"Then you'll be wantin' the key, zur." He took a key from his pocket and gave it to me. "I was going up there myself before dark. There's a row of potted chrysanthemums'd do with a drink."

"I'll give them a drink and save you the trouble," I told him.

After a while I added cautiously: "Jonquil, if you've any ideas about Fabian and arson, you'd better confide in me. I want something to trip him with."

He took out his pipe and squirted nicotine into the harbour.

"Have you heard anything?" I asked.

"From time to time, zur. From time to time."

"Do you think there's anything behind it?"

"Don't ask me, zur, what's behind the things Fabian says, damn and blast his stinkin' hide. I've heard him say if a single house in Rhuine caught fire, it'd be the end of the village."

"You've heard him say that," I said. "And Mrs. Dukas tells me the same thing. So why hasn't somebody been to the police about it?"

I'd already answered that one for Mrs. Dukas, but I thought there could be no harm trying it on Jonquil.

"What good would that do, zur? D'you think they'd take any notice?"

"Isn't that what they're there for?"

"Now look here, zur, you and me sees this from one angle and the police see it from another. We know Fabian's a dangerous man. He's never been crossed in his life till now. But his wife's crossed him, you have, I have, and a lot more besides. That's what we know. But the police sit up there at Shilstone, zur, and see all this from a distance. Fabian's a gentleman, and gentlemen don't burn villages down, no more than they keep harlots in their wives' cottages and kill innocent fisher-folk like me."

There was sense in that, of course. The moment the Fabian case became the business of Authority, it would look and smell different. Fabian would be the injured party; a man whose wife had twice tried to kill him, a man responsible for two unpleasant children not his own, with half the local population of oafs and reactionaries making violent demonstrations against his benevolent, enlightened plans for the district.

"Take my word for it, zur, the way to trip Fabian isn't to tell the police he's threatened arson," Jonquil said. "They'd laugh at you."

We had another pint, then I left Isaiah and walked up the hill and along the alley to the Liquorice Gardens.

I unlocked the gate and the shed. The chrysanthemums were looking sorry for themselves. I found a water-can, filled it half a dozen times at a pool in the stream, and gave them their promised drink. Everything else about the place looked as if it would last till Luke came back.

I put the can away and looked for the hammer. I found it under the bench. I swung it over my shoulder. The shaft was stout and tight. I looked forward to standing on top of the safe and swinging at that door.

I wrapped the hammer in sacking and locked up. I left the Gardens by way of the hole in the hedge and the one-man track through the wood, and so back to the house, where I left the hammer in the hall and went looking for Sheila.

"The cold war's over," I said to her, "and the shooting war's just starting. I don't think Fabian, even with his thick hide, will feel like staying in Rhuine after tomorrow. I think he'll quietly fade away. I'm going to smash the safe open."

"He won't fade," Sheila said. "I know him better than you do. He'll want a blaze of glory to go out in."

"He'll be damned lucky if he gets it. I'm going up now for a bath and a shave. Then I'm going to tackle the safe. Keep your chin up, Sheila. We're nearly through."

We were. But not in the way I imagined then.

I went upstairs. For half an hour I relaxed in hot water. Then I shaved, put on clean underwear and a clean shirt. I felt a lot better after that. I grinned as I twirled the loose button between my fingers. I'd get Sheila to look after that right now. It would be nice to have something to remember Rhuine by, if it was only a stitched button.

I went downstairs. I asked at the baize door for Dillon, but he wasn't there. Cook said the police had asked him a lot of questions that morning, and he had been upset all day. He had been still more upset, I thought, after talking to me a little while ago. It was his evening off, Cook said, and he had told them he was going into Shilstone and might not be back till morning.

That suited me. I told them they might hear a lot of noise in the next half-hour, but they were to pay no attention to it. Then I went into the hall and took the hammer out of the sacking.

I was going to enjoy myself.

But I wasn't. As I was opening the study door, I heard the telephone ring. I waited a moment to see if Sheila came, but she couldn't have heard it. So I lifted the receiver and heard the Poskett's voice.

"Mrs. Fabian?" she asked.

"No," I said, "it's Cardew."

"Cardew, good! You're the one I wanted. I think you'd better come down here. . . . Soon as you can. To Lora's. Yes, it's odd, don't you think? She's the only one you haven't met yet. I told you you should."

"I've work to do here," I said. "Can't Lora wait?"

"I wouldn't like to risk it. Fabian left there about half an hour ago and he's up at the Galleon. I see a lot from my window. I saw Lora run after him into the Score. She doesn't do that sort of thing normally, so I followed her back to the cottage to see why."

I waited.

"I don't know what's been happening, Cardew. Maybe Fabian's been using her to compensate for his troubles in other directions. But she says she's going to kill herself. And she means it. I think you should come down."

I put the receiver back. I looked regretfully at the hammer. Then I took it back to its corner and wrapped the sacking round it again.

It looked as if I wouldn't be using it for a while.

As a matter of fact, I wasn't going to use it at all.

CHAPTER EIGHT

NOCTURNE

IT WAS nearly dark when I reached the foot of the Score. My imagination might have been running amok, but I could have thought there was a feeling of suppressed excitement all about me, as if Rhuine knew something was going to happen in the near future. I felt excited myself, and couldn't tell why.

I was going towards Lora's cottage when I saw the Poskett. She looked like part of the night in that shapeless blue garment, and I mightn't have recognised her if she hadn't called out to me in her masculine voice.

"I've just been in," she said. "I might have stayed, but I thought it was better to leave the coast clear for you. New brooms sweep clean."

I said that was kind of her.

"What's wrong?" I asked. "What's brought her to suicide point all of a sudden? Surely she's wise to all Fabian is before this?"

"It's probably a cumulative effect," she said.

I turned into the little sunken garden outside Lora's cottage. I stared moodily at the usual hydrangea that sprouted from the angle of the walls. I had started with considerable admiration for hydrangeas. Now, I felt, I should never want to see one again after leaving Rhuine.

I took my first good look at Lora through the window before I went in. She wasn't putting on any act for me, because she couldn't have known I was looking. There was a cloth on the table, a folk-weave she had probably bought from the Poskett, and she was clawing at it with her crimson mandarin-spike nails. I could see where the threads pulled up. I couldn't see her face for the witch-bowl in the middle of the table. I couldn't have seen much of it anyway, because it was down in the crook of her left arm.

I counted ten, then pushed open the door. It let me into the little stone-flagged kitchen where Fabian and I had attended to each other's injuries. There was no light, and I had to fumble with the catch of the inner door. The noise I made must have roused her, because when I went in, blinking, she was staring up at me.

"What do you want?" she asked in a flat hard voice, and as I pulled the door shut behind me I said it was a fine night for a good cry, but she should draw the curtains. A lot of men, I said, couldn't resist beauty in distress.

Then I got my first real close-up, and I could have whistled. Till then, I'd been resenting all this as an interruption. But now I forgot the hammer and relaxed, my mind at rest and my eyes doing everything necessary.

She was all the seven-pound-ten-shilling a week glamour girls rolled into one, good points and bad both. Her hair was half-way between what a sovereign used to look like in Good King Edward's golden days and a half-crown looks like now, and it was brushed straight down to her shoulders in a heavy sweep, where it curled under so that you didn't see any loose ends. She even smelled right—not the gin-and-Woolworth I was accustomed to in most girls of her liberal ideas, but the clean, dry body-smell they ought to bottle and label *Fastidious* and sell at a guinea a drachm.

Her features were good and her teeth brushed. She was

thin in the right places and nicely-moulded in the others. I could tell that without trouble, because if she was wearing anything besides a quilted wrap I didn't notice it. Anyway, I could see the whole of one breast, tastefully decorated, and three parts of the other. Aside from that she looked intelligent, and her eyes were good. I tried to be my age and concentrate on the eyes. . . .

She was the sort of girl, if I'd been in Fabian's shoes and had his ideas, that I should have picked for—well, what he'd picked her for.

Quite suddenly she looked down and pulled the wrap across, like closing a door.

"Thanks," I said. "You needn't have troubled, but that makes it easier to concentrate."

"What do you want?" she asked again, "and who are you?"

"I thought everyone in Rhuine knew who I was by this time. You needn't worry your head with details. I'm one of your few friends, if you want one. Do you?"

She didn't say. "How long has Fabian been gone?" I asked.

She didn't answer that one either. "It doesn't matter," I said. "The Poskett saw him leave. That was only a feeble effort at polite conversation."

I could see she was shivering. The breeze was off the water again that night, and Rhuine can be chilly after sundown, as I had discovered in the summer-house. There wasn't any fire, but a two-bar radiator stood in the hearth, and I switched on both elements. Then I stood looking round, checking Fabian's taste in love-nest furnishings.

He hadn't spent a lot on non-essentials. There was a divan in the corner, with a spring overlay. There were three shiny hardwood chairs that reminded me of my office, and the table under the folk-weave cloth was shiny hardwood too. On a round, three-legged stand was a cheap radio. There was rush matting on the floor and a wool rug in front of the radiator.

181

There were three film-fan magazines on the divan, and the walls were bare except for a signed photograph of Bing Crosby.

Between the chimney-breast and the outer wall was a sagging book-shelf. A chintz curtain hung from the edge on a flexible wire runner. The curtain was pulled half-back, and I could see two other shelves underneath, littered with shoes. They were mostly town shoes—wedges and cuban heels. Fairly cheap stuff. I wasn't much interested in the shoes, but the books on the top shelf were worth looking at.

No Orchids for Miss Blandish, Miss Otis had a Daughter, Kiss the Blood off my Hands, somebody's *Technique of Love and Sex,* the *Awful Disclosures of Maria Monk,* and a brace of Monsieur Paul Renan's classics for makeweight.

I began to feel rather sorry for Lora.

"What has Fabian's line been tonight?" I asked. "So different from usual? Why is this the first time you've talked about killing yourself?"

"Who says I have?"

"The Poskett, and I've a great respect for the Poskett's knowledge and judgement."

I sat down, still watching her. I felt tired.

"Look," I said, "I have a lot of troubles of my own. Recently, I took on some of Sheila Fabian's. They've grown and multiplied till I don't know what's going to happen next, or why. So far, I've left you out of my calculations. But now you've begun to talk like this, I have to take a hand whether I feel like it or not."

"Why?" she asked. "If I want to kill myself, can't I do it without your interference?"

"The law says no," I told her, "and all citizens are supposed to uphold the law as far as possible. Mind, I think you've got something when you complain about my interference. It does seen a strictly personal matter. If anybody wants to put

182

his or her head in a gas-oven, why shouldn't he or she? It's his or her life and his or her oven, so what?"

"So what?" she repeated. "So why don't you go away and let me alone?"

"Because what I've just said is all right only so long as you live on a desert island. For all I know, you've got relations. Maybe an old mother who puts the candle in the window. Maybe a van-driver or a clerk or a drapers' assistant you threw over when you decided to try your luck with Fabian. Even if I'm on the wrong tack there, someone would find you and have to clean up the mess. You've no right to inflict your private grievances on other people. They have their own."

She drooped her head over her arm again.

"There's Sheila Fabian," I said. "There's the Poskett. There's me. It's going to worry us quite a lot if you kill yourself." I leaned across the table. "But Fabian, the person you want to worry, won't care a damn. All he'll do is find another blonde. When a man's income is three thousand per or over, blondes like you are four a penny and nine for twopence."

"That's what he said," Lora moaned into the crook of her arm. "In nearly those very words."

"Well, what did you expect him to say?"

She didn't tell me that.

"Look, Lora, you don't have to put on any act with me. I was born in the big city, too. You don't have to pretend to be the shrinking innocent who only let Fabian pay your expenses because you thought he was going to make an honest woman of you. You came here with your eyes wide open, didn't you? You let him fix you up in the cottage. You let him flaunt you in front of Rhuine to humiliate his wife."

"All right!" she flung at me. "All right! I'm not making excuses. . . . But everybody's turned against him. He hasn't a friend left. Every plan he made, it's gone wrong. And I

183

thought when he came up against that, when he knew he was alone, he'd want me to stand by him. And I would have done. . . . I would."

That was a new slant. I tried to feel cynical about it but couldn't, quite.

"Did you tell him this?" I asked.

"Yes." Her voice dropped. She stared at the opposite wall, biting her lip. "You see—there's something about him."

"Maybe his hairy chest," I said. "Or his beautiful soft skin. Or even his kind, gentle personality."

"I don't know. . . . But I told him whatever went wrong, he had me. I'd keep to the bargain. And he—he laughed."

"He laughed," I said. "Yes, he would."

"So I don't care what happens to me now."

"You may, tomorrow morning," I said. "The sunshine makes a lot of difference."

"I just want you to leave me. I'm going to—well, I know what I'm going to do. The Poskett shouldn't have interfered."

"But she did," I said. "Send her a Christmas card for that every year, Lora. To let her see you haven't forgotten her kindness. And to remind yourself that you were once fool enough to think of suicide for a handsome, white-haired rat who bought most things you had at a bargain price and then wouldn't take your loyalty for nothing."

I took her chin in my hand and jerked it up.

"Let me look at you," I said. "The Poskett says you're beautiful. And when young Peter was half-delirious the other day at Jonquil's cottage, it was Lora he wanted. He said Lora was a smasher. That should be worth something from an experienced young Lothario of seven."

She smiled at that, a faint but recognisable smile.

"Oh, Peter!" she said. "Peter's very fond of me. Funny, isn't it?"

"Why funny? And keep that smile. Remember your appearance. You've a duty to your public."

I got up and prowled about the room. Maybe she thought I was just curious. If so, she was wrong. I knew there was no gas-oven, because gas isn't laid on at Rhuine. And electricity didn't worry me. You don't deliberately fry yourself on two hundred and twenty volts.

But there might be other easy ways out.

I went into the kitchen. It was the size of a matchbox, and I saw it had been cut in two so as to provide another matchbox of a bathroom beyond a lath-and-plaster partition. I went into that bathroom. On a shelf was something promising, one of those mini-razors that girls use for—well, that girls use. I unscrewed the handle and slipped the blade from under the guard. There was also a green-tinted bottle of disinfectant. I emptied that down the bath waste-pipe and gave it a quick flush for luck.

I went back to her. She was still shivering, though the radiator was turning the place into an oven.

"We'd better get one thing straight before we leave," I said to her. "I'd like to know how you propose to do the deed. It's low tide. You'll have the devil's own job to drown yourself before morning. It'll mean taking out a boat. Besides, it'll spoil the look of you."

"What do you mean?" she asked.

"If I were you, I'd use this instead." I tossed the razor-blade on the table. "It'll make a mess to clean up, but you'll look prettier for the police cameras."

She didn't move. The razor-blade shone between us like a bit of sharp flat evil on the folk-weave cloth.

"Or," I said, "you could give up the whole idea and behave like a rational being. You could lock the door if you heard Fabian coming again. You could catch the first bus out in the morning. You could be in London by three o'clock."

"I never want to see London again," she said. "Not now. . . . I've nothing to live for."

"Only fifty or sixty years of future," I said. "That's worth

185

quite a lot. Many a dying man would think so, anyway. And why not now? Where's the difference?"

"You know," she said. "You must know."

"I could guess. You've been a naughty girl, haven't you? But when Fabian sold you the ~~idea~~ of coming to Rhuine, you knew you were going to be naughty. And you thought it was cute. It probably was. I'm no puritan. But now it's in the past instead of the future, it doesn't seem so hot, does it?"

The mandarin spikes stiffened and trembled. "It's been rotten," she sobbed. "It's been—filthy."

"So what? It's just turned out that way. But you're still the same. The real you, underneath. Don't tell me about having nothing to live for. Some day you'll meet some ordinary, nice fellow—"

"No!" she said violently.

"—and he'll marry you, and just about as quick as the laws of nature allow you'll become the mother of half a dozen bouncing babies. And in twenty years' time you'll have forgotten Fabian's name and what he looked like."

She began to whimper into the folds of the quilted wrap. I let her cry it out.

Meanwhile I went to look for coffee. I thought she needed some. I couldn't find any in the kitchen cupboard, but there was some of the tinned muck the Emancipated Woman uses in lieu thereof. I poured some milk into a saucepan and lit a pressure-stove that was lying handy. There didn't seem to be a hot-plate. Probably Fabian hadn't thought she was worth that much expense.

I waited for the milk to heat up, my eyes roving the matchbox kitchen. I don't know what made me curious about what might be under the sink. There was a curtain across the space. I pushed it aside with my foot. Underneath was a can of some kind.

I bent down. It was a jerrycan. I supposed she kept her paraffin in that. I unscrewed the cap and smelt. . . .

And then Lora stopped being just a disconnected incident between Sheila's story and breaking open the safe.

It wasn't paraffin. It was petrol.

And behind the jerrycan were two others. And at the side of the sink was a fourth. And all of them were full.

I glanced at the milk, then went to the door of the living-room.

"Lora," I said, "why is all this petrol in your kitchen?"

"Petrol?" she repeated. "It—it's his."

"But why should Fabian store petrol here?"

She hesitated a moment. "He said he'd bought it off-coupon. He didn't want to take it home or his wife might find out about it."

I went back to the kitchen. I tried to imagine Fabian, at the start of a journey in either of Sheila's cars—which he didn't seem to drive anyway—walking through the street of Rhuine with four spare jerrycans. The picture didn't make sense.

I sat on the edge of the sink, thinking. Thinking about the coach-house and Mrs. Dukas and Isaiah Jonquil. And of other things even farther back in Fabian's history. It wasn't merely rumour now. It wasn't a fantastic joke. Right here at my feet was the means. The means to transform a nasty possibility into nightmare reality.

I couldn't be sure, of course. But faced with a thing like that, you can't take chances. I saw Lora's cottage in flames. I saw the offshore wind sweeping the blaze up the Score as if it were a gigantic chimney.

No, I couldn't be sure. You can't be sure when a man is pointing a pistol at your head. It may not be loaded. Even if it is, he may be joking. . . .

But no insurance company would cover the risk.

I unscrewed the first jerrycan and emptied it in the bath. Then the three others. The stench was terrific. I even forgot to turn out the pressure stove while I did it, which may show

187

how far gone I was. But the last drops gurgled down the waste-pipe without the house disappearing in a cloud of black smoke. I only hoped to God that no one threw a lighted match into the harbour where the drain came out.

She must have thought I was a long time making that coffee. Because when the petrol was emptied, I still sat on the edge of the sink, trying to pull myself together. My medals for courage are all leather ones.

At last I put some of the coffee powder in a jug and poured on the boiling milk. I rummaged in the cupboard for sugar and carried the jug and a cup into the living-room. I watched her sip the scalding stuff, watched the colour come back into her face.

"Lora," I said, "how old are you?"

"I'm twenty," she said.

I lit a cigarette. I thought about Fabian and Peter. About the safe at Edward's Bounty. I thought of what might have happened to Rhuine, what might happen to Jonquil tomorrow morning. And Lora was twenty. . . .

"I sometimes think," I said, talking more to myself than to her, "that I'd like to kill Fabian. Just for pleasure. I'd like to push him over that low wall on Yeo's Jinkin and see him turn two somersaults before he landed in Mrs. Crummett's yard with his back broken."

I was still holding the cigarette packet. "Sorry," I said, and gave her one.

"Thanks," she said. "I gave my last packet to him."

She didn't call him Stuart, I noticed. Maybe she couldn't bring herself to pronounce the name.

"Lora," I said, "to please me, will you postpone killing yourself for twenty-four hours?"

"You shouldn't have come," she said.

"Would you like me to take you over to the Poskett's studio? You could sleep there."

"It isn't necessary."

188

"It isn't if you give me your solemn promise not to do anything foolish."

"I promise."

"Good girl! I'll fix things for you, Lora. If you feel you can't go back to London, we'll think of something else. Now, come and lock the door after me. And don't unlock it again tonight."

She came with me to the door. And there she put her hand on my arm.

"It's difficult to say things, isn't it?"

"Always," I said. "Especially things that mean a lot."

"I just want to say . . . thanks."

I felt rather good as I walked up the Score. As if for once in my useless life I'd done something worth-while.

I went slowly uphill, to the Galleon. I went into the bar. Fabian was there. I didn't know why I'd come or what I planned to do. I told myself I only wanted to satisfy myself that he was there, so that I could go back to Edward's Bounty knowing I had time to crack the safe in comfort.

I stood well back in the corner. Mackender wasn't present, but several others were around Fabian, all strangers to me. He had seen me come in, of course, but it was ten minutes before he looked across.

Then he said in a voice as normal as ever I had heard him use: "We've decided to call a truce, Cardew."

I hadn't intended speaking to him. I made some sort of flippant reply about not knowing there was a war on.

"Tomorrow night, at the meeting, we're going to bury the hatchet," he went on. "All of us. Jonquil and Boldry and Mackender and me. All of us. Dear old pals, jolly old pals. Each for all and all for each."

He had had a lot to drink. "That's nice going," I said. "Have you told Jonquil and Boldry yet?"

"Not yet. It'll be a pleasant surprise for them."

189

The barman polished a glass. "They say Mr. Fabian's being sent to the Tower," he remarked with a sardonic leer. "One of his logs sunk a battleship in mid-Channel this afternoon."

"It might even come to that," I said.

I looked at the clock above the bar. I hadn't realised it was so late. Five minutes to ten . . . There wasn't time for much more of this light-hearted chatter. If Fabian was going straight home, there wouldn't be a chance to open the safe till morning. It looked as if I'd had it after all.

The last rounds were being ordered. I didn't want any more. I wondered what to do. I felt wide-awake now and very alert. If Fabian went home, should I follow him, act as if nothing had happened, and spend the night there?

I couldn't make up my mind. I didn't want to do that. But it might be the best thing. At least I should be in the house if he started any rough stuff. And he might.

So I stayed in the corner till he drank up. He hung on another few minutes, talking to his cronies, then went out, rock-steady. And as he passed me he gave me a glance I neither understood nor liked.

I waited a quarter of a minute, then followed him into the Score. I could make out his figure a hundred yards away. He must be carrying a good load, I thought, in spite of the way he was holding it, because he didn't take the footbridge over the ravine. He was making towards the sea. He passed Lora's cottage without pausing or even looking in its direction. That was one relief at least.

When he reached the harbour and turned over the bridge, I lost sight of him. I walked a little quicker. There wasn't a soul about. I came to the stream. It seemed to be making a lot of noise tonight. Maybe, I thought, because there were no competing sounds. I began to walk by the tubular rails that protected the footpath from the sharp drop to the river-bed, peering ahead for another glimpse of Fabian.

Then I saw him. But he wasn't ahead. He was in the road

to my left, ten feet away. And he was coming towards me.

I stood, waiting for him. He had a torch. He flicked it on and it shone in my eyes, blinding me.

"Well, well!" he said. "Good-evening!"

"I thought we'd met earlier," I said, as coolly as I could, trying to figure out just where he was behind the light.

"On the contrary," he said, "we're meeting for the first time. Or shall we say, I'm meeting you for the first time! The real you. That's why I didn't address you by name. . . . Because you're not Harry Cardew, are you?"

"Then who am I?" I asked, playing for time and wondering if I could get in a blow at the light that was dazzling me.

"I'm not quite sure about that. I've not yet been able to find out. Someone, obviously, brought by my wife to spy on me. That was a mistake, for both of you."

I took out a cigarette and lit it. Someone might hear. Someone might come. If they didn't, the next ten minutes weren't going to be so good.

"I wonder how you found out?" I said.

"Through Dillon in the first place," he replied evenly. "Dillon is a very complex character. I've never been under any illusions as to his faithfulness. He plays with me or against me purely to suit his own ends. But the time of your first arrival coincided with a period of devotion. He reported to me something that he thought suspicious about your clothing. So I took the precaution of cabling Sydney."

"Smart of you," I said.

"I'm gratified that you think so. I was informed, of course, that my wife's cousin Harry Cardew is still busily engaged there earning his living."

"It just shows," I said, "how careful one has to be."

"Yes. . . . So in those circumstances, you won't be coming back to Edward's Bounty tonight."

"Everything considered, I don't think I will."

"You see, I still have a low opinion of your mentality. And

of your physique. You lack guts, my boy. Whatever my failings, I don't. You remind me of Hamlet; you're quite incapable of making up your mind. You've more than a suspicion, for instance, of what's going to happen to your friend Isaiah Jonquil. It probably will happen. . . . But you don't do anything about it, do you?"

"I may have done quite a lot," I said.

"I don't think so. Now, of course, it doesn't matter if you do make up your mind. It's too late. You shouldn't have followed me out of the pub. You shouldn't have waylaid me. You shouldn't have compelled me to defend myself. Because, if Jonquil should go the way of all flesh, you'll scarcely be a reliable witness to go to the police, will you?"

"Waylaid you?" I said. "Did I get that right?"

"Oh yes, quite right! I'm going to be quite rough with you. You're going to be hurt very badly, all in self-defence, of course. So if you go to the police with some ridiculous story tomorrow, it will so obviously be a malicious invention, won't it?"

His voice was very low. I knew what was coming, unless I did something about it. I pulled hard on the cigarette.

"You can't get away with this, Fabian," I said. "You shouldn't try."

And then I flung the glowing cigarette with all my strength, just where I thought his eyes should be. But I was a fraction too late or I'd got the wrong range. Something hit me in the groin, and I staggered back across the footpath and fetched up against the tubular rails.

I stayed there sobbing for breath till there was enough air in my lungs for movement. Then I got up. The light was still in my eyes. I flung myself forward, head down. . . .

It wasn't any use. Something hit me again and again and again. In the same place every time. In the stomach.

I folded up. I didn't see the light now. My eyes were shut. But I had to have another try.

It was the last one. His brogue got me in the middle of my chest. This time, it seemed a long way back to the rails. I found the middle one with the small of my back, the top one with my head.

I didn't move now. I was still conscious. I wished I wasn't. I heard him walking away.

I thought my back was broken. I was certain he'd ruptured me. But I got to my knees. It wasn't pluck. I was dying. So how I died didn't seem to make any difference. And I was in such searing agony that movement didn't make it any worse. It couldn't.

Or perhaps it was because I wasn't consciously thinking and moving any more. I don't know.

I don't know, either, why I moved after him. But I did. I saw him stop to light a cigarette. He didn't know I was following. He thought I was finished. I hugged the shadows. At the foot of the Score he turned up Yeo's Jinkin. Then I trod on a loose cobble, and he turned round.

He probably thought I was a ghost. I don't think he realised it was me. I wanted him down. I wanted him down on the ground so I could grind my feet into his face, so that I could grind out that grin that had mocked Sheila and Peter and Jonquil and Lora. I wanted that before I died.

And I think I should have got him down, because I was crazy with pain and rage. My head and shoulders and arms went like a battering-ram for his knees. I saw the light come on again, and knew that if once he found my eyes with that beam, it was curtains. I struck up at the torch. Fabian, who must have been astonished at the fury of that tackle, took three steps back to gather himself for a counter-attack.

He shouldn't have done that. . . . One hand shot towards me, scrabbling at my jacket. The torch went up in the air, flashing in a wide arc. And Fabian screamed.

I went limp. I remember thinking that Mrs. Crummett must have gone to bed.

Sometimes I've grinned to myself on reading that the accused stated he couldn't remember what happened after that. But I don't grin now. I've often tried to remember, but I can't. Or maybe my subconscious doesn't want to.

There's a nightmare picture in my mind, all blurred in colours of black and violet, of going back down Yeo's Jinkin and finding my way into Mrs. Crummett's back-yard, and feeling in Fabian's pocket for the keys I had to have. I couldn't have been more than half-conscious when that happened.

Next thing I remember is staggering up Church Staithe and turning in at the gate of Edward's Bounty. The door was locked. I daren't ring the bell. There was a light in the big living-room. I could see Sheila there, and tapped on the window. She opened the door, very quietly, and I fell forward into her arms.

She half-carried me in. I looked at myself in the mirror as we passed through the hall. My face didn't seem to be damaged. All the serious damage was between my neck and my thighs.

She got me into the living-room and pulled the curtains across. I nodded towards the whisky. She didn't speak. She poured a half-tumbler and I drank it neat. I choked and spluttered. She tried to make me sit down, but I wouldn't, because I knew if I sat down I shouldn't get up again.

"I'll get Dr. Warren," she said, moving towards the hall.

"No," I said, "I'll be all right. I don't want anybody to know."

But I think she understood, even then.

I stood there a minute, letting the whisky get down to my feet. Then I moved off along the corridor, shuffling like a crippled crab. I went into Fabian's study and unlocked the safe, thinking how much easier it was to use a key than a hammer, even a fourteen-pound hammer. I don't know whether I expected to find anything in that safe or not. But there was something, in a fitted drawer, also locked, which I opened with another key on the ring. There were three envelopes. I pulled them out and slit them open with my thumb.

I didn't believe it till then. I saw Fabian's writing. I saw Dillon's signature, a shaky one. I saw a report from a chemist, typed on a business letter-head bearing a Central London address.

I saw something else too. Something that shook me almost as much as Fabian's blackmailing of his wife. But that would have to wait till I could think it over.

I closed the safe again, very carefully, then took the envelopes and their contents to the fireplace and burnt them. I waited till every scrap had gone, then pounded the ash to dust and swept it among the logs that had been laid on the flat hearth ready to light.

Then I went back to Sheila. I told her that I had to go out again and would be back, I hoped, in a quarter of an hour.

I was. It took me just that time to crawl back to Yeo's Jinkin and put a dead man's keys back in a dead man's pocket.

When I came back that second time, I had the chance to look into Sheila's eyes. I looked into them a long while.

"He hasn't come back," she said.

"No? It wouldn't be the first time he's stayed out."

"But he went to Lora's early. That's why it's so odd. When he goes early, he always comes back here to sleep. It's only when he goes to Lora's after the Galleon closes that he stays all night."

"It's convenient," I said, "when you can even chart a man's immoralities. You know where you are."

Her face was just a mask.

"Sheila," I said, "it's over. You don't have to be afraid any more. The safe's empty."

I saw the tautness go out of her.

"And Dillon," I said, "is Stuart's illegitimate son. He

worked in Stuart's office. He embezzled three thousand pounds of Stuart's money."

Her eyes went wide now. . . .

"But Stuart didn't prosecute," I said. "He preferred to have a slave. Dillon's signed confession was in that safe, too."

I could have explained a lot more. I could have told her how that tied up a lot of ends. That was the reason, of course, why Dillon had joined up with Jonquil and Lora and tried to get hold of Fabian's keys. He had as much interest in that safe being opened as they had.

That, also, might explain his assault on Luke Jonquil. Luke might have said that Peter was at breaking-point and he wasn't waiting any longer. He was going to confide in Lee Vaughan, Mrs. Fabian's cousin, and get some action. And Dillon didn't want that. Dillon wanted to open that safe himself or let it stay shut.

But I didn't go into that with Sheila. I was used up. I was past caring about anything. I asked if she had any rolls of bandage, any iodine.

There was iodine in the bathroom cabinet, she said. And she would find some bandages. I waited till she brought them.

"Harry," she said, using the name from force of habit, "why are you hurt? What have you been doing?"

"I took a header over the harbour bridge," I told her.

"I don't believe that," she said.

I couldn't argue. I climbed upstairs. I was stiff now. I couldn't move my legs without hellish agony. And tomorrow, I had to walk as if nothing had happened. My life might depend on that.

I ran the bath full of scalding water and lowered myself into it, inch by inch. I was glad the children were not in the nursery and the radio was on in the kitchen below, because I couldn't keep back the grunts and groans. I lay in that water for an hour. By that time I was light-headed, I fancied myself as that fellow Marat, and kept looking over my

196

shoulder for Charlotte Corday, expecting to see her coming for me with a knife.

When I pulled myself out of the bath, I took a bottle of liniment that chanced to be in the bathroom cabinet, and while the pores were open I rubbed and rubbed till I was sweating like a service bull in a heat-wave. Then I unwound the rolls of bandage and strapped my body up tight. Once into my pyjamas, I found I could walk and use my arms fairly well. The trouble was that I felt stiff as a mummy. I couldn't even turn my head.

Well, I thought, I'd two chances now. . . . To live or die.

I got into bed. And while I lay there staring at the ceiling, Charlotte Corday came in. But she wasn't carrying a knife. She'd brought something hot and steaming in a beaker. She told me to drink it up. I did. She smiled and went out.

After a while I slid into a rocking, drowning sea that was neither sleep nor waking. I couldn't move, and yet there was a flicker of something in my brain that kept me aware of things.

I was aware, for instance, that someone came into my room.

I didn't know who. I didn't care. . . . And ten or twelve thousand years later, I smelt burning. Or perhaps I had fire on the brain. Perhaps the house was afire or Rhuine burning after all.

I slept then. But when I wakened, I could still smell burning. A queer smell, like smouldering cloth. I thought of that because a cigarette-stub had once set my pants alight.

And next time I opened my eyes it was morning. A watery sun was shining into my room, and somewhere a heartless bird was singing.

I didn't want to get up. All I wanted was to lie there for ever, half-asleep, with the bird singing and the breeze swaying the curtains. But there is seldom any close affinity between what you want to do and what has to be done, and I tried to get out of bed.

I had forgotten my bandaged torso. I had to try again, and again, and finally slid out in a sort of solid block. I had to lie on the floor to pull on my socks, and my shirt defeated me for a quarter of an hour.

Then I noticed something.

My trousers and jacket were not where I had left them last night. They were on the same chair, but in a different position. I wouldn't have noticed, perhaps, but when you're a bachelor you get finicky about such things. You probably don't vary the position by an inch in a year.

I sat on the bed, trying to tie up that fact with the somebody who had come into my room last night. With that smell of smouldering cloth.

But I couldn't. There seemed no connection at all.

I crawled into the bathroom and shaved. I tried to do a few exercises. I had to limber up. I had to be sprightly. If it killed me, I had to limber up.

I did exercises for ten minutes, then dressed and went into the corridor. There wasn't a sound anywhere. When I got down to the hall, I saw one of the maids, dusting. Usually, the girls smiled and said good-morning, or whatever it was. This time she didn't. She just looked at me.

I found Sheila in the living-room. She looked ten years older. There were purple rings under her eyes and all her colour had gone.

"It's only eight o'clock," she said. "I didn't expect you down yet. I was letting you sleep."

"I'm probably tougher than I imagined," I said.

"They've found him." She moved away from me, to the window. "They've found Stuart."

"Where?" I asked, like somebody saying a line in a play.

"In Mrs. Crummett's back-yard. With his neck broken."

I went to the coffee pot. Whatever happens, we seem to go on eating and drinking.

"Who told you?" I asked.

"The boy who brings the morning papers. They'd found Stuart just as he was coming past."

"No one else has been yet?"

"Not yet. I suppose when the police arrive . . ."

"Yes. They'll come and give you the news officially."

I hadn't any cigarettes. I went to the box to get one of Fabian's. But I let the lid drop again. There are limits.

"What are you going to do?" I asked. "I suppose you ought to go down there."

"I don't think that would be in character." She passed her fingers over those swollen, purple eyes. "Would it?"

"Probably not. But the police may not appreciate that. Especially if they come from Shilstone. They may not be as well posted in Rhuine's recent history as we are."

"Still, I can't go down," she said. "I can't help it what they think."

"Then you'd better have some coffee," I said.

I poured it for her and took it to the window, walking like a mummy and hoping she didn't notice.

"Did Dillon come home last night?" I asked.

"I don't think so."

From the window we could see down the drive. The watery sun had gone. There was a drizzle of rain. The trees and flowers hung like limp fingers. We drank our coffee and kept our eyes on the curve of the drive. We waited like that for half an hour before we saw him. A big, slow-moving constable who looked acutely conscious of his errand.

Instinctively we moved apart as Rose showed him into the room. He opened his mouth twice before he could find words. Then Sheila interrupted him and spared his further embarrassment.

"I know," she said. "I heard a little while ago."

"Instantaneous," he offered comfortingly.

Sheila looked vaguely round the room. "I suppose one ought to be glad of that."

"I'm very sorry, Mrs. Fabian."

She pulled herself together.

"You must be wondering, Mr. Tasker, why I'm not more upset. . . . I am upset really. Though perhaps not quite in the way I should be."

"It'd seem hypocritic," the constable rumbled heavily, "if you was, Mrs. Fabian."

"Hypocritic?" she repeated. "Oh yes!"

"I don't think there's many in Rhuine won't understand how you feel."

"I hope they do."

He twirled his helmet.

"I daresay you'll be having the Inspector to see you sooner or later, Mrs. Fabian. He's a very understanding gentleman. You won't have nothing to fear."

"Of course not," Sheila said. After a pause she added: "I didn't hear any details. . . ."

"There aren't many. Instantaneous, as I said. Some time before midnight, they think." He breathed noisily, looked through the window and addressed the lawn. "I don't like to worry you at this sorrowful time, Mrs. Fabian, but if there's any details I could give the Inspector—?"

"I'm quite willing to tell you all I know. But I'm afraid it amounts to very little."

His expression brightened. He produced a notebook and pencil. Not the grubby notebook and inch-stub of fiction, I noticed. Quite a shiny affair, with a sharply-pointed soft lead. And he didn't lick it.

"Mr. Fabian went out about two o'clock yesterday and I didn't see him again."

"Two o'clock . . . You wouldn't know where he went, Mrs. Fabian?"

"Not with certainty. Probably to see a lady friend in the village." She said it quite unemotionally.

The constable registered compassion. "You don't have to

mention no names," he said.

"Later," I volunteered, "he was at the Galleon. He left shortly before I came out myself. At a few minutes past ten."

"Few . . . minutes . . . past . . . ten. Thank you, sir." He looked at me curiously.

"My cousin," Sheila supplied. "Mr. Cardew. He's been staying with us since last Sunday."

"Ah yes! Mr. . . . Cardew!" He made a little row of dots in the shiny notebook. "You didn't see anything of Mr. Fabian after you left the Galleon, Mr. Cardew?"

"No," I said. "And I came home by the same route. Or I imagine so, if it's true that he was found in Yeo's Jinkin. There would be two or three minutes between us, of course."

"Yes," he said, looking at me thoughtfully.

I looked back at him. Thoughtfully.

"There's one other question I ought to ask," he said, "though under the circumstances, as you might say, it seems redundant. But would you say there was anyone—"

He stopped, fumbling again for appropriate words.

"Any resident of Rhuine who might have liked to nudge him into the next world?" I said. "Probably seven to eight hundred. That's roughly the population, isn't it?"

"There was the Mischief Night business," he said sadly. "Very bad that was. Bad for everybody, sir."

"Very bad," I agreed. "But I don't think you're on the right track there. I couldn't have been far behind. If there'd been any fracas, I should have heard it."

"That's very likely." He made another row of dots. "In your opinion, sir, was the deceased incapacitated? Or to put it in plain English, the worse for drink?"

"That's a difficult question to answer," I said. "Fabian seemed to have the sort of constitution that can soak up a lot of alcohol without showing it. But how far it would affect his judgements I'm not prepared to say. That's something for your doctor to decide."

He nodded. "It's a very low wall," he said reflectively.

"And Fabian was a very tall man and it was a very dark night, but for all that we're guessing, aren't we?"

"That's so, sir. Ah well, time will tell!"

He looked benignly at Sheila. I almost thought he was going to pat her hand.

"There's nothing to be afraid of," he said. "You'll find the Inspector very pleasant and understanding. Quite a gentleman, in fact."

I don't think either of us realised that he had backed from the room. Not till we saw him walking down the drive, holding the helmet he had apparently forgotten to put on.

Ten minutes later, I was on my way to the village myself.

I didn't want to go. But I felt it looked indecent for none of the household to show any interest in Fabian's death.

It was a solemn occasion and I could walk slowly. I hoped no one noticed my stiffness. That was a thing I had to risk. I didn't like going down Yeo's Jinkin, but that had to be done too. So I put a good face on it and went towards the wall. It was lined with silent people, all looking down through fifty feet of space at nothing.

Nothing, that is, but another policeman who was standing selfconsciously against Mrs. Crummett's chicken-house, trying not to look at a tarpaulin sheet that covered the middle of the yard.

I was told that Mrs. Crummett had made the discovery when letting the chickens out, and run screaming for her neighbours on both sides. The constable had been informed while breakfasting, and had arrived fastening his tunic and with his bootlaces still flapping.

Feeling too conscious of curious eyes, I walked in the direction of the Brickhole. But I didn't go in to see the Jonquils. I could see Luke sitting at the door of his cottage, and Peter playing beside him. A nice tit-bit for the reporters, that! The Mischief Night fracas, Fabian's death, the meeting that was to be held tonight . . . And Peter Charles, heir to all Rhuine playing in the Brickhole. I wondered what they would make of it all.

I rested my aching body against the harbour rails till I felt capable of walking the hundred yards from there to the Poskett's studio. I'd thought about calling to see Lora, but didn't. It would have been a waste of time anyway, for when I reached the top of the stairs and tapped on the Poskett's door, Lora was there with her.

Lora looked different this morning. She looked a sad and lovely child, not at all like the strapless blonde I had seen last Sunday. She had been going to leave this morning, she told me. The Poskett was lending her money to get away. But now all this happened, she supposed she would have to stay till everything was cleared up.

"That goes for all of us," I said.

I wandered about aimlessly for half an hour, then hobbled back to Edward's Bounty. It was still raining, a deathly day. Dillon had come back, been told the news, and had given a satisfactory explanation of his absence. He had stayed with a man he knew in Shilstone, a motor haulier who would like Dillon to join him in business if he had any money. That was Dillon's story, and if it lacked anything, it wasn't my job to question him.

Then, at three o'clock, the Inspector came.

I was in my room when he arrived. I went down and found him with Sheila. He had brought a sergeant with him. They were sitting with their backs to the door when I went into the room. The Inspector turned in his chair and gave me an interested glance.

He was a thin man, very ordinary-looking. Fortyish. Slightly bald, slightly grey. Nondescript, you might have said, except for his eyes. He was wearing a blue uniform, rather shabby for an Inspector. Last time I had seen him, he had worn a rather shabby suit.

He smiled at me.

"Smith's the name," he said in a soft, burring voice. "Inspector Smith . . . One of the Shilstone Smiths."

PREVENTIVE HOMICIDE

WE WENT through the preliminaries. He asked most of the questions the constable had asked, and the tired-looking sergeant made an occasional note. I watched him closely. A lot might depend on Inspector Smith. He was diffident of manner but firm of purpose. Not obviously inquisitive, but missing nothing.

After a while he stopped asking questions. He sighed, and stared through the window so long that I thought he had gone to sleep.

"Why do you want to know all this, Inspector?" Sheila asked. "Surely you don't think—"

"We don't think anything, Mrs. Fabian," he replied pleasantly. "We're just trying to be quite sure."

He looked through the window again.

"Is there anything else?" Sheila asked. "If not, may I go?"

"Of course you may go, Mrs. Fabian. I can't think of anything else just now. If I do, perhaps you'll spare me another five minutes before I leave the house?"

She went out of the room quickly. But Smith didn't say I

could go. So I stayed, sitting by the table with my legs crossed, smoking a cigarette.

"One of the Shilstone Smiths!" I said bitterly.

His smile was as soothing as a cool hand on a headache. "We're quite a big family round these parts, Mr. Cardew. I was born in Rhuine. I'm fond of Rhuine. That's why I chanced to be in several places just about the time you were there. You see, I've been waiting. . . . Not for this, exactly. But for something like this."

"The wait's been justified," I said.

"Now, Mr. Cardew, according to our local man—"

"I'm not Mr. Cardew," I told him.

The sergeant's head came round sharply, but Smith's expression didn't change.

"My name is Lee Vaughan," I said. "I'm not Mrs. Fabian's cousin. I never heard of Fabian, wife or husband, till she walked into my Covent Garden office a few days ago and asked me down here to make certain inquiries."

Smith looked interested. "So you're a private agent? Mr. Vaughan, did you say?"

"I'm not exactly that. I've no professional status. But quite a lot of people get themselves into jams and need a little outside help. Things the police wouldn't care to worry about. That's what I've been doing. Clearing up jams."

"Well," said Smith, "there are all sorts of ways one can earn a living."

"In my case it wasn't a very good living."

"No?"

"No. I was on the point of applying for a street-cleaning job when Mrs. Fabian came in."

"As bad as that! And exactly what did Mrs. Fabian want you to do?"

"Come to Rhuine, judge the situation for myself, and do what I could about altering it."

"What situation?"

"The same one that's kept you prowling about Rhuine in plain clothes, watching everything with a fatherly eye when you could have been playing golf," I said. "Fabian's idea that Rhuine would make a good Margate if it was hotted up."

Smith never pounced. There was always a little gap of silence between answer and question. But only a little one.

"And why did you adopt a false name, Mr. Vaughan?"

"As Vaughan, I couldn't easily have been entertained here at Edward's Bounty," I said. "So I slid into the identity of one Harry Cardew, a cousin of Mrs. Fabian's who's now in Australia. That gave me a standing."

Smith glanced at the sergeant. The sergeant had a leather-like face. A crease appeared in the leather. It was probably his idea of a smile.

"I appreciate frankness," Smith said. "And you've been very frank." He added, blunting the compliment slightly: "On this point whatever else. I think I might tell you that a cable from Australia was found in Mr. Fabian's pocket. It stated that Mr. Harry Cardew was neither in England nor contemplating an early visit."

I took a deep breath. "I'd like to ask a question."

"Why not? I might even answer it, but I can't promise."

"When did Fabian receive that cable?"

"Yesterday morning."

"I was wondering," I said, "why he hadn't acted upon it. But that explains. I was in the village till after he had left for Lora's cottage. And after that I only saw him at the Galleon."

"Exactly!" Smith nodded. "That will be the reason you weren't thrown out earlier. You weren't here to throw out."

He gathered his thoughts, looking at me all the while. "You saw him at the Galleon. . . . That would be the last time, of course. As he was leaving. A few minutes after ten, you told Constable Tasker."

"That was the last time," I said.

He looked through the window again. The sergeant took a

digestive tablet from a cellophane tube and put it in his mouth. I lit another cigarette.

"What conclusions have you reached since you came here, Mr. Vaughan?"

"That things were pretty much the same as Mrs. Fabian had led me to believe. I suppose you know all about the will and Mrs. Fabian's second marriage before she knew she had inherited Rhuine?"

"I know all there is to know about that."

"I decided that Fabian was prepared to go a long way to make his wife suffer."

"Did you decide why? Personally, I think I should cherish a woman who had inherited a place like Rhuine. Wouldn't you?" Smith asked the question conversationally.

"I would. But we're normal men, Inspector. I don't think Fabian was."

"You'd no personal animosity towards him, I take it? Or had you?"

"I'd plenty. Fabian was the nastiest specimen of manhood I've encountered since I left school, and that's a long time ago. But I had Fabian taped without having to pitch him over a wall, if that's what you're getting at. Mrs. Fabian paid me two hundred advance expenses and promised another cheque if I could put a spoke in Fabian's wheel. It might have been another two hundred, or more. But before I accepted a murder commission I should want five thousand down in cash."

The sergeant chuckled, and Smith frowned.

"I wasn't accusing you of anything," he said gently.

"No, but I thought I'd put in a word for myself. You don't mind?"

"Not at all. . . . In point of fact, I don't think we regard you as a suspect. Several people appear to have genuine motives. And you appear to have none. You can comfort yourself with that."

"Thanks a lot," I said.

"What about the children?" he said absently. "One, I hear, has been sent away. The other is living with Luke Jonquil, and I'm told that his mother hasn't been down to see him."

"All that," I said, "is wrapped up with whatever was between Mrs. Fabian and her husband. I'd say that Mrs. Fabian left Peter with Luke Jonquil because she thought it was a healthier atmosphere there than here."

"Probably Peter knew something about his step-father's association with this girl in the village?"

"He probably did," I agreed dryly.

"And Jonquil . . . The gardening brother, I mean. It was you, of course, who found him injured in his hut."

"It was."

"And went with all speed for Dr. Warren. . . . Odd that you should have been mixed up in that, too."

"Just as odd," I said, "as that you happened to be less than fifty miles away at the same time. We'd the same interests, Inspector. That brings people together. Like football matches and symphony concerts and leg-shows and libraries. And why mixed up . . . ? I found the old man, yes. I went for the doctor, yes. And that's all I know about it."

"And it was an accident. The old man had fallen against something." He tapped his nails on the table. They were well-kept nails.

"He said it was an accident."

"And your opinion, Mr. Vaughan . . . ?"

"I haven't one. Mrs. Fabian was paying me to deal with her husband, not find out whether a market gardener fell against a stove or didn't."

I knew what he was thinking. So I put it into words, well aware that he wouldn't.

"If you imagine," I said, "that Fabian attacked Luke Jonquil, and Isaiah Jonquil revenged himself on Fabian because of that, you're wrong."

"Am I?"

"I know you are. You don't have to tell me there was bad blood between Fabian and Isaiah. Everybody knows that. But there's a Cromwellian streak in Isaiah. He believes he's God's chosen instrument to defeat Fabian's machinations. They played an elaborate game, Fabian and Isaiah. I think each had the idea that the outcome was pre-ordained."

And I went on to tell Smith of Fabian's arrangement with Jonquil to go fishing that morning.

"I warned Jonquil not to go," I finished. "You see, Jonquil can't swim."

"A number of people who go down to the sea in ships can't swim," mused Smith. "It seems odd, but there you are."

I nodded. "But he wouldn't listen to me. He didn't under-rate the danger, don't think that. He knew it and was prepared to meet it."

"So it wasn't Jonquil because he believed in Fate rather than in the strength of his own right arm," Smith returned. "There's probably something in what you say. And yet, Mr. Vaughan, when everyone in Rhuine from his wife to Mrs. Dukas wished him dead, it seems odd that Fabian should accidentally fall over a wall and break his neck."

"These things happen," I said. "You mentioned his wife, Inspector. She's my client. So naturally, I say she could have had nothing to do with his death."

"Oh, naturally!"

"But if I didn't say it, I think she would be able to prove she never left the house about that time."

"I hope so."

He tapped his nails again. The sergeant patiently doodled.

"You know, Mr. Vaughan, as I come to think of it, you yourself could have had a motive. Don't you agree?"

"I'd like to hear of it," I said.

"If Fabian had told you of the cable . . . If he had been prepared to expose the fact that you were here under false colours, . . ." His voice trailed away. He smiled pleasantly.

"I don't want to produce my answers too pat," I said, "or you might get the idea that I've thought them up in advance. But that cat won't jump, Inspector."

"No?"

"No! Whatever Fabian had found out wouldn't have cost me any sleep. At the worst, it would have meant dropping the case. Not even that, I think, because he hadn't even the authority to turn me out of the house. It was his wife's. But if he had, I should simply have gone home and Mrs. Fabian would have paid me just the same. That isn't a motive."

"I don't understand why you did so badly at your chosen profession," he said. "I think you're very astute, Mr. Vaughan."

"Thanks," I said. "I appreciate that. I'll put it on my office stationery."

When he made no reply, I went on:

"You're spending a lot of time on me, Inspector. So I'll tell you something. Or shall we say I could tell you something. I could probably tell you a lot of things. I haven't been going around Rhuine with my eyes shut. I'd give you my information with no conditions attached, but I'm conscientious. Mrs. Fabian's suffered enough. I'm no lawyer. I'm not even a private detective within the meaning of the act. But I'm all she has."

He gave me a keen glance.

"And I'm anxious to do all I can for her while I'm here. Now I'm an outsider. I can help a lot. Providing you help me."

"It is the duty of all citizens," he said, "to assist the police. Without attaching conditions."

I nodded. "Theoretically, yes. But that doesn't compel a man to open up his mind if he doesn't feel like it. Or remember things he could easily forget."

"You want me to strike a bargain?"

"I want to be in on the ground floor."

He moved round slightly in his chair, so that the light from the window didn't catch his eye.

"I'm surprised at you, Mr. Vaughan. It's only in fiction and films, surely, that the gifted amateur and the plodding policeman act in friendly rivalry."

"I want neither friendship nor rivalry," I said. "All I want is a chance to hear what people say to you when you ask questions. I may be able to throw a different slant on it. Out of my knowledge, I might even be able to prevent a miscarriage of justice."

"Kind of you," Smith said.

I don't think he swallowed it. I don't think, either, that he suspected my real motive. Which was, of course, to know everything that was going on behind the scenes for my own advantage. No, I don't think he suspected that. I think he was just puzzled.

"I'm the only outsider," I went on. "I haven't any axe to grind."

"Not even keeping Mrs. Fabian out of trouble?"

"That's understood. She pays me."

"And you would defend even a murderess if she paid you?"

"I would. Doesn't any defending counsel? But she isn't a murderess. Fabian's death wasn't murder. Even if he didn't die by accident, I still say that."

"You mean he was probably killed in self-defence?"

"It could be that," I said. "There's another alternative that doesn't seem to have occurred to you. Is it murder to kill a homicidal maniac?"

"Was Fabian that?"

"He was."

"That might be a difficult thing to prove."

"If you talk to the Argus editor you might get something on his case-history. If you haven't got it already. Aside from that, I'm willing to prove it."

"Yes?"

"It ties up with the information I said I'd give you. You haven't promised yet to let me in on the ground floor. I'll trust you that far. If my information's worth it, I shall expect my reward."

I settled back in my chair. Partly because I wanted to look self-satisfied and partly because my whole body was racked and aching.

"I'm talking about the rumours," I said, "that Fabian was going to burn down Rhuine. You know all about that, don't you? Wasn't that in your mind when you mentioned keeping him indoors on Mischief Night?"

"Not altogether," Smith said. "I was merely communicating a vague and quite unofficial fear. Whether for Rhuine or for Fabian, I'm not quite certain. But the recollection of these rumours you mention may have had something to do with it. Certainly they had come to my ears. Didn't I mention Mrs. Dukas just now?"

"But you didn't attach much importance to them?"

"Frankly, no."

"Then can you tell me why Fabian had salted away sixteen gallons of petrol in Lora's cottage?"

The sergeant suddenly stopped doodling.

"Can you prove that he did?" Smith asked evenly.

"You'll have to take my word for it. There's probably enough of the stuff left in the jerrycans he used for storage to indicate that I'm speaking the truth. I found it last night and poured it down the bath waste-pipe."

I sat farther back, feeling good for once.

"That's my information, Inspector. And now I'll tell you my case. I don't know whether or not Fabian was drunk when he left the Galleon last night. But I do believe he was beside himself with frustrated rage. I believe the Mischief Night episode, the knowledge that practically everyone's hand was against him, and finally Isaiah Jonquil's handling of the protest meeting arrangements had sent him over the line. I believe that his repeated threats to set Rhuine alight, coupled with his past record and the hoard of petrol found in Lora's cottage, stamp him as a homicidal lunatic on a grand scale. I believe he fell over the wall. But if I'm wrong on that point, then the person who pushed him over was acting in self-defence, as you hinted, or else—"

"Or else?" the Inspector repeated patiently.

"The alternative I just mentioned. One that may be novel to you. Or that person was acting as a public guardian and benefactor by killing Fabian before Fabian could kill Jonquil and burn down the village."

He didn't reply. He just sat and looked at me.

"Personally," I added, "I don't think we need go as far as that. I think he went over accidentally."

"And I think you're wrong," Smith said, a new, slightly harder note in his voice. "I'll tell you why, Mr. Vaughan. The reason I suspect murder, or manslaughter, or—to include your own curious alternative—preventive homicide, is just one of those trivial clues. In this case, a button. An ordinary button. It was found within a few inches of Fabian's right hand. A jacket button."

I felt a loud singing in my ears. The room swam round. I just had the presence of mind not to glance down.

"That's different," I said, trying to keep my voice steady. "But not conclusive. There are plenty of buttons around. You might find one in any yard in Rhuine."

"We might. I've thought of that."

"Makes it interesting," I said. "A good, honest-to-God clue comes nice among so many slabs of psychology."

"I agree. But don't underrate your own contribution, Mr. Vaughan. These rumours have been a disturbing factor all the time. I was afraid that if I discussed them with my superiors, they would dismiss them as fantastic inventions. Your version, backed, of course, by the discovery you made in Lora's cottage, makes them much more credible."

I felt the way a mouse probably feels when the cat comes back. Pleasantries didn't add up to much if the middle button of my jacket was missing.

"As for your request, I think it might be granted. I've no objection to your being here when I interview Dillon. And I think you might go with me to see this girl Lora, and Miss Poskett. The Jonquils too. . . . But you must give me your word to repeat nothing you hear."

"Gladly," I said.

"I don't know what my superiors would say. But then, they haven't the matter to deal with, have they?"

He craned his neck so that he could see the sergeant's notes. "I think," he said, "we should have Dillon in now."

The sergeant went out. I shifted my position just far enough to see my reflection in the wall mirror. I expected to see threads hanging where the button had been. I expected to see a cold gleam in Smith's eye before he pounced. . . .

But the button was there.

Feeling for my cigarettes, I gave it a sharp tug. Fast as a house! And it had been hanging loose. I tried to think when last I had worn my blue suit, when Sheila might have fetched this jacket down from my room and stitch on the button. I tried to remember whether the button had been fast or loose yesterday, or the day before.

But I couldn't remember. I felt myself sweating with relief. The operative fact was that it was fast now.

The door opened. Dillon followed the sergeant into the room and looked studiously at the top of Smith's head. He didn't even glance in my direction. Smith couldn't have seen him. He asked the first questions without troubling to look up.

"How long have you been with Mr. Fabian, Dillon?"

"Four years, sir."

"Since quite a time before his marriage, in fact?"

"His marriage to Mrs. Charles, yes sir."

"So Mr. Fabian was married before?"

"Twice, sir."

"Widower?"

"Divorced, sir."

Now Smith looked up. "Where were you last night?"

"In Shilstone, sir." And he gave Fabian the details I had already been told.

"I gather you were Mr. Fabian's personal servant in a household otherwise devoted to his wife. That puts you in a rather special position. You must have talked to him when he came in late after his visits to the local pubs, for instance. What was his condition on those occasions?"

"Quite often—tight, sir."

"You mean, actually drunk?"

"I couldn't say as to that. But his eyes were always brighter and he breathed quicker."

"How did he react to the Mischief Night business?"

Dillon didn't reply, and Smith patiently repeated the gist of his question.

"I heard you, sir. I was trying to think."

"By all means, Dillon. Don't let me prevent you."

"I'd say something cracked in his mind. He realised he was up against it."

"Against what?"

"You might say everything, sir. His wife. People like Jonquil. And now the whole crowd was after his blood."

"Has he ever made threats against Isaiah Jonquil in your hearing?"

"I've heard him say, sir, he should have to put Jonquil in his place."

Smith looked more intently at Dillon.

"I want you to think carefully before you answer the next question. Don't be influenced by rumours you may have heard. Have you ever heard Fabian threaten to burn Rhuine?"

Dillon's bloodless face contorted. "Several times, sir."

"Specifically or generally?"

"I beg your pardon?"

"You know quite well what I mean."

"I'd say both, sir. I've heard him say it would be a good thing for everybody if Rhuine went up in smoke like it did once before. I've also heard him say that one of these days he'd set fire to the bloody town. Those were practically the words he used, sir."

"Do you think he meant them?"

"I don't know, sir. But there was the coach-house. I believe Mr. Fabian did that. I think he wanted to see how easy it was to start a big fire. Or how difficult, sir."

Odd, I thought, how closely that coincided with what Sheila had said to me.

"You haven't any proof of that, naturally?"

"No sir. But I was on the spot, and I saw the expression on his face."

"Difficult to admit as evidence," Smith said, "but far be it from me to discount it on that account."

He suddenly changed his tactics.

"Have you any personal opinion as to how Mr. Fabian may have died last night, Dillon?"

"I haven't, sir. Wasn't it an accident?"

"I wonder if there's such a thing," murmured Smith, "as preventive homicide?"

That seemed to confuse Dillon. He looked at the sergeant, and back again to Smith. "To—to prevent what, sir?"

"The death of Isaiah Jonquil. The despoiling of Rhuine. The burning of the village. The continuing deflowering of foolish innocence. The humiliation of his wife . . . Or perhaps other things of which, being an outsider, I am in ignorance."

Somewhere in the house a clock struck four. The sergeant glanced at the watch on his wrist.

"I don't think there's anything else, Dillon. Not just now. Will you ask Mrs. Fabian if she can spare me a moment?"

216

Until Sheila came in we sat quite still, nobody speaking. Then Smith stood up and took a bunch of keys from his pocket. They were attached to a long, flexible metal cord.

"These are your husband's keys, Mrs. Fabian. At this stage, I may not be lawfully entitled to examine his effects. This is a kind of tentative inquiry. But if there is any reason for his death that may have escaped us, we shall possibly find it in his desk or his safe. . . . Perhaps a threatening letter. Would you have any objection to my looking?"

"None at all," she said in a voice I scarcely heard.

Dillon was standing outside the door as we went into the corridor. He must have heard what was being said. He followed us to the study, again standing where he could hear—and this time see, for Smith did not close the door.

He went, unhurrying, to the writing-desk. He inspected each pigeon-hole and drawer, glancing at various papers and putting them aside for further reference. Then he crossed to the safe and opened it.

I looked back at Dillon. He was like a man already dead. I could have felt sorry for him if I had known less about him. The same thought probably occurred to Smith, for he told him to come into the room instead of standing there in the hall.

He turned again to the safe. He took out a deed-box that I had ignored the night before, put it on the table, and unlocked it.

"Mostly relating to various properties," he said. "In Surrey and Sussex. A maisonette in Quince Mews, Hertford Street . . . A cottage at Selsey. You will know all about those, Mrs. Fabian."

"I've never heard about them," she said.

He closed the box. Now he unlocked the fitted drawer in the safe. He emptied the contents, item by item, on to the safe floor. For two or three minutes he didn't speak. There was silence till an odd, stifled sound came from Dillon's throat.

"What did you say, Dillon?" asked Smith.

"N-Nothing, sir. I was wondering if I might sit down?"

"If Mrs. Fabian doesn't object, I most certainly don't."

He continued to turn over the contents of the drawer. He half-turned to the attentive sergeant.

"A bundle of five-pound notes—let me see, twenty-three. Seventeen pounds in singles. A little loose change. A cheque-book and a bank statement. I think that's all."

I could have told him that was all.

He closed the safe and went back to the papers he had taken from the desk.

"Insurance policies," he said, "and a few old letters." He skimmed through the first three with an expression of distaste. "I think you would be well-advised to burn these unread, Mrs. Fabian. . . . Well, we haven't learned much, have we?"

Dillon was still looking at the safe. A man in front of a firing-squad who finds they have just shot off blanks at him and he's still alive would probably feel very much as Dillon felt then. And you couldn't have said that Sheila herself was composed. She took the keys from Smith with a murmur of thanks.

Smith seemed to be thinking something over.

"One point before I leave," he said. "It appears that Mr. Cardew is actually Mr. Lee Vaughan, a somewhat eccentric type of private agent," he said. "Could I have your version of his presence here, Mrs. Fabian."

"I wanted him to look after my interests," she said. "My husband . . . But you must know all about his ideas for Rhuine."

"I think I do."

"I couldn't fight any more. I could have fought an outsider. But it's different in the case of one's own husband."

"Quite!" murmured Smith. "The enemy within the gates." He glanced in my direction. "And has Mr. Vaughan carried

218

out the commission to your satisfaction?"

"Oh yes! He's given a lead, you see. Until he came, I think my people thought I was letting things slide."

"My people!" repeated Smith with a curious little smile. "I know how you meant that, Mrs. Fabian. But the way you said it was quite—queenly."

I saw a flush come into her cheeks.

"I've thought of them in that way," she said. "As people I had to protect, even from my husband. Perhaps that is why all these things have happened."

He lifted her limp hand from the table and held it a moment between his own. "I hope you reign over your kingdom a long time," he said.

Then, more briskly, he turned to me.

"I'm going back to Shilstone for tea, Mr. Vaughan. Afterwards, I'd like to see the Jonquils, Lora, and anyone else you can think of who might help to clarify the situation. Will you meet me at the top of North Score at—say half-past six?"

I said I would, and followed by the sergeant he took his leave.

I saw them to the door and then went back to Sheila.

"Do you mind," I said, "if we don't talk about all this till Smith's finished with us?"

"Will he ever have finished with us?" she asked.

I was still wondering that when I left the house at ten minutes past six and went to the top of the Score. Smith had arrived in a police car, left it just above Boldry's house, and was waiting for me. Rhuine was packed with visitors that evening. They were probably running extra coach-trips.

"It's good for trade," Smith said. "You'll notice I'm in mufti this evening, Mr. Vaughan. I don't want to advertise my presence too much."

Accompanied by the leather-faced sergeant, we made for the Brickhole. Luke Jonquil's door was closed now; the rain had apparently driven him indoors. I knocked and we entered. Luke was sitting by the window. Isaiah and his wife were standing belligerently in the middle of the room. And between them stood Peter.

I told them, unnecessarily, that this was Inspector Smith. . . . I had never before seen Peter look awed. But he did now, slightly.

"I think you'd better go and play," I said to him.

"It's raining."

"Perhaps there's another room?" suggested Smith. "We may be talking about things slightly above his head."

"I doubt it," I said.

"The sergeant has two children. I happen to know he has a way with them."

The sergeant's face turned the colour of fine old brick-work. "Lay off it!" he growled. Those were the only three words I heard him utter in all my association with him.

Smith turned to Peter. "This is the sergeant. He can make noises like a duck and give a convincing imitation of the elephants in the Zoo. I suppose you're good, too. Would you like to take him into the kitchen and show him a few tricks?"

"Go with the sergeant, Peter," said Luke Jonquil.

And he went. It's wonderful what you can do with people if you handle them properly.

"Well, Mr. Jonquil," said Smith, "how's your head?"

"Practically better now, zur."

"Had a nasty accident, I hear."

"Getting over it nicely, zur."

"Personally," said Smith, "I wouldn't like to stop a crack from a man like Fabian was."

"No, zur. Neither would I."

Smith gently rubbed his chin. "No getting past you, is there, Mr. Jonquil?"

I liked Smith's mufti suit. It was a nice shade of grey. He took out a tobacco pouch and slowly filled his pipe. I wouldn't have believed that filling a pipe could take so long.

"After spending his young life among the emotional stresses of Fabianism, Peter must have found your garden a pleasant refuge."

"He did, zur."

"And his mother must have a high opinion of you, Mr. Jonquil, to let her son stay with you. They tell me she hasn't even been down to see him."

Luke said nothing. And Smith, with a patient sigh, turned to Isaiah.

"Have you postponed your protest meeting tonight?"

"No, zur. Why the hell should I?"

"I can think of no adequate reason."

Smith now lit his pipe. That also took a long time.

"Unless we admitted *de mortuis nil nisi bonum* as a reason."

"I don't quite follow you, zur."

"A Latin tag which tells us that we should pretend the dead were all saints and heroes. . . . You didn't happen to see anything of Fabian last night, after he left the Galleon at ten or thereabouts?"

"I was in bed, zur. I get up early in the mornings, and I like to get my sleep."

"Of course." Smith's eyes flickered to Mrs. Jonquil. "You bear out that statement?"

"I do!" she said.

"Even if it were untrue, you'd still bear it out?"

"I would, zur," she affirmed stoutly. "I'm his wife. But it's not untrue. He was in bed at half-past nine last night."

"I hear you were to have taken Fabian fishing this morning?"

"If you can call it fishing, zur. He didn't know much about it."

"Had the thought crossed your mind, Jonquil, that Fabian might be unbalanced?"

"I know he was, zur."

"You also know that he regarded you as the spearhead of the opposition to his efforts?"

"He'd every reason to, zur. I was. And am."

"You had been warned, I believe, that Fabian might lose control of himself and attack you?"

"I should have been ready for him, zur."

"But you must have known that this morning's proposed trip in your boat might be, shall we say, more significant than others preceding it? That it would probably be Fabian's last opportunity to be rid of you?"

"I realised that, zur. I'd have been a fool if I hadn't."

"Yet you ignored the warnings."

"It would have been him or me, zur."

"It seems foolhardy, Jonquil."

"Maybe it was, if you look at it that way. But as I told Mr. Cardew there, nobody was never going to say that a Jonquil and a Rhuine man bred and born ever turned his back on a bloody foreigner."

"Unofficially, that's a spirit I admire," Smith said. "But it comes perilously near to taking the law into one's own hands."

"What, zur, being prepared to defend yourself against a bloody maniac? Where'd you be, zur, if every man who thought somebody might take a running jump at him came yelping to you for protection? Why, zur, you wouldn't have no time for point-duty and organising the Constabulary Sports."

"*Lese majeste*, Jonquil."

"I wasn't the aggressor, zur. And I'd no bloody mind to be." Jonquil was visibly annoyed. "But if Fabian had tackled me, he'd have stopped a packet. He'd have got the heavy end of the oar in his guts."

"Even that might have been less painful and permanent than a broken neck," ruminated Smith. "Then you've no idea who might have attacked him last night?"

"I haven't, zur. And if I had, I wouldn't tell you. But if you'd seen what happened on Mischief Night you might have ideas of your own. Young hooligans they were, though heaven bless 'em for what they did. I cheered as loud as the next when that wagon went over Haldom Cliff. But they were out for blood. If Fabian was thrown over that wall and didn't fall over it in his own blind rage, you'll find whoever did it among them, zur."

"It's a point worth considering," Smith admitted. "I suppose you've no particular individual in mind?"

"I haven't, zur, or I'd send him a letter of congratulation."

"Sorry I mentioned it." Smith placidly smoked. "Did Fabian ever make any general threats against Rhuine to your knowledge?"

"Now we're back to it!" said Jonquil, and spat into the fire. "You mean did he ever say he'd burn the place down? He did. Not once, but twenty times."

It went on for quarter of an hour, over ground that was painfully familiar to me by now. Then Smith abruptly switched to Lora.

Jonquil spat again. "That's nothing to do with me, zur. I'm a broad-minded man, and if anybody wants a nice bit of 'ome-work, that's his look-out." He glanced warily towards his wife. "In a manner of speaking, that is," he added placatingly.

Smith also glanced at Mrs. Jonquil. "I think a feminine opinion might help," he said.

"I'm not broad-minded," Mrs. Jonquil said. "Women can't afford to be. To my mind it's sin and there's no getting away from it. But I've nothing against the girl. She's been a victim of circumstances, zur."

"You're barking up the wrong tree if you think Lora tipped Fabian over the edge," Jonquil said flatly. "He could have picked her up with one finger."

"And yet, if hate lends strength as fear is said to do—"

223

murmured Smith, but forbore to pursue the matter.

He called the sergeant from the kitchen, surprising him in the act of walking on all fours with Peter on his back. Peter and the sergeant, in fact, seemed quite reluctant to part. We said goodbye to the Jonquils, Isaiah giving me a sly wink behind the Inspector's back, and went up the Score to the Poskett's studio.

"Do you know anything about art?" asked the Inspector as we went up the stairs. "I always have an inferiority complex where artists are concerned. They have their own jargon, their own morals, their own code of conduct. Last time I had official dealings with one was a case of alleged abduction. Fellow cohabiting with his model, age sixteen just plus or just minus." Smith knocked out his pipe against a brass bedwarmer. "I got pulled into a discussion on pre-Raphaelitism and clean forgot what I'd gone to see them about."

"Was it abduction?" I asked absently.

"Oh, yes. But she abducted him."

In the studio, the Poskett was surrounded by a further six studies, this time of Rhuine from the Harbour. And on the window-seat overlooking the street, almost flattened against the panes, was Lora.

"I've been expecting you all day," grunted the Poskett. "You don't mind if I work while we talk? By the way, Smith, that's Lora. Have you met?"

"I'm always glad to accommodate myself to local conditions," Smith said. He went to the window, holding out his hand. "No, I don't think I've met Lora. In fact, I'm sure I haven't. I should have remembered."

The sergeant dropped weightily on the model's throne. "It's always nice to meet someone you've heard a lot about," Smith went on. "Your name's been cropping up constantly. How d'you do, Lora."

She timidly took the outstretched hand.

"Let me make it perfectly clear," Smith said, "that I don't

suspect you of killing Fabian."

"Don't frighten the child," said the Poskett from the donkey.

"The child isn't frightened. Is she?" Smith said, his eyes still on Lora. "Let's clear up one thing right away, Lora. Are you glad or sorry Fabian's dead?"

The Poskett lifted her brush and frowned.

"I'm not glad," Lora said. "I couldn't be glad anyone was dead. But somehow—somehow I can't feel sorry either."

"That's a very balanced view to take. How long have you been in Rhuine, Lora?"

I didn't catch her reply. But I saw that a pink flush was turning to vivid scarlet.

"Lora," said Smith, "I may not be much of a terror to evil-doers, but in my opinion there's a lot more than that to a policeman's job in a place like this. I like to think of myself as one of those people who help to make the world a cleaner, safer place to live in. Do you know, you've caused me a lot of worry. I've often wished I could break up whatever was between you and Fabian."

"But why?" she asked. "Why should you worry about that?"

"I have a teen-age daughter, Lora. The things she does and would like to do keep me awake at night. She's quite a good girl, but she tries to be hard-boiled. I think it's highly probable that if she'd been earning her own living in London, and an attractive man like Fabian had made the same suggestions he made to you, she would have fallen for them. But that doesn't alter the fact that she's fundamentally a good girl."

He spoke slowly, patiently. "And she isn't as beautiful as you are, Lora. I suppose beauty must make you feel very powerful. Does it?"

There were tears in her eyes. "I—I don't know," she stammered. "I've never thought about it."

"No? Well, you've had your experience and lived through it. So don't feel like the Scarlet Woman. Try to think about the Lora who did these things as someone else. A rather foolish someone who doesn't exist now."

My admiration for Smith was growing. I knew he couldn't have sized up Lora with a glance. I saw him as someone who had been watching, thinking, waiting . . . And who now was going about Rhuine admonishing here, encouraging there, and generally patching up the scars Fabian had left to fester and disfigure. I sat there for half an hour while he put his questions to Lora. The Poskett, meanwhile, worked with savage energy or sat astride the donkey, biting a hog's hair brush.

When he had brought her almost up to date, he glanced at me.

"So that's why you dropped in to see her!" he said. "I'd been wondering about that. Luck for you that he did, Lora. Now, what's this I hear about Fabian storing petrol in your kitchen?"

"I didn't think there was any harm in it," she said.

"Not much," he murmured with gentle sarcasm. "Few people seem to have scruples about the black market. Still, I think we can let that slide. What reason did he give you for keeping the stuff there?"

"He said we could go for a long holiday when the season here was over. Perhaps to Scotland. He said we should want a lot of petrol for that."

"So you would, of course . . . Did he ever mention any other possible use for it?"

"I don't think so. Unless . . . Oh no! That was only a joke."

"I'm inclined to think," Smith said, "that Fabian's jokes had sometimes a grim core."

"I once heard him say there was enough petrol under the sink to burn Rhuine to sea-level."

"But you didn't think he was serious about it?"

"Of course not! What good would that have done him?"

"Not as much good as going to Scotland with you, I agree. But the mind of man is capable of infinite twists and subtleties."

Smith glanced at the sergeant, who had spent this interlude staring open-mouthed at the Poskett's sextuple activities. "I wonder," he said to the Poskett, "if you could throw any light on this business?"

"I'm just a working woman," she retorted.

"In fact, you didn't know Fabian at all?"

"You don't throw a pint of beer in the face of a man you don't know. Not unless you're drunk. And I wasn't."

"I was wondering if you'd see fit to mention that little episode," Smith said. "Why did you do it?"

I held myself tight. If she told him the real reason—that we had come from Jonquil's house after seeing Peter and realising what Fabian had done to him—that would open up new vistas. God only knew what might come out.

But her broad shoulders lifted indifferently under the blue smock. "I do not like thee, Dr. Fell, Pell, or Snell," she said. "Fabian commissioned me to do a picture of him. I did it, he didn't like it, and hasn't paid me. And I'm a poor woman."

"So Fabian sat for you?"

"He did. It would have been worth the fifty guineas he didn't pay to listen to his talk."

"What did he talk about?"

"Sex and death."

"Nothing else?"

"Sex and death," said the Poskett firmly.

"A curious combination . . . Or is it?"

"It was probably normal to him. I listened every morning, Inspector, to the tally of his conquests. I gathered that he had been luring maidenhood to its full fruition since he was fifteen."

"But death . . ." said Smith. "Would you say he was a suicidal type? Or a homicidal?"

"I refuse even to speculate. But Fabian, I think, had a streak well-known to psychological science. The man who throws himself off the Eiffel Tower, Inspector, is seeking safety on the ground below. The fact that he'll be dead when he reaches it doesn't occur to him. I believe I'm right?"

"Substantially, I think you are," Smith admitted.

"Fabian was dissatisfied with himself. His marriage to Sheila had shocked and shaken his ego. He wanted death . . . The death of Jonquil, of his wife, of himself, even of Rhuine."

"Interesting. But why had his marriage shocked and shaken his ego?"

The Poskett began work on six hydrangeas on six pictures. After half a minute she paused long enough to reach a photograph from the chest behind her. "Take a look at that," she invited.

Smith looked at the photograph. Over his shoulder, so did I. It was a postcard blow-up of an amateur snap. It showed Sheila in a beach-costume, with a good-looking, fair-haired man whose arm was round her shoulders. She looked seventeen. Smiling and radiant.

"Sheila," said the Poskett, "with Godfrey Charles, her first husband. That was taken at Estoril during the war. That was the girl Fabian married after Godfrey was killed. A little older, perhaps. Not quite so gay. She had two children by then. But young and pathetically alone and malleable. That's how Fabian liked them, Inspector. Malleable."

Smith handed the photograph back.

"It was very nice for Fabian," went on the Poskett. "Behind him were thirty years of youthful seductions and sophisticated lechery. Sheila was handed to him on a plate—the nuts and wine of a varied and satisfying meal. He had the money. Sheila would look up to him, helpless and dependent, grateful for his protection, excusing his faults. Even if she

228

found out what he was, she would endure it for the children's sake. What a situation for Fabian to enjoy!"

The Poskett limned in the cottage windows.

"Then came the shock. Overnight, Sheila became the uncrowned queen of Rhuine, with enough money to buy up all her husband had. And more then that, Inspector—"

The Poskett jabbed Smith with her brush.

"—more than that, she developed strength of character and a tremendous sense of responsibility. She wasn't malleable any more. She was a woman with a trust, and a determination to be worthy of it."

"What you are telling me," said Smith, "though you may not realise it, is that given the opportunity Sheila Fabian might easily have killed her husband for the sake of Rhuine."

"Don't be thick-skulled," said the Poskett. "What I'm telling you is that Fabian was so humiliated by that change in his wife's fortunes and so dismayed by the change in her character, that he started a downward trend of introspection, megalomania, drunkenness and promiscuity that finally led him over Mrs. Crummett's wall."

Smith eyed the six canvases thoughtfully.

"I suppose you didn't kill him yourself? You're strong enough, I imagine. And one must dislike a man very strongly to empty a pint of beer down his neck at the price it is today."

"If you're working on those lines I wish you luck," she said cheerfully. "You'll need it. I don't think anyone would have seen me walking from here to Yeo's Jinkin. And if they had, Inspector," she finished with gusto, "I'm quite sure they wouldn't tell you. They'd have a house-to-house collection and give me a cheque." She put an exploring finger in her mouth. "I could do with it, too. I need a new top set."

Smith took something from his pocket. It was a button. He began to toss it in the air and catch it again. He looked at me sideways.

"Seems we're up against it, Mr. Vaughan. We're back to

our one certainty. You're the only one known to have been in this part of Rhuine about the time Fabian died. I suppose we shall have to overlook the fact that you're an outsider with no motive, and pull you in."

"No!" said Lora sharply, and his eyebrows rose into bland question-marks.

"It seems you have a champion, Mr. Vaughan." He smiled at Lora. "Regarded as a whole, the police are a pretty solemn lot. Solemn and sometimes grim. But an occasional Inspector can pull an occasional leg, Lora."

"I should plead manslaughter," I said. "I should claim that he attacked me and I defended myself."

"You wouldn't get away with that. Now, if you'd a cracked rib or a broken nose or a black eye . . ."

He picked up his hat and dusted it off. "I think we ought to be going."

"I suppose you'll be coming back?" said the Poskett. "I'd like you to sit for me sometime. You've a very peculiar face, Inspector Smith."

"I'll be delighted, Miss Poskett."

"And have some coffee before you leave."

"The sergeant and I never drink or smoke when we're on duty, do we, Sergeant?" He sat down, carefully hitching up his trousers. "Have a cigarette, sergeant. . . . I do hope it's real coffee, Miss Poskett?"

CHAPTER TEN

SEE THE CONQUERED HERO GOES

I LEFT Smith outside and went back to Edward's Bounty. I told Sheila what had happened. I almost asked her about the button, but shied at the last moment. Whatever came next, I felt, was out of my hands. It had probably been out of my hands all the time. Something—the impersonal force some of us label Fate or the personal influence others call Providence —had just been moving me about a board.

And if that was so, there were certain things I still had to do before the final move which might sweep me right off the table.

Next morning, I went to see Luke Jonquil and asked if he felt well enough to walk up to the Liquorice Gardens. He would like that, he said. Did I want to go up that way now?

"No," I said. "But I want to take Peter home to see his mother. I thought it might sugar the pill to say we're going to meet you up there and we'll call round home on our way. I'll bring him along later."

Peter was in Isaiah's house next door. I called him in.

"Peter," I said as casually as I knew how, "Luke's going up to the Gardens this morning. I think we'll walk up. But we'd better call round and tell your mother first. She may come this way to see you and wonder where you've gone."

"I don't want to go home," he said sullenly.

"I'm not very keen myself, Pete. But we all have to do a lot of things we don't want."

We walked up. I tried to seem quite unconcerned. Sheila met us at the door. I hoped she wouldn't fuss over Peter or cause a scene. She didn't.

"Luke Jonquil's feeling better," I said to her. "He's going up to the Gardens. Can't trust me to look after his plants any longer. I'm taking Peter up there now."

We all went inside. "And that reminds me," I said, as we came to the study door. "I've a note to write. Can I help myself to paper and an envelope?"

She started to say something. "Come in and wait for me, Pete," I said.

"I don't want to go in there," he said.

His face was chalk-white. I remembered he was still being looked after by Dr. Warren. It was drastic treatment, but I had to go through with it. I glanced at Sheila, who was standing at the door.

"Why don't you want to come in?" I asked Peter sharply. "What's wrong with you, Pete?"

"I won't go in," he repeated stubbornly.

"There's nothing to be afraid of," I said. I watched him a minute and added: "Old Horny's dead."

"I know. Somebody pushed him over Mrs. Crummett's wall. I wish I'd been there to see."

"If you're as brave as all that," I said, "sit down and wait for me."

He crawled into the room, hugging the wall like a blind cat. I hadn't any letter that needed writing, but I wrote one that didn't. I sat at the desk, looking up at him from the writing-block. He couldn't keep his eyes away from the safe.

"Some day," I said, "I'm going to buy a safe like that."

Sheila was still at the door. "Can I borrow the key?" I asked. She came to the desk, took the key-ring from a drawer, and gave it to me. I walked over and put the key in the lock. And as I pulled at the handle, Peter screamed.

A thin, piercing scream. I pushed back the door. He stood with his feet splayed out, his hands shoving something away. But there was nothing in the safe. It took him a minute to realise that. Then he screamed again, but differently this time. It was something being released, something that had been under high pressure a long time. He ran to his mother. I watched him bury his face in the soft flesh of her neck. Then I turned away, staring at the safe, feeling hot and dry, like something used up and thrown away.

I slammed the door shut. As I passed Sheila I said, throwing down the keys, "Well, I've earned the money."

I walked up the hill, alone, and found Luke at the Liquorice Gardens. He asked me where Peter was.

"With his mother," I said.

I sat down on the wall beside the stream. I sat there all day. Nobody could see me. It was a little world of its own behind those high thorn hedges. And there would never be a hotel built there now. I felt I had the right to sit there as long as I wanted.

I returned to Edward's Bounty to sleep. There was an inquest on Monday and I would have to be there. But I didn't have my meals with Sheila. There are limits to what a man can do. Especially a man with no great reserves of physical or moral courage.

I didn't even enquire what had happened at the Protest Meeting. The only conversation I had over the week-end was with Dillon, as I was leaving the house on Sunday morning for a snack at the Poskett's studio.

It was a Dillon I hadn't seen before. Even the pallor of his face was less deathly. He looked like a man not entirely lost.

"So there was nothing in the safe?" he asked.

I could have grinned, in spite of the way I felt. I could have told him there would have been plenty for Smith to find if I hadn't found it first.

"You're quite right," I said.

"I don't understand it, Mr. Cardew."

"The name's Vaughan," I reminded him. "I'm no relation."

"But that night . . . The night he made me sign."

"And that other night, four years ago, when he made you sign something even more damning," I said softly. "That confession of your embezzlement. A confession that you'd stolen from your own father."

He stared at me so hard I thought his eyes would come out.

"Don't ask me how I know. That's why I came here—to find things out."

"He was a devil!" he said hoarsely. "I'd rather he'd have prosecuted. I'd rather have gone to prison."

"But that wasn't Fabian's way," I said.

"It was in the safe," he said, still staring at me and shaking his head. "He's tormented me about what was in that safe, just as he tormented his wife."

"It wasn't in the safe," I told him. "Tell yourself that till you believe it. Fabian double-crossed you as he double-crossed everybody. Including himself. He wouldn't dare keep stuff in the safe that might have incriminated him as a moral blackmailer of that calibre."

I dug my thumb against his chest. "Just tell me two things for my own peace of mind. You hitched up with Lora and the Jonquils because you thought that in getting that chemist's analysis out of the safe you could also get your own confession. Isn't that right?"

He nodded. "I—I'd tried myself. I thought they might have a plan."

"Strength in numbers, eh? . . . And you tried to silence Jonquil because you thought the boy's distress would drive Jonquil to the point of confiding in me, and I might have a go at the safe. And find things in it about you as well as about

234

Fabian's wife. Right again?"

"I—yes, that's right. I must have been crazy."

"Then forget it. A bad dream's over. Don't think about the safe again. Or about what happened at the Liquorice Gardens. Jonquil's forgotten what you did to him. He kept quiet for the boy's sake. You owe Peter something too, Dillon. And his mother. You let Fabian get away with it. You hadn't the guts to protest. Well, Fabian's dead and the safe's empty. But don't forget what you owe them."

I thought he was going to break down, and a snivelling Dillon would have been the last straw. I was moving away.

"If only I could do something," he said.

"You probably can. Ask Mrs. Fabian if she wants you to stay on. If she does, be her good and faithful servant. And give Jonquil a hand in the Gardens sometimes. It'll do you good. Later, you might teach Peter to ride a bicycle."

I turned away.

The inquest was opened on Monday afternoon, in the Methodist Schoolroom that was to have been the scene of Fabian's rout. After formal evidence, it was adjourned. The Coroner was a Shilstone lawyer, and he sat with a jury.

So for a week longer I stayed at Edward's Bounty, got up every morning early, spent the day walking, eating and drinking at the Dolphin, sitting on the beach or in the Liquorice Gardens, watching the Poskett paint. All morning she painted her two stock pieces. All afternoon she painted Lora. I think it was an excuse to give the girl money. She was trying to persuade Lora to stay in Rhuine and help her run the cafe. I sat on the model's throne, watching and listening. We never talked about Fabian.

Fabian was buried on Tuesday afternoon. I don't know who went to the funeral. I didn't.

And all that week, two hard-faced men moved quietly in and out of the Rhuine cottages, asking questions. I knew what they were asking. They wanted to find someone who

235

had been in the vicinity of the harbour bridge or Yeo's Jinkin on the night of Fabian's death. Someone who might have seen him—and probably someone else with him or close behind. They were asking about a button, too.

I didn't see Smith again till the adjourned inquest. It lasted two and a half hours. The Divisional Surgeon gave his evidence. Mrs. Crummett gave hers. I gave mine.

The Coroner sat in a patch of sunlight. It made his bald head seem like a monk's tonsure. He had a thin grey face and looked tired as Lora told of the way Lee Vaughan had emptied the jerrycans. He didn't even show interest when Inspector Smith mentioned the button found by Fabian's body, and said there was no article of clothing owned by Isaiah Jonquil or Lee Vaughan from which a button was missing.

The jury returned a verdict of Accidental Death. And they wished to add . . .

The Coroner looked up.

". . . that the wall on Yeo's Jinkin should be built higher, and that the thanks of the people of Rhuine should be expressed to Mr. Lee Vaughan . . ."

The Coroner glanced at me dubiously.

". . . for his prompt action in removing the possible cause of a fire which might have destroyed the village."

"Yes," said the Coroner absently, and Inspector Smith, across the room, coughed gently.

I sat there till everybody moved away. Then I went into the sunlight. I went past Edward's Bounty and the church, along by the stumps of Maldwyche Avenue, and when I was out of everybody's sight I sat down and looked at the sea. I had been looking at the sea a long time when I heard a step behind me. It was Smith.

"Nice after the rain," Smith said, softly and gently.

"Warm in the sun." I made room for him on the stump. "Don't sit too close. Anybody seeing us from a distance might think we were handcuffed together. I wouldn't like that."

"I'm glad to see you're getting some of your native humour back, Mr. Vaughan," he said. "I've seen you several times this week. I thought you seemed dispirited."

He crinkled his eyes at the horizon. "What are you going to do now, Mr. Vaughan?"

"Go back to London if you've finished with me."

"I've no power to prevent you."

"But your enquiries will go on, I suppose?"

"Isn't it generally believed that the police never close a case?"

"That's what I've heard."

"I suppose that if someone came forward even at this late hour to say they had seen this or that . . ."

"It seems improbable," I said. I was feeling tired. Yet I didn't want to get up and walk away. There was something I wanted to ask him.

"I like to have my definitions right," I said. "What exactly is murder?"

Smith considered a few seconds.

"That you did, on the night of etc. etc., feloniously and of your malice aforethought, kill and murder one Stuart Durward Fabian," he said.

That was cutting near the bone. I felt a nerve jump in my jaw.

"And manslaughter?"

"That's a wider matter. You can commit manslaughter in a car by knocking down someone you've never heard of. Or by hitting too hard in the course of a quarrel."

"And what about justifiable homicide?"

"Wider still," Smith said. "To employ a melodramatic allegory, if you found a burglar with his hands round your wife's throat, and you put the bread-knife through his backbone, that, I think, could roughly be defined as justifiable homicide."

"And the preventive homicide you mentioned?"

"That you mentioned," Smith corrected mildly. "Wasn't that purely an invention to fit certain imaginary circumstances?"

"Could we elaborate it?" I said. "Suppose that the burglar's hands were not actually round my wife's throat, but I knew of a certainty they would be if I did nothing about it? How far would action with the bread-knife be justifiable then?"

He took his time. Smith can spend five minutes looking at the blue horizon while he fills his pipe and wastes half a box of matches lighting it. Some day I'm going to smoke a pipe.

I got tired of waiting for him.

"Fabian, according to the evidence, told a number of people he should have to kill Jonquil. Also, that he intended burning down Rhuine. His spare-time job was driving his wife into an asylum, and it was one of his minor ambitions to send the heir of Rhuine to a home for delinquent children," I said. "So—"

"So we're back to the question I asked Dillon," Smith said. "Whether some man or woman killed Fabian before he could make good his promises."

"You couldn't very well blame him," I said. "Or her."

"That's the layman's view," Smith pointed out. "A highly improper one. In such circumstances, the correct course was to pass on those threats to the proper quarter."

"Meaning the police," I said. "And what would you have done? Suppose Fabian's wife or Mrs. Dukas or the Poskett or Isaiah Jonquil had come to you? Sheila's ideas you'd have put down to domestic misunderstandings. Mrs. Dukas would have been a crazy old woman, the Poskett a malicious gossip. Jonquil, you'd have said, was a known enemy of Fabian's trying to get him on the wrong side the law. Oh, you'd have questioned Fabian! But it would have ended in laughter all round and drinks and Fabian handing you a cheque for the Benevolent Fund."

238

Smith looked faintly worried.

"I wish I could say you're absolutely wrong."

"Or suppose," I went on, "that any one of these people had come to you after the event? Suppose Jonquil had been drowned? Suppose Fabian had swum ashore after gallant efforts to rescue him and the Poskett had told you it was murder? Suppose Rhuine had gone up in smoke and Fabian had been one of the heroic fire-fighters as he was when the coach-house was burnt down. Would you have listened if someone had said it was calculated murder and arson instead of accident?"

"You're driving me into a corner," Smith said plaintively.

"It's a technical ruling I'm after," I said. "How long must elapse between a murderous deed and its forcible prevention to change manslaughter into justifiable homicide?"

Smith smoked in silence.

"In other words," I said, "if Fabian was tipped over that wall, in payment for past misdeeds and to prevent worse ones in the immediate future, where do you stand?"

"In the uncomfortable position of having to arrest whoever it was. You don't need me to tell you that the law doesn't take the victim's character into account."

Smith took a button out of his pocket and turned it over in his palm. "Sentences for manslaughter," he remarked, "are often quite light."

"I'll try to think of someone who might have done it," I said, "and tell them that."

Smith was looking across the bay. The sun glinted on the water; between us and Haldom head the sea was a great sheet of silver.

"We see the surface," he said. "The play of light and shade. But there are depths beneath. . . . It's easy to acquire facts and correlate them. Less easy, though, to penetrate the hidden places. Especially in a small, tight community like this. I'm often conscious of that, Mr. Vaughan, even in minor cases.

239

The sort of thing we get down here much more often than murder."

"I often feel that way too," I muttered.

"A surface of facts," he said almost in a whisper, "and beneath it—what? Agonies of the heart, lost dreams."

"Stick to facts," I said, feeling choky. "They're safer to deal with in the long run."

He seemed to be talking to himself. But he wasn't. Smith was clever. He was talking to me.

"So many odd things. The accident to Jonquil that wasn't an accident. Something connected with Dillon I couldn't quite place. The hammer I saw in the hall at Edward's Bounty that wasn't anywhere on the premises when I looked for it again . . ."

There was sweat on my forehead.

"The fact that Sheila Fabian didn't visit her sick son at Jonquil's house. A little pile of burnt papers among the logs in the study fireplace. A smell of burning cloth that everybody but Sheila Fabian noticed on the night of her husband's death. . . ."

My nails were digging into my hands. Not only because of what he was saying. But because I couldn't have helped him there even if I'd wanted.

"All under the surface!" Smith said. "Ah well . . . ! Some day, a few years from now, you'll have to drop in and see me. Perhaps we'll have a chat about old times."

We got up. We sauntered like old friends back to the foot of the Score. And there we shook hands.

"May I say," he murmured with his hand still in mine, "that I like you and think you're a very good fellow?"

"Thanks a lot," I said. "I feel the same way about you."

I turned back to the Dolphin. I could buy brandy anywhere, I thought. So I'd have cider. Rough cider, like I'd had on the first day. It seemed ten years since.

I went round that evening and said goodbye to everybody I knew. To the Poskett and Lora. Isaiah and his wife. The little man in the Dolphin who was like an educated monkey. I went up to the Liquorice Gardens and said goodbye to Luke, and stayed there till it was dark.

When I got back to the house I said goodbye to Dillon. I intended being away early next morning. I looked in at the night-nursery, and saw an arm flung out, a tousled little head. Peter, asleep. . . . But I didn't sleep that night.

I was up at six. I moved quietly about the house. My cheap fibre case was packed. I drank half a bottle of milk I found in the kitchen, and helped myself to a slab of cake and a packet of biscuits. Then I got my raincoat out of the cloak-room and stood a minute in the hall.

I was listening to ghosts playing the piano. But that heart-breaking tune of Liszt's was only in my mind.

I went to the door. But I hadn't been quiet enough. Maybe it wouldn't have mattered how quiet I had been. Sheila Fabian was on the half-landing. She came down quickly, she almost ran to me.

"You didn't tell me you were going!" she said.

She had on a long crimson housecoat, with a high, Tudor collar. She reminded me of a picture I had once seen of Dorothy Vernon.

"There's no point in staying," I said. "I should have gone last night if there'd been a train."

"But there are things to clear up," she said. "There are things—"

"There's nothing," I said.

"Even your—your fee," she said desperately.

"I've had my fee," I told her. "Two hundred pounds and free board for a fortnight. That's not too bad."

She came nearer. "Harry . . ." she said. Then, on a lost, high note: "I don't even know what to call you."

241

"Lee Vaughan's the name."

"You can't go away like this. Promise you'll come back. Some time. . . . Some day."

"There'd be all this to go through again," I said. "Do I have to say what I'm thinking?"

I bent down. . . . Then I moved away quickly and opened the door. I didn't look back. I struck through the wood, away from the village, away from the little path Peter had trodden to the Liquorice Gardens. I wasn't conscious of walking. I was only conscious of a sort of blindness and numbness, because I knew I was living through the first few minutes of something that was going to last a lifetime.

When I came to a clearing, I dropped the fibre case and turned round.

I could see it all. Haldom Head, the Downfall across the bay. The sea, with the sun shining flatly over it. The harbour. . . . I could even see things moving. Figures right down there below, little black dots.

I looked away. I had to.

For a long time I stared at nothing. I don't know how I came to notice the thread. . . . It was funny, that. It took my mind back to Sheila's work-basket, to the embroidery over her knees, to those dozens of reels—silks and cottons and threads, all colours of the rainbow.

Thread. . . . Button thread.

My raincoat was unfastened. Under it, I was wearing the Donegal suit. Odd, but you can wear a suit for two years, as I had worn that, without knowing the colour of the buttons. I couldn't have sworn, even then, that they were not the buttons that had been on the suit when I bought it.

Just as I couldn't have sworn, on any of those occasions when Smith had toyed with the button found in Mrs. Crummett's back-yard, whether it was mine or not.

But for some crazy reason, I had known the kind of thread those buttons were sewn on with. Black thread.

But now, my buttons were sewn on with a kind of grey-brown that matched the cloth.

Not one of them. All of them.

I pulled open my jacket. My trouser-buttons had been sewn on with different thread, too.

I lowered my haunches on to the grass bank and sat there a long time, thinking.

There had been a loose button on my jacket.

That night, when I came in, that button must have been missing.

I sat there on the grass, working that out. It took a long time.

That night, while I had been travelling through those ten thousand years of sleep, someone had come into my room.

I'd known that, hadn't I? And next morning, my things weren't just where I had left them.

I went on working it out.

There's a button missing from someone's jacket. You're afraid it may mean something. Something you daren't admit even to yourself . . . There isn't another button to match.

So what do you do?

If you can't match the missing button, you have to replace them all, haven't you? But how?

By cutting the buttons from another suit. One that belongs to another man in the same house. A man who won't be wanting that suit, or any other, ever again. You have to do that. Trouser buttons as well. They all have to match.

But someone may come looking. Someone may find that other man's suit with all the buttons missing.

So what do you do about that?

You burn that other man's suit. It takes you all night, and there's the danger that someone may smell it burning. But that's a risk you have to take. There's no other way.

That's what you do, I figured out.

That's what you do if you're brimming with a great thankfulness, haunted by a great fear, shining with a great loyalty.

I looked back towards Rhuine. For the last time now. It had been worth it all.

Jonquil, soon, would be walking up the Score to the Liquorice Gardens. Ninian would be coming home. Sheila would grow old there, old and well-loved as Mary Louisa Charles had been. Some day Peter would reign there in her place. Lora was safe from Fabian and herself. Life would go on.

Life, I thought without any great originality, always goes on.

Some of the chimneys were smoking now. I looked and looked till I couldn't see anything. Nothing but a blue, swirling emptiness in front of my eyes.

Then I bent down, plucked a buttercup, and put it in my buttonhole; the only thing of Rhuine I was taking with me.

I turned and walked away towards the Shilstone road.

THE PERENNIAL LIBRARY MYSTERY SERIES

Delano Ames

FOR OLD CRIME'S SAKE (*available 12/82*)   P 629, $2.84

MURDER, MAESTRO, PLEASE (*available 12/82*)   P 630, $2.84
"If there is a more engaging couple in modern fiction than Jane and
Dagobert Brown, we have not met them."   —*Scotsman*

E. C. Bentley

TRENT'S LAST CASE   P 440, $2.50
"One of the three best detective stories ever written."
          —Agatha Christie

TRENT'S OWN CASE   P 516, $2.25
"I won't waste time saying that the plot is sound and the detection
satisfying. Trent has not altered a scrap and reappears with all his old
humor and charm."   —Dorothy L. Sayers

Gavin Black

A DRAGON FOR CHRISTMAS   P 473, $1.95
"Potent excitement!"   —*New York Herald Tribune*

THE EYES AROUND ME   P 485, $1.95
"I stayed up until all hours last night reading *The Eyes Around Me*,
which is something I do not do very often, but I was so intrigued by the
ingeniousness of Mr. Black's plotting and the witty way in which he spins
his mystery. I can only say that I enjoyed the book enormously."
          —F. van Wyck Mason

YOU WANT TO DIE, JOHNNY?   P 472, $1.95
"Gavin Black doesn't just develop a pressure plot in suspense, he adds
uninfected wit, character, charm, and sharp knowledge of the Far East
to make rereading as keen as the first race-through."   —*Book Week*

Nicholas Blake

THE CORPSE IN THE SNOWMAN   P 427, $1.95
"If there is a distinction between the novel and the detective story (which
we do not admit), then this book deserves a high place in both catego-
ries."   —*The New York Times*

Nicholas Blake (cont'd)

THE WHISPER IN THE GLOOM   P 418, $1.95

"One of the most entertaining suspense-pursuit novels in many seasons."
—*The New York Times*

THE WIDOW'S CRUISE   P 399, $2.25

"A stirring suspense. . . . The thrilling tale leaves nothing to be desired."
—*Springfield Republican*

THE WORM OF DEATH   P 400, $2.25

"It [The Worm of Death] is one of Blake's very best—and his best is better than almost anyone's."   —Louis Untermeyer

John & Emery Bonett

A BANNER FOR PEGASUS   P 554, $2.40

"A gem! Beautifully plotted and set. . . . Not only is the murder adroit and deserved, and the detection competent, but the love story is charming."   —Jacques Barzun and Wendell Hertig Taylor

DEAD LION   P 563, $2.40

"A clever plot, authentic background and interesting characters highly recommended this one."   —*New Republic*

Christianna Brand

GREEN FOR DANGER   P 551, $2.50

"You have to reach for the greatest of Great Names (Christie, Carr, Queen . . .) to find Brand's rivals in the devious subtleties of the trade."
—Anthony Boucher

TOUR DE FORCE   P 572, $2.40

"Complete with traps for the over-ingenious, a double-reverse surprise ending and a key clue planted so fairly and obviously that you completely overlook it. If that's your idea of perfect entertainment, then seize at once upon *Tour de Force*."   —Anthony Boucher, *The New York Times*

James Byrom

OR BE HE DEAD   P 585, $2.84

"A very original tale . . . Well written and steadily entertaining."
—Jacques Barzun & Wendell Hertig Taylor, *A Catalogue of Crime*

Marjorie Carleton

VANISHED   P 559, $2.40
"Exceptional . . . a minor triumph."
—Jacques Barzun and Wendell Hertig Taylor, *A Catalogue of Crime*

George Harmon Coxe

MURDER WITH PICTURES   P 527, $2.25
"[Coxe] has hit the bull's-eye with his first shot."
                    —*The New York Times*

Edmund Crispin

BURIED FOR PLEASURE   P 506, $2.50
"Absolute and unalloyed delight."
           —Anthony Boucher, *The New York Times*

Lionel Davidson

THE MENORAH MEN (*available 10/82*)   P 592, $2.84
"Of his fellow thriller writers, only John Le Carré shows the same
instinct for the viscera."   —*Chicago Tribune*

THE NIGHT OF WENCESLAS (*available 10/82*)   P 595, $2.84
"A most ingenious thriller, so enriched with style, wit, and a sense of
serious comedy that it all but transcends its kind."
                    —*The New Yorker*

THE ROSE OF TIBET (*available 10/82*)   P 593, $2.84
"I hadn't realized how much I missed the genuine Adventure story
. . . until I read *The Rose of Tibet*."   —Graham Greene

D. M. Devine

MY BROTHER'S KILLER   P 558, $2.40
"A most enjoyable crime story which I enjoyed reading down to the last
moment."   —Agatha Christie

Kenneth Fearing

THE BIG CLOCK   P 500, $1.95
"It will be some time before chill-hungry clients meet again so rare a
compound of irony, satire, and icy-fingered narrative. *The Big Clock* is
. . . a psychothriller you won't put down."   —*Weekly Book Review*

Andrew Garve

THE ASHES OF LODA   P 430, $1.50
"Garve . . . embellishes a fine fast adventure story with a more credible
picture of the U.S.S.R. than is offered in most thrillers."
                                        —*The New York Times Book Review*

THE CUCKOO LINE AFFAIR   P 451, $1.95
". . . an agreeable and ingenious piece of work."   —*The New Yorker*

A HERO FOR LEANDA   P 429, $1.50
"One can trust Mr. Garve to put a fresh twist to any situation, and the
ending is really a lovely surprise."   —*The Manchester Guardian*

MURDER THROUGH THE LOOKING GLASS   P 449, $1.95
". . . refreshingly out-of-the-way and enjoyable . . . highly recommended
to all comers."   —*Saturday Review*

NO TEARS FOR HILDA   P 441, $1.95
"It starts fine and finishes finer. I got behind on breathing watching Max
get not only his man but his woman, too."   —Rex Stout

THE RIDDLE OF SAMSON   P 450, $1.95
"The story is an excellent one, the people are quite likable, and the
writing is superior."   —*Springfield Republican*

Michael Gilbert

BLOOD AND JUDGMENT   P 446, $1.95
"Gilbert readers need scarcely be told that the characters all come alive
at first sight, and that his surpassing talent for narration enhances any
plot. . . . Don't miss."   —*San Francisco Chronicle*

THE BODY OF A GIRL   P 459, $1.95
"Does what a good mystery should do: open up into all kinds of ramifica-
tions, with untold menace behind the action. At the end, there is a
bang-up climax, and it is a pleasure to see how skilfully Gilbert wraps
everything up."   —*The New York Times Book Review*

THE DANGER WITHIN   P 448, $1.95
"Michael Gilbert has nicely combined some elements of the straight
detective story with plenty of action, suspense, and adventure, to produce a superior thriller."   —*Saturday Review*

FEAR TO TREAD   P 458, $1.95
"Merits serious consideration as a work of art."
                                              —*The New York Times*

C. W. Grafton

BEYOND A REASONABLE DOUBT   P 519, $1.95
"A very ingenious tale of murder . . . a brilliant and gripping narrative."
                              —Jacques Barzun and Wendell Hertig Taylor

Edward Grierson

THE SECOND MAN   P 528, $2.25
"One of the best trial-testimony books to have come along in quite a
while."   —*The New Yorker*

Cyril Hare

DEATH IS NO SPORTSMAN   P 555, $2.40
"You will be thrilled because it succeeds in placing an ingenious story
in a new and refreshing setting. . . . The identity of the murderer is really
a surprise."   —*Daily Mirror*

DEATH WALKS THE WOODS   P 556, $2.40
"Here is a fine formal detective story, with a technically brilliant solution
demanding the attention of all connoisseurs of construction."
                              —Anthony Boucher, *The New York Times Book Review*

AN ENGLISH MURDER   P 455, $2.50
"By a long shot, the best crime story I have read for a long time.
Everything is traditional, but originality does not suffer. The setting is
perfect. Full marks to Mr. Hare."   —*Irish Press*

TENANT FOR DEATH   P 570, $2.84
"The way in which an air of probability is combined both with clear,
terse narrative and with a good deal of subtle suburban atmosphere,
proves the extreme skill of the writer."   —*The Spectator*

TRAGEDY AT LAW   P 522, $2.25
"An extremely urbane and well-written detective story."
                                                 —*The New York Times*

UNTIMELY DEATH   P 514, $2.25
"The English detective story at its quiet best, meticulously underplayed,
rich in perceivings of the droll human animal and ready at the last with
a neat surprise which has been there all the while had we but wits to see
it."   —*New York Herald Tribune Book Review*

THE WIND BLOWS DEATH   P 589, $2.84
"A plot compounded of musical knowledge, a Dickens allusion, and a
subtle point in law is related with delightfully unobtrusive wit, warmth,
and style."   —*The New York Times*

Elspeth Huxley

THE AFRICAN POISON MURDERS   P 540, $2.25
"Obscure venom, maniacal mutilations, deadly bush fire, thrilling climax compose major opus.... Top-flight."

—Saturday Review of Literature

MURDER ON SAFARI *(available 8/82)*   P 587, $2.84
"Right now we'd call Mrs. Huxley a dangerous rival to Agatha Christie."   *—Books*

Francis Iles

BEFORE THE FACT   P 517, $1.95
"Not many 'serious' novelists have produced character studies to compare with Iles's internally terrifying portrait of the murderer in *Before the Fact,* his masterpiece and a work truly deserving the appellation of unique and beyond price."   —Howard Haycraft

MALICE AFORETHOUGHT   P 532, $1.95
"It is a long time since I have read anything so good as *Malice Aforethought,* with its cynical humour, acute criminology, plausible detail and rapid movement. It makes you hug yourself with pleasure."

—H. C. Harwood, Saturday Review

Michael Innes

DEATH BY WATER   P 574, $2.40
"The amount of ironic social criticism and deft characterization of scenes and people would serve another author for six books."

—Jacques Barzun and Wendell Hertig Taylor

HARE SITTING UP *(available 9/82)*   P 590, $2.84
"There is hardly anyone (in mysteries or mainstream) more exquisitely literate, allusive and Jamesian—and hardly anyone with a firmer sense of melodramatic plot or a more vigorous gift of storytelling."

—Anthony Boucher, The New York Times

THE LONG FAREWELL   P 575, $2.40
"A model of the deft, classic detective story, told in the most wittily diverting prose."   *—The New York Times*

THE MAN FROM THE SEA *(available 9/82)*   P 591, $2.84
"The pace is brisk, the adventures exciting and excitingly told, and above all he keeps to the very end the interesting ambiguity of the man from the sea."   *—New Statesman*

Thomas Sterling

THE EVIL OF THE DAY   P 529, $2.50
"Prose as witty and subtle as it is sharp and clear. . .characters unconventionally conceived and richly bodied forth. . . . In short, a novel to be treasured."   —Anthony Boucher, *The New York Times*

Julian Symons

THE BELTING INHERITANCE   P 468, $1.95
"A superb whodunit in the best tradition of the detective story."
                      —August Derleth, *Madison Capital Times*

BLAND BEGINNING   P 469, $1.95
"Mr. Symons displays a deft storytelling skill, a quiet and literate wit, a nice feeling for character, and detectival ingenuity of a high order."
                      —Anthony Boucher, *The New York Times*

BOGUE'S FORTUNE   P 481, $1.95
"There's a touch of the old sardonic humour, and more than a touch of style."   —*The Spectator*

THE BROKEN PENNY   P 480, $1.95
"The most exciting, astonishing and believable spy story to appear in years."   —Anthony Boucher, *The New York Times Book Review*

THE COLOR OF MURDER   P 461, $1.95
"A singularly unostentatious and memorably brilliant detective story."
                      —*New York Herald Tribune Book Review*

THE 31ST OF FEBRUARY   P 460, $1.95
"Nobody has painted a more gruesome picture of the advertising business since Dorothy Sayers wrote 'Murder Must Advertise', and very few people have written a more entertaining or dramatic mystery story."
                      —*The New Yorker*

Dorothy Stockbridge Tillet
(John Stephen Strange)

THE MAN WHO KILLED FORTESCUE   P 536, $2.25
"Better than average."   —*Saturday Review of Literature*

Simon Troy

THE ROAD TO RHUINE   P 583, $2.84
"Unusual and agreeably told."   —*San Francisco Chronicle*

Simon Troy (cont'd)

SWIFT TO ITS CLOSE   P 546, $2.40
"A nicely literate British mystery . . . the atmosphere and the plot are
exceptionally well wrought, the dialogue excellent."   —*Best Sellers*

Henry Wade

THE DUKE OF YORK'S STEPS (*available 8/82*)   P 588, $2.84
"A classic of the golden age."
  —Jacques Barzun & Wendell Hertig Taylor, *A Catalogue of Crime*

A DYING FALL   P 543, $2.50
"One of those expert British suspense jobs . . . it crackles with undercur-
rents of blackmail, violent passion and murder. Topnotch in its class."
                                                              —*Time*

THE HANGING CAPTAIN   P 548, $2.50
"This is a detective story for connoisseurs, for those who value clear
thinking and good writing above mere ingenuity and easy thrills."
                                          —*Times Literary Supplement*

Hillary Waugh

LAST SEEN WEARING . . .   P 552, $2.40
"A brilliant tour de force."   —*Julian Symons*

THE MISSING MAN   P 553, $2.40
"The quiet detailed police work of Chief Fred C. Fellows, Stockford,
Conn., is at its best in *The Missing Man* . . . one of the Chief's toughest
cases and one of the best handled."
            —Anthony Boucher, *The New York Times Book Review*

Henry Kitchell Webster

WHO IS THE NEXT?   P 539, $2.25
"A double murder, private-plane piloting, a neat impersonation, and a
delicate courtship are adroitly combined by a writer who knows how to
use the language."   —Jacques Barzun and Wendell Hertig Taylor

Anna Mary Wells

MURDERER'S CHOICE   P 534, $2.50
"Good writing, ample action, and excellent character work."
                                    —*Saturday Review of Literature*

Anna Mary Wells (cont'd)

A TALENT FOR MURDER   P 535, $2.25
"The discovery of the villain is a decided shock."   —*Books*

Edward Young

THE FIFTH PASSENGER   P 544, $2.25
"Clever and adroit . . . excellent thriller . . ."   —*Library Journal*

If you enjoyed this book you'll want to know about
THE PERENNIAL LIBRARY MYSTERY SERIES

Buy them at your local bookstore or use this coupon for ordering:

Qty	P number	Price

postage and handling charge $1.00
_____ book(s) @ $0.25

TOTAL

HARPER & ROW, Mail Order Dept. #PMS, 10 East 53rd St., New York, N.Y. 10022.

Please send me the books I have checked above. I am enclosing $_____ which includes a postage and handling charge of $1.00 for the first book and 25¢ for each additional book. Send check or money order. No cash or C.O.D.s please

Name_____

Address_____

City_____ State_____ Zip_____

Please allow 4 weeks for delivery. USA only. This offer expires 4/30/8
Please add applicable sales tax.